TEAM TAEKWONDO #1

ARA'S ROCKY ROAD TO WHITE BELT

Master Taekwon Lee & Jeffrey Nodelman
Illustrated by Ethen Beavers

RODALE KIDS

An Imprint of Rodale Books
400 South Tenth Street, Emmaus, PA 18098
Visit us online at rodalekids.com

Text © 2017 by ATA International
Illustrations © 2017 by ATA International

Rodale books may be purchased for business or
promotional use or for special sales. For information,
please e-mail: BookMarketing@Rodale.com.

Printed in China
Rodale Inc. makes every effort to use acid-free ∞, recycled paper ♲.

Book design by Tom Daly

Library of Congress Cataloging-in-Publication Data
is on file with the publisher.

ISBN 978–1–62336–882–1 hardcover
IBSN 978–1–62336–880–7 paperback

Distributed to the trade by Macmillan

2   4   6   8   10   9   7   5   3   1   hardcover
2   4   6   8   10   9   7   5   3   1   paperback

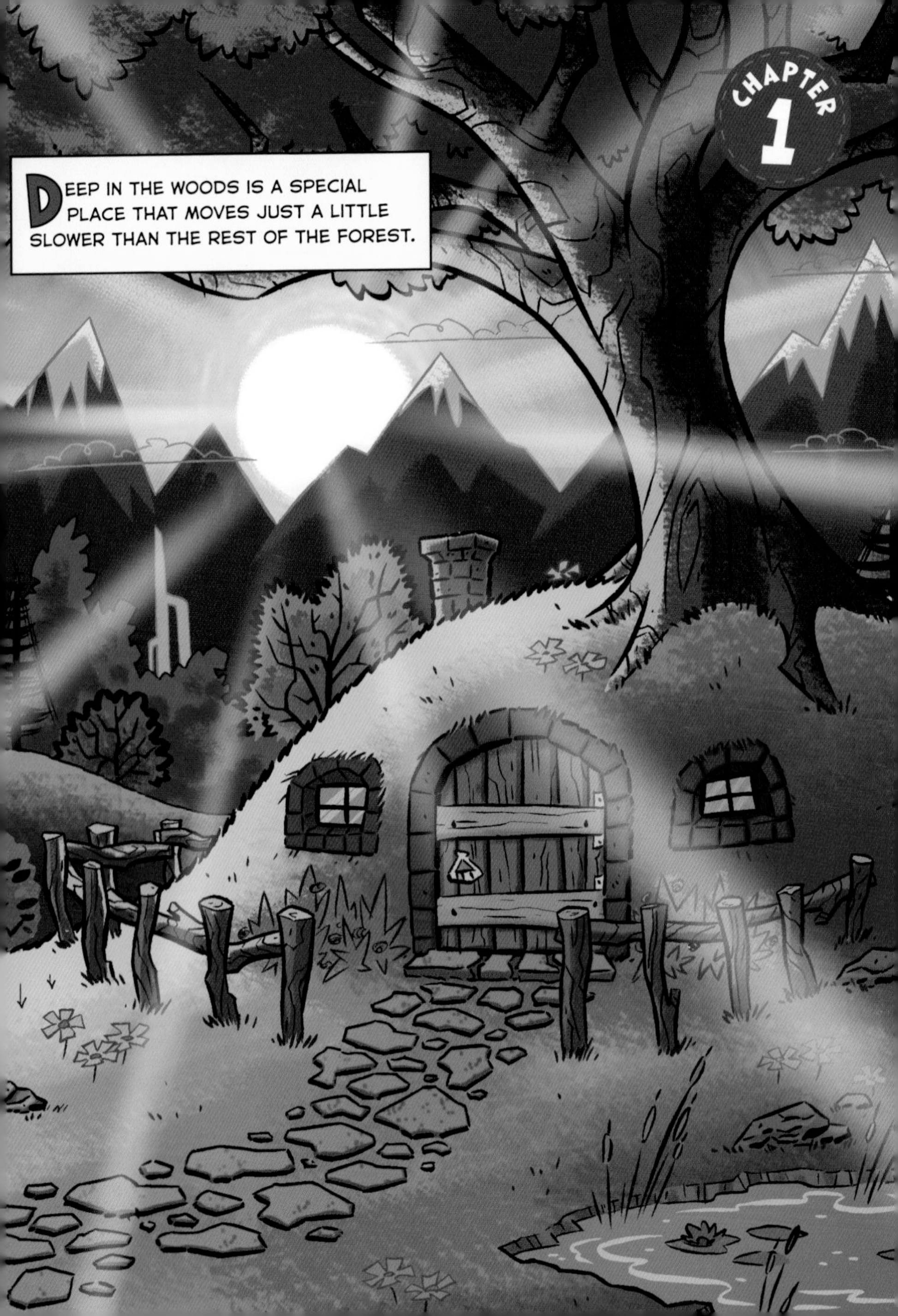
CHAPTER 1
DEEP IN THE WOODS IS A SPECIAL PLACE THAT MOVES JUST A LITTLE SLOWER THAN THE REST OF THE FOREST.

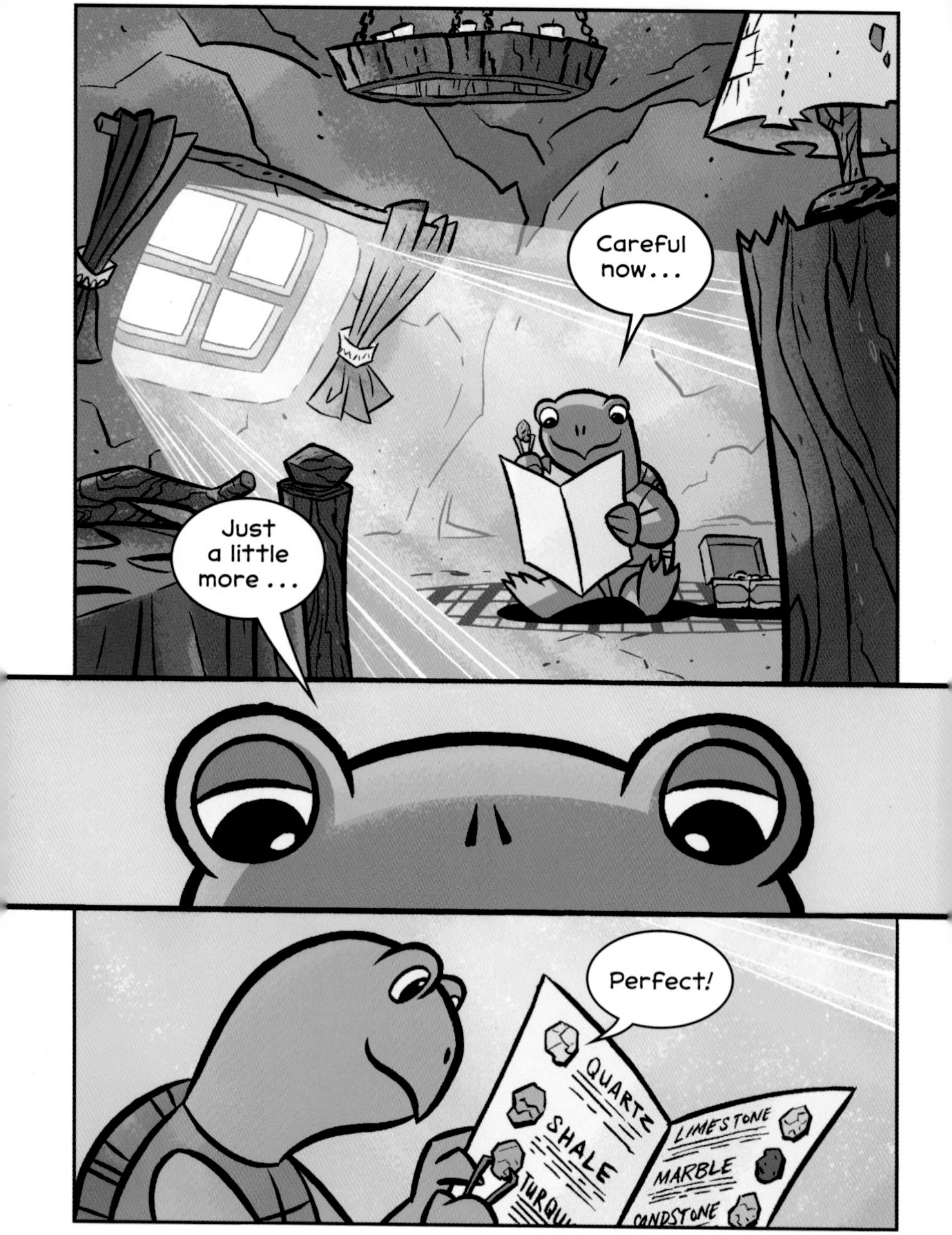
Careful now...
Just a little more ...
Perfect!
QUARTZ
SHALE
LIMESTONE
MARBLE

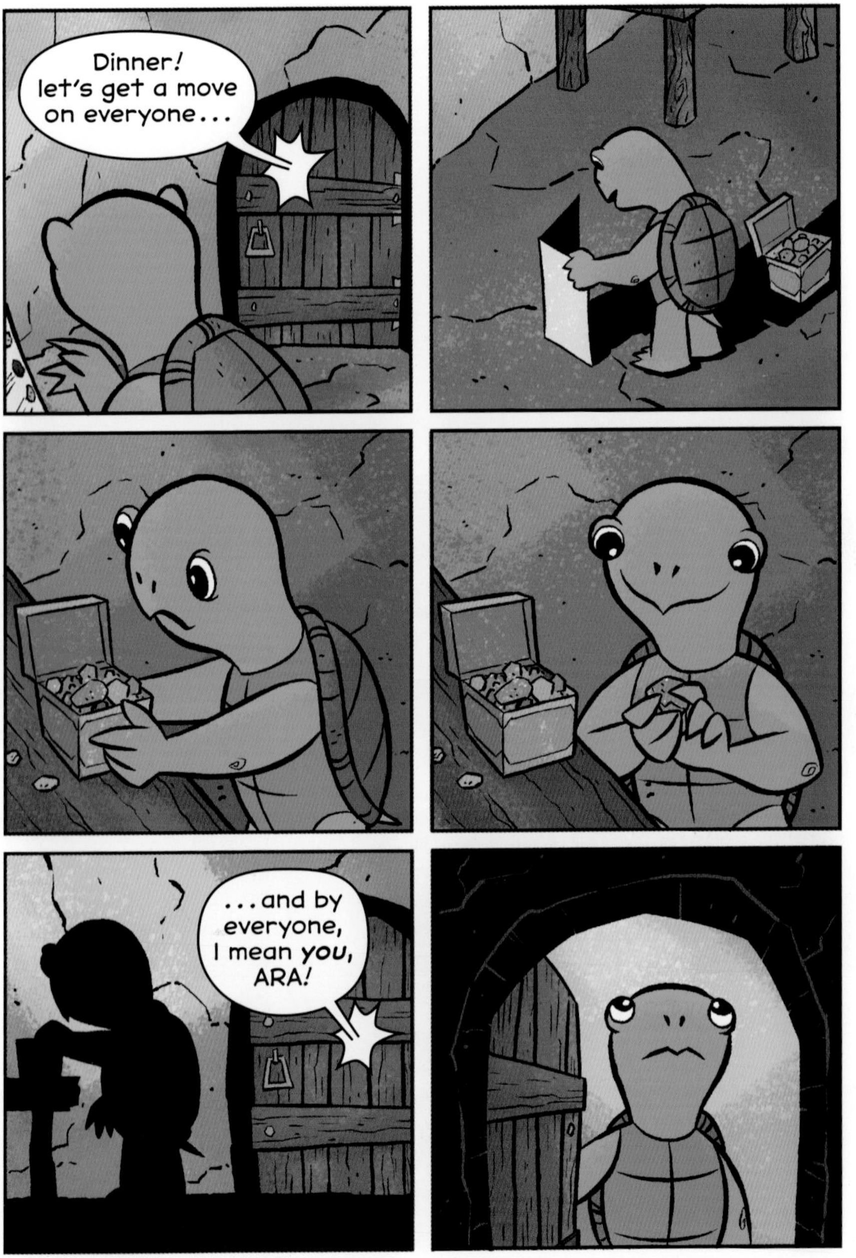
Dinner! let's get a move on everyone...
...and by everyone, I mean *you*, ARA!

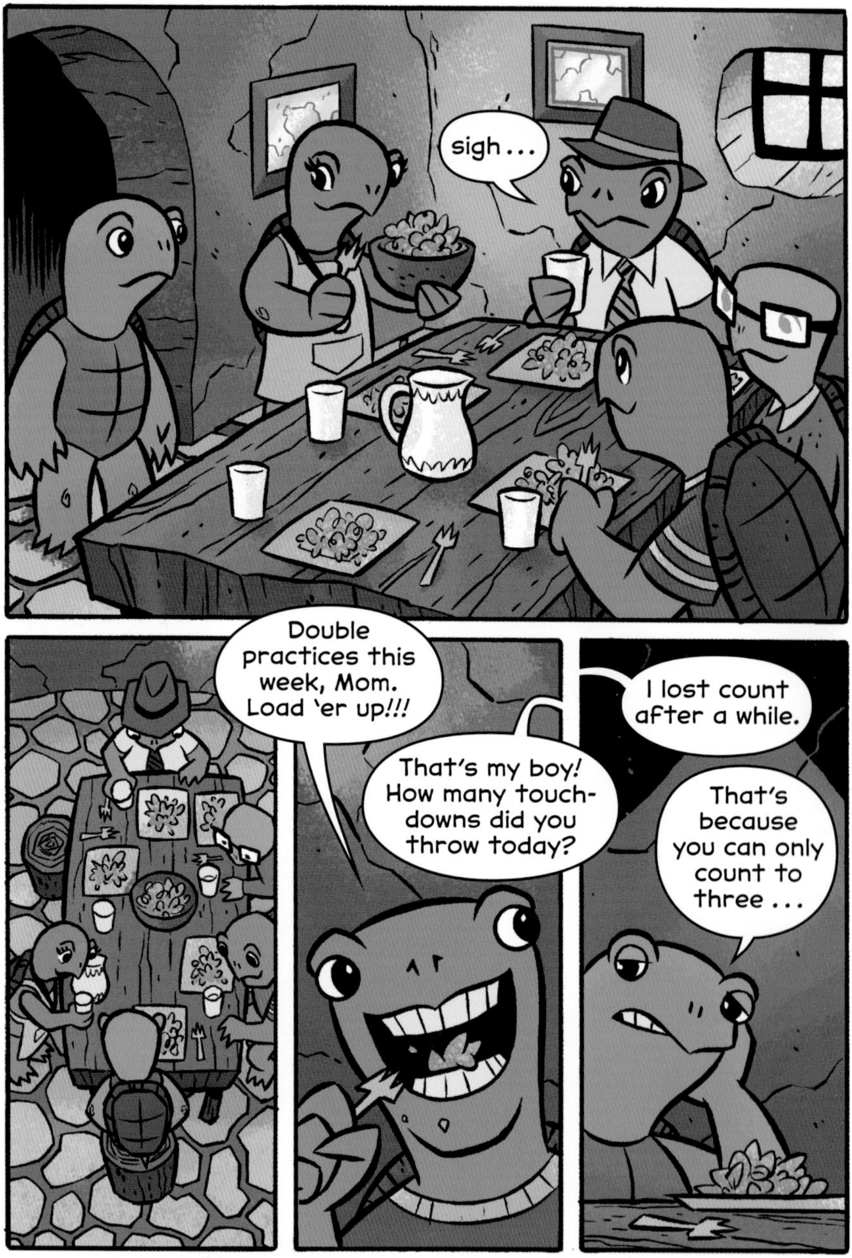
sigh . . .
Double practices this week, Mom. Load 'er up!!!
That's my boy! How many touch-downs did you throw today?
I lost count after a while.
That's because you can only count to three . . .

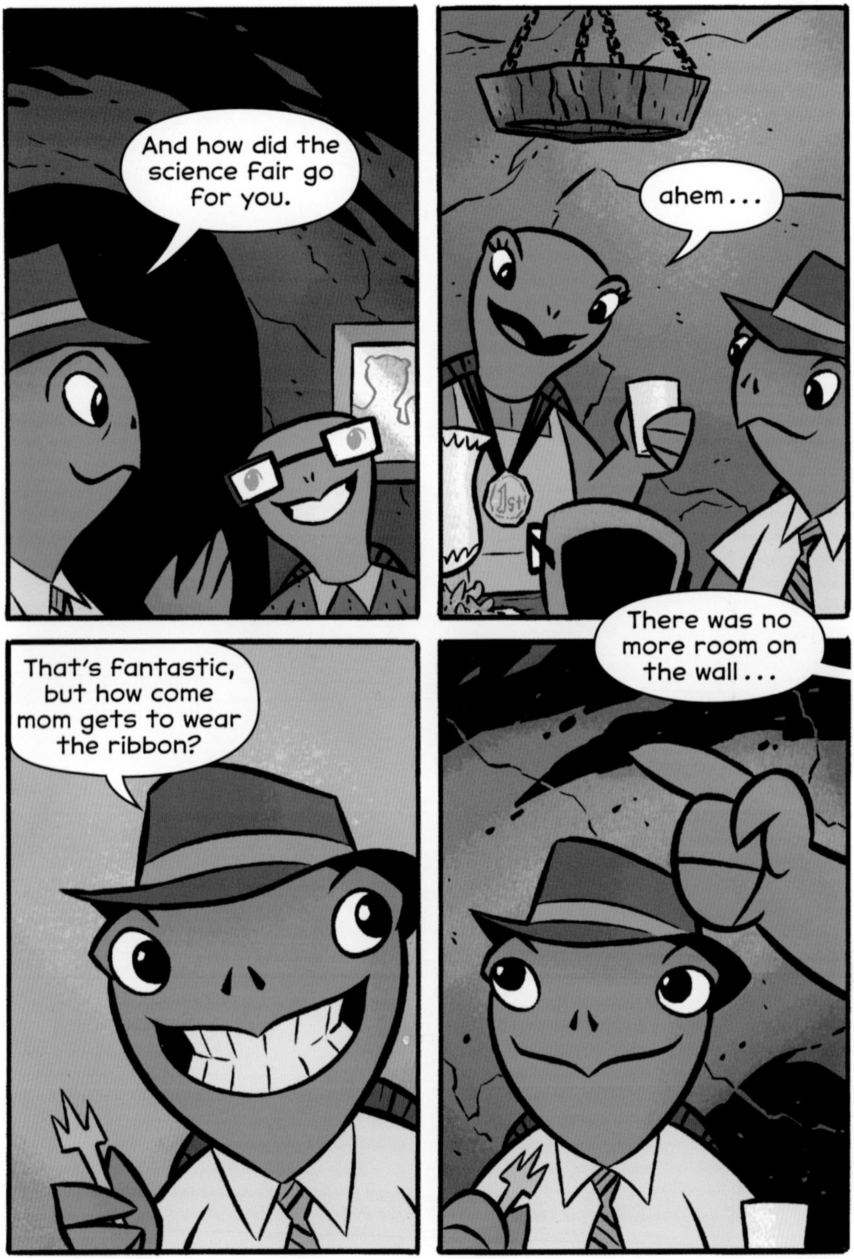
And how did the science fair go for you.
ahem...
That's fantastic, but how come mom gets to wear the ribbon?
There was no more room on the wall...
1st

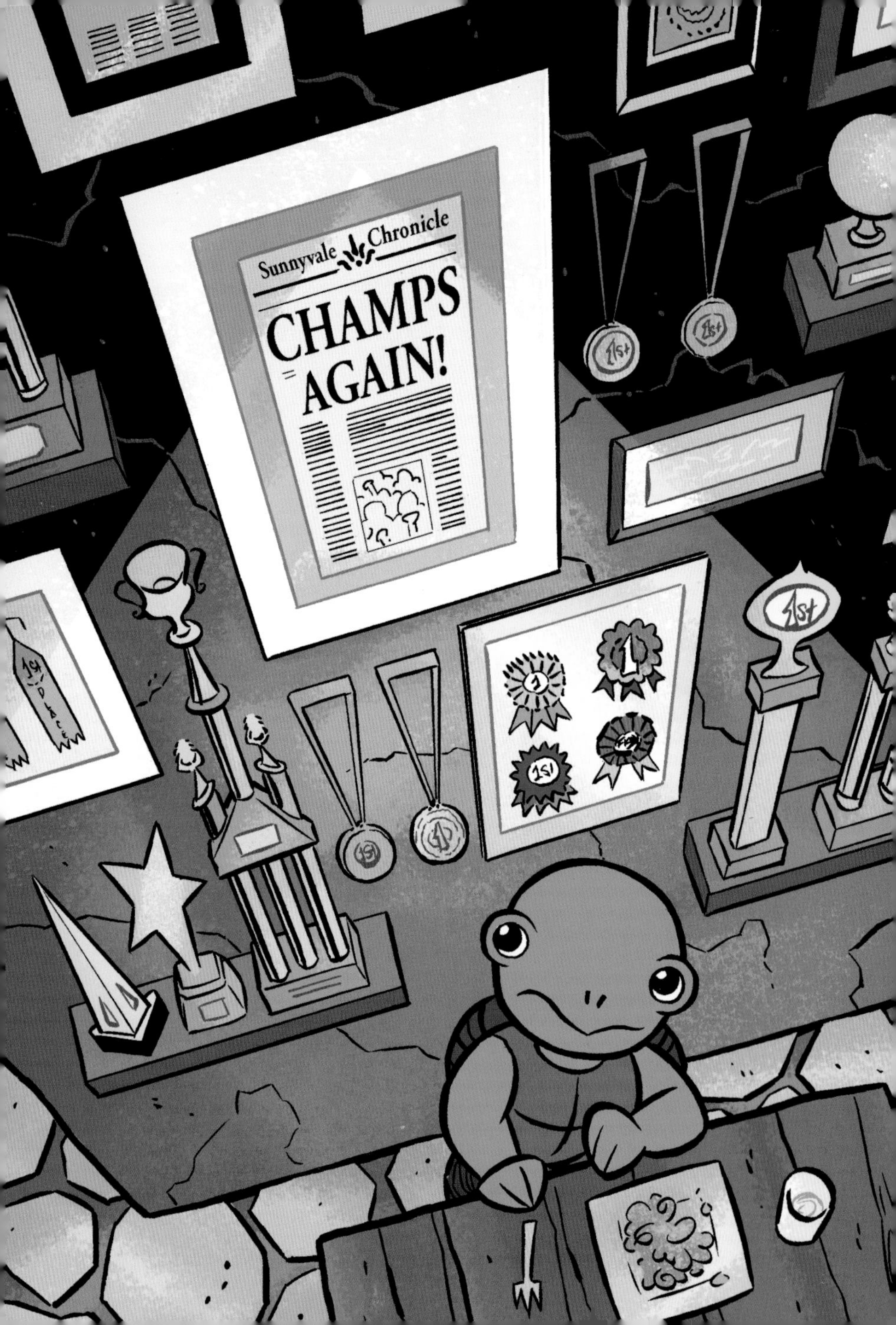
Sunnyvale Chronicle
CHAMPS AGAIN!
1st

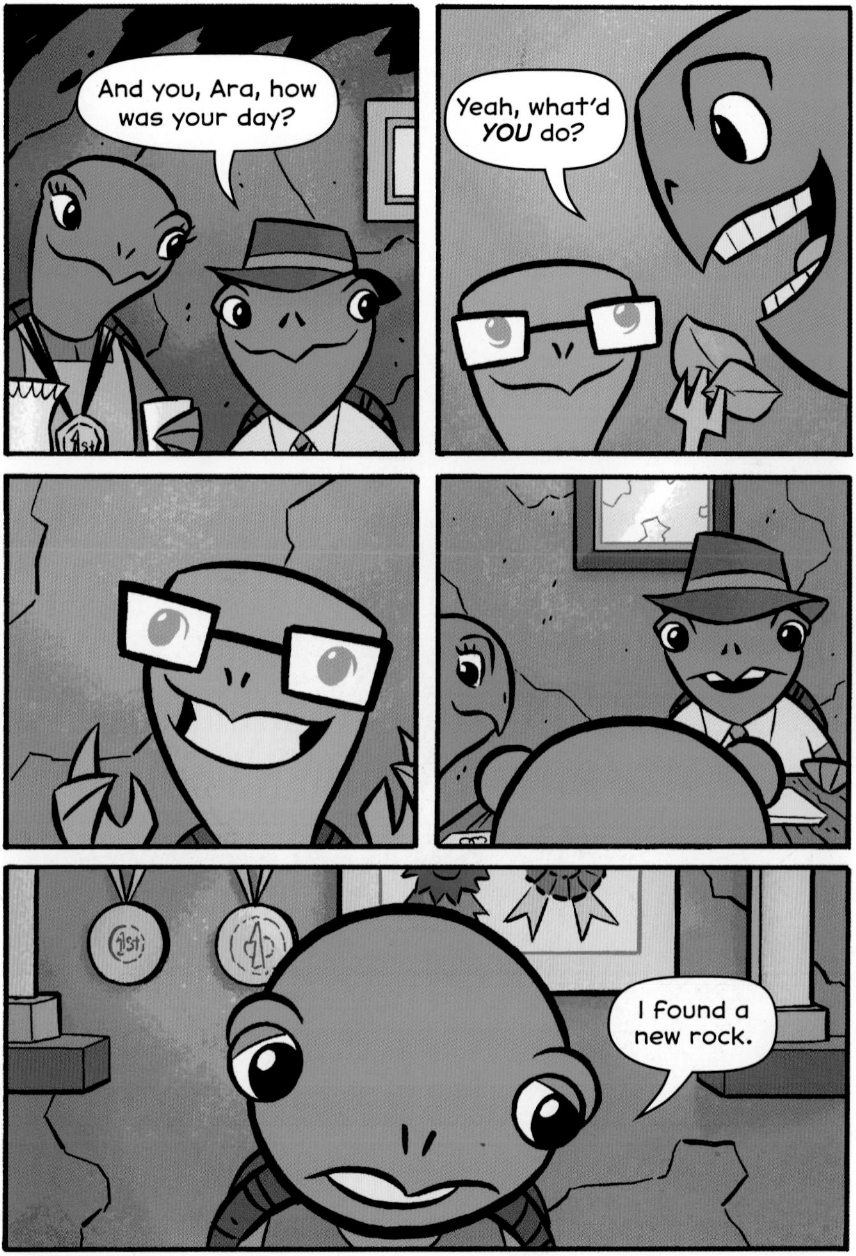
And you, Ara, how was your day?
Yeah, what'd *YOU* do?
I found a new rock.

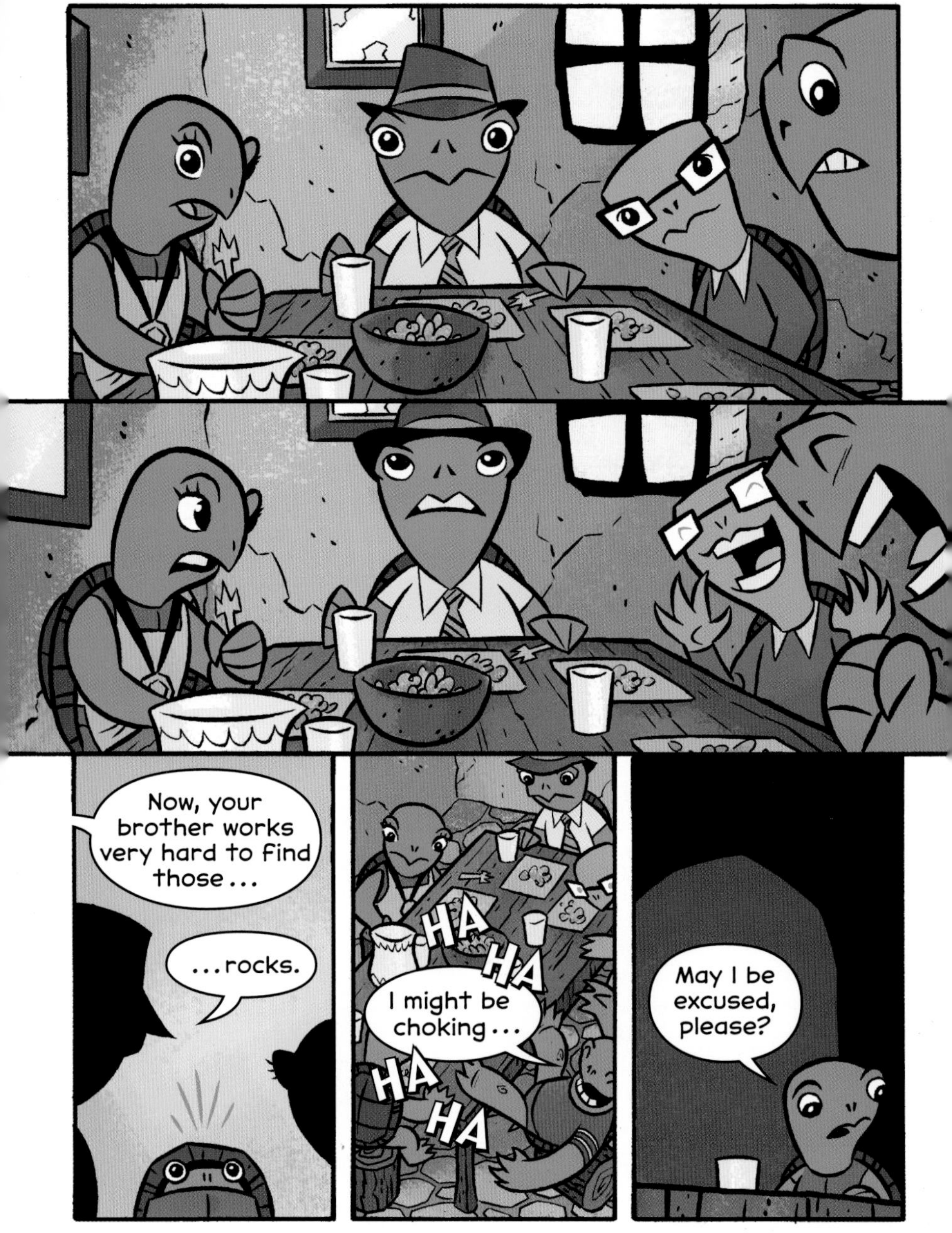
Now, your brother works very hard to find those...
...rocks.
HA
HA
I might be choking...
HA
HA
May I be excused, please?

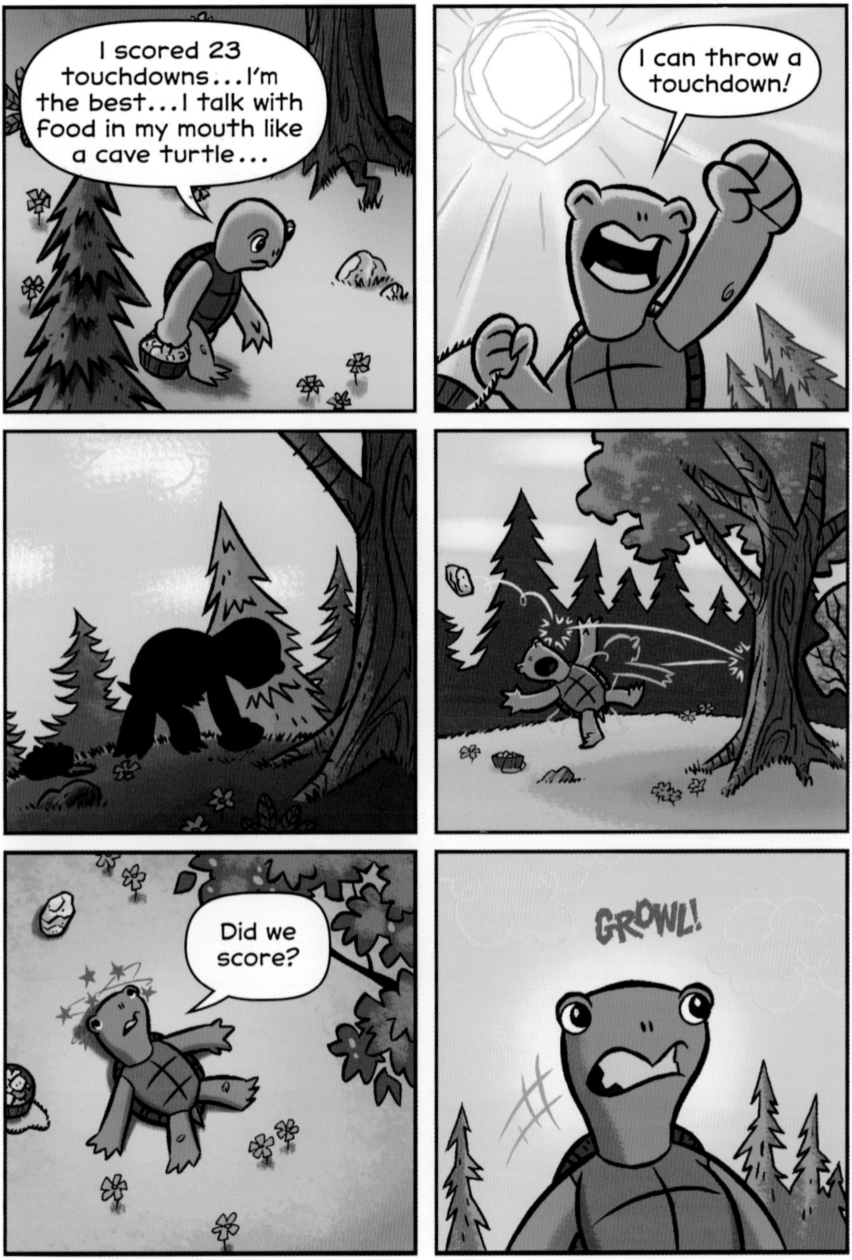
I scored 23 touchdowns...I'm the best...I talk with food in my mouth like a cave turtle...
I can throw a touchdown!
Did we score?
GROWL!

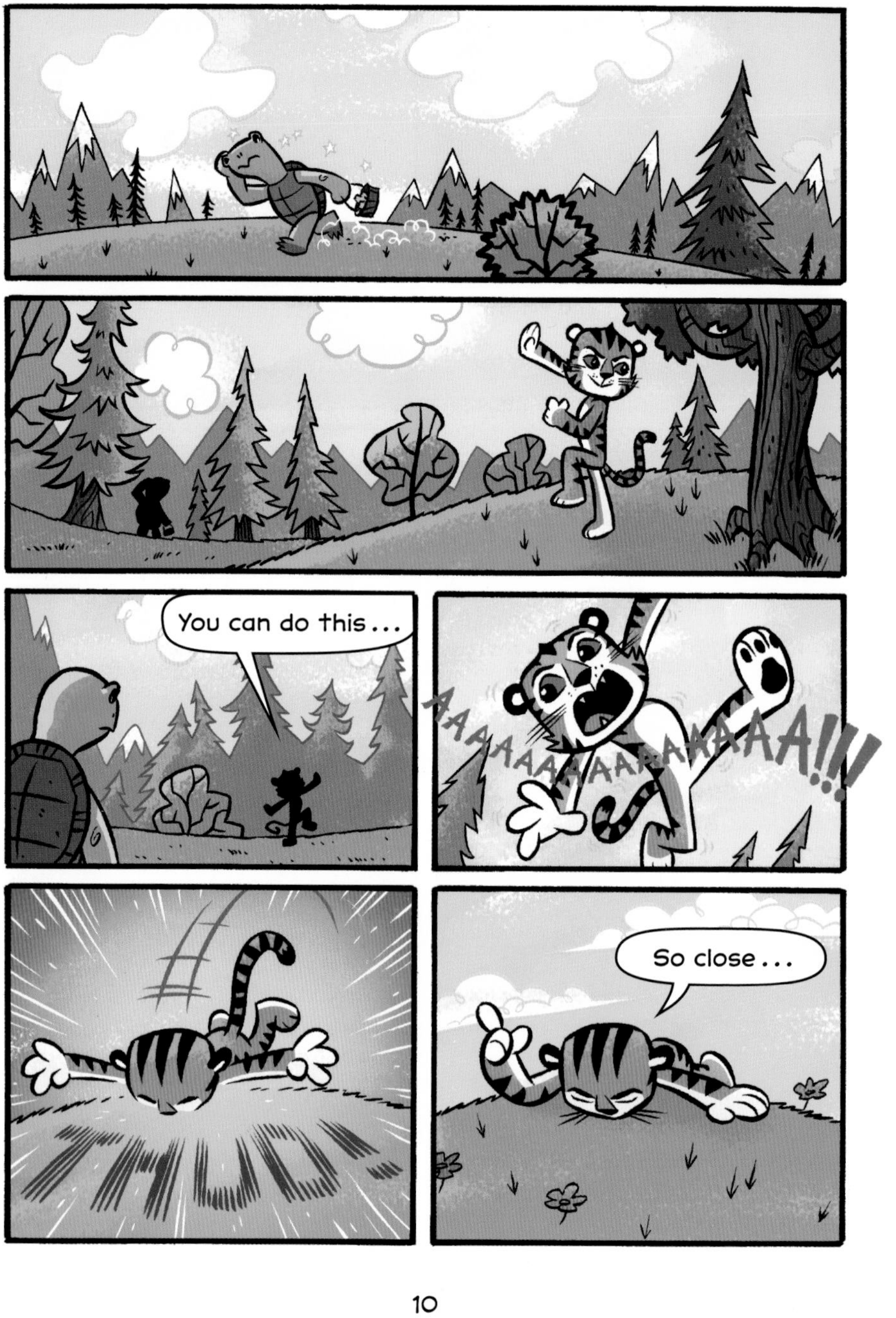
You can do this...
AAAAAAAAAAAAAAA!!!
THUD!
So close...

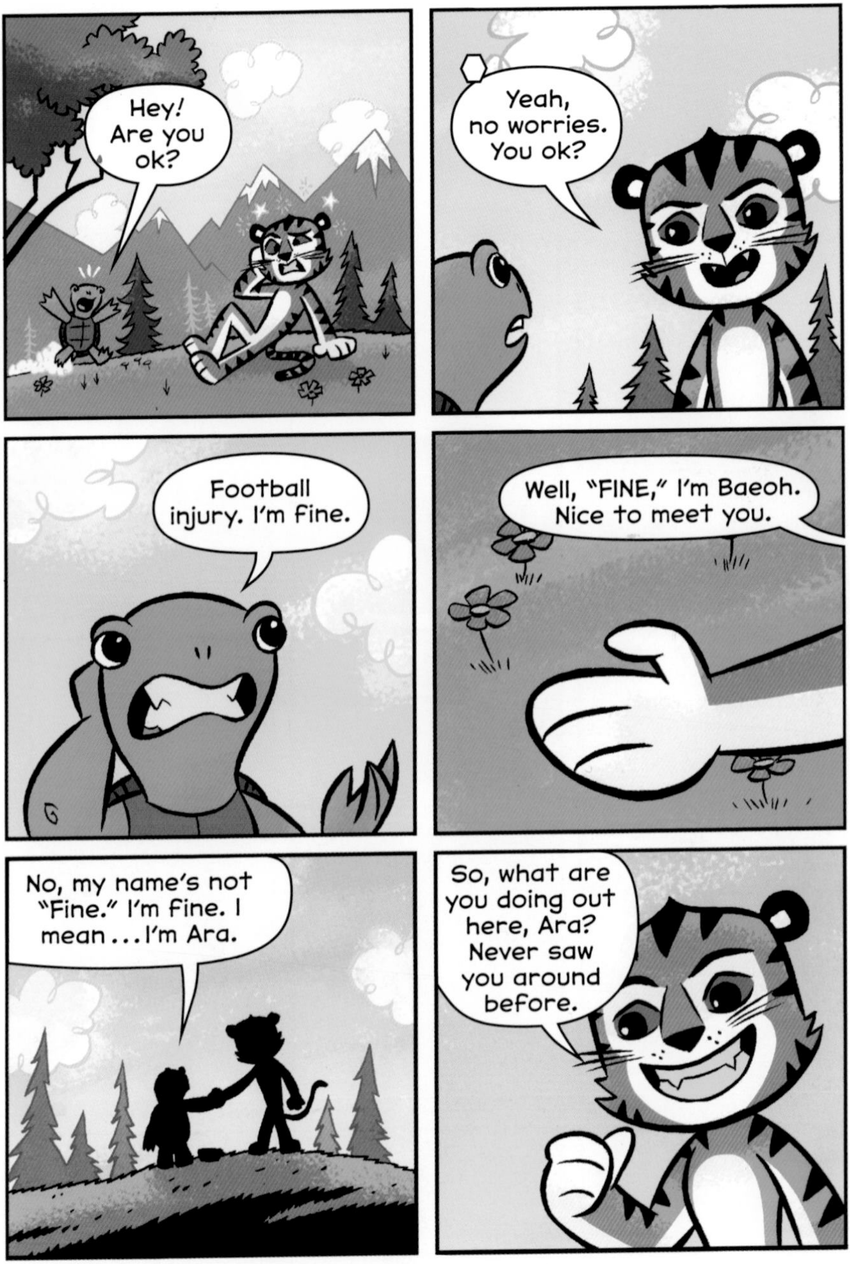
Hey! Are you ok?
Yeah, no worries. You ok?
Football injury. I'm fine.
Well, "FINE," I'm Baeoh. Nice to meet you.
No, my name's not "Fine." I'm fine. I mean . . . I'm Ara.
So, what are you doing out here, Ara? Never saw you around before.

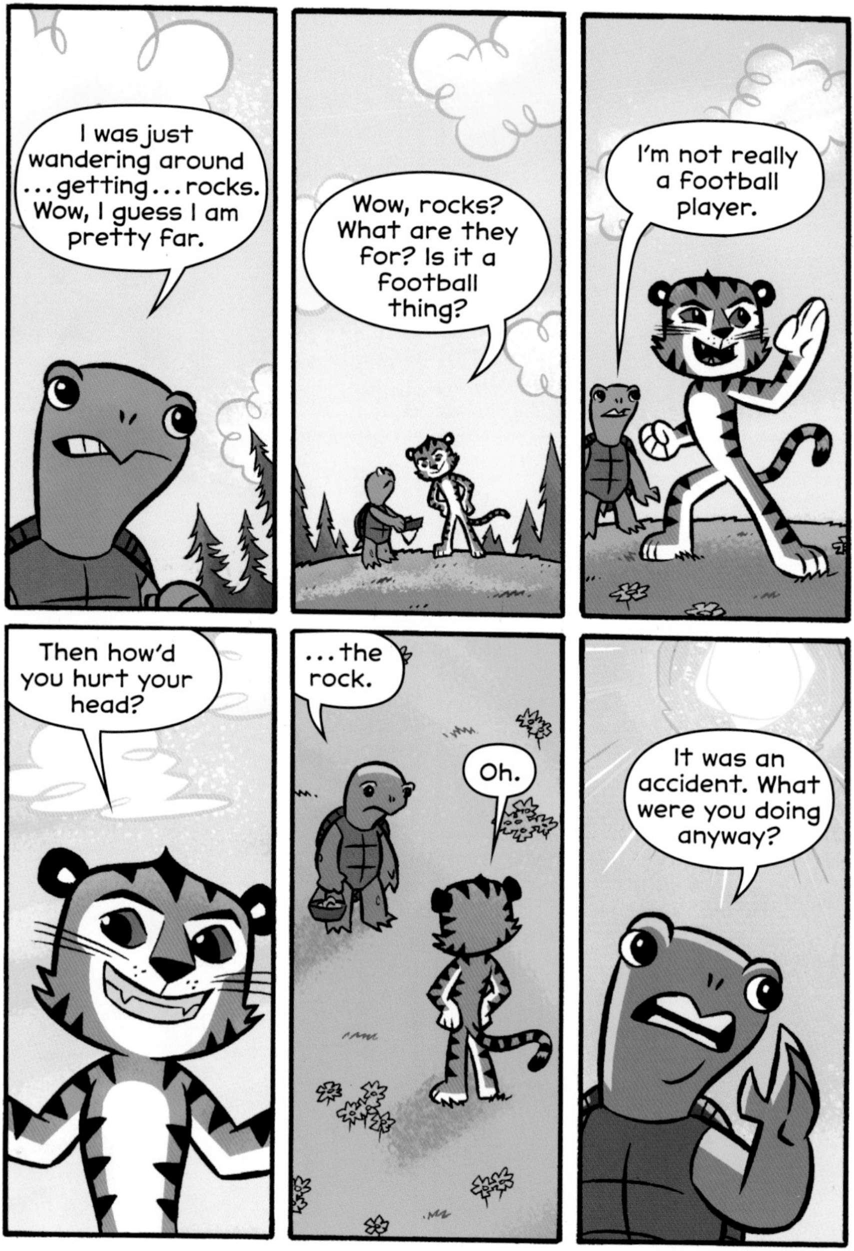
I was just wandering around ...getting...rocks. Wow, I guess I am pretty far.
Wow, rocks? What are they for? Is it a football thing?
I'm not really a football player.
Then how'd you hurt your head?
...the rock.
Oh.
It was an accident. What were you doing anyway?

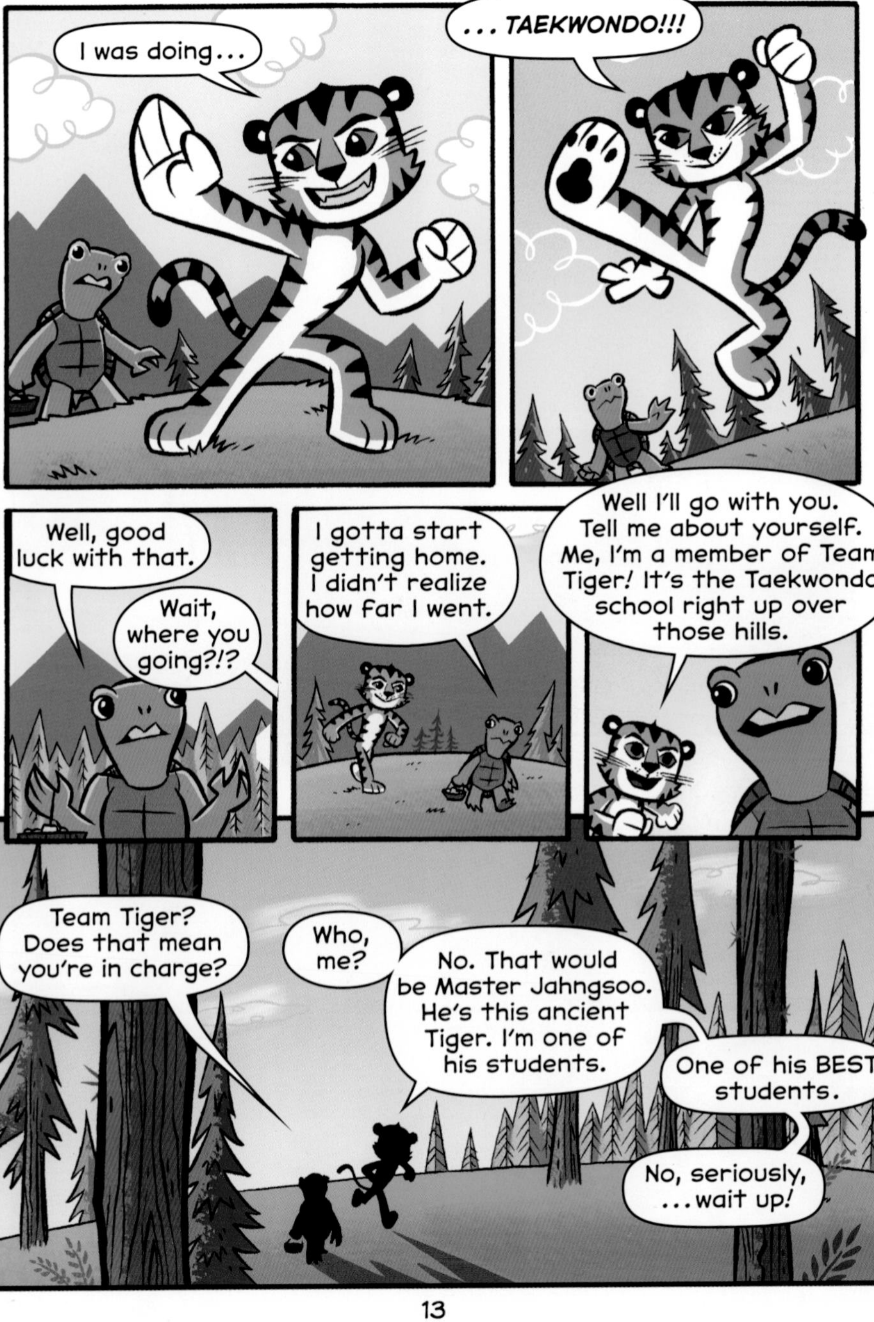

I was doing...
...TAEKWONDO!!!
Well, good luck with that.
Wait, where you going?!?
I gotta start getting home. I didn't realize how far I went.
Well I'll go with you. Tell me about yourself. Me, I'm a member of Team Tiger! It's the Taekwondo school right up over those hills.
Team Tiger? Does that mean you're in charge?
Who, me?
No. That would be Master Jahngsoo. He's this ancient Tiger. I'm one of his students.
One of his BEST students.
No, seriously, ...wait up!

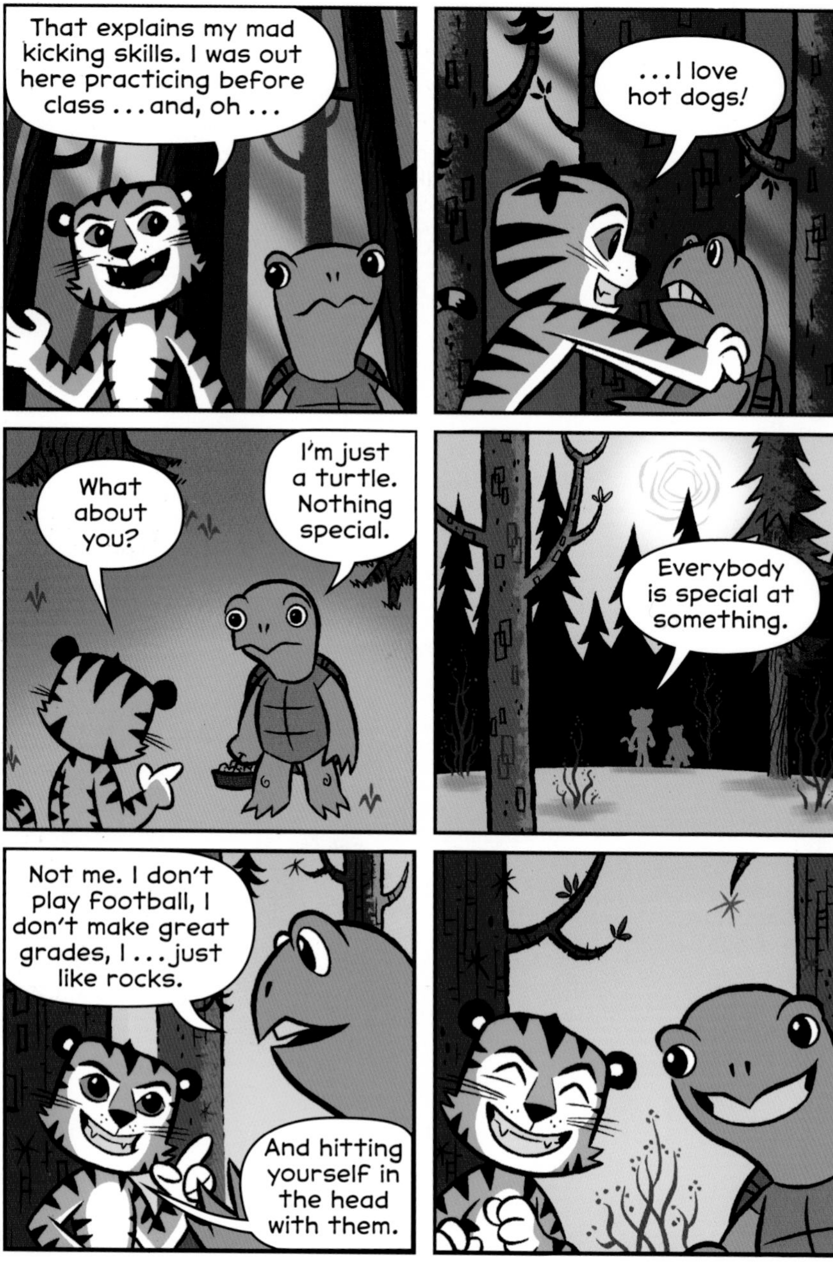
That explains my mad kicking skills. I was out here practicing before class . . . and, oh . . .
. . . I love hot dogs!
What about you?
I'm just a turtle. Nothing special.
Everybody is special at something.
Not me. I don't play football, I don't make great grades, I . . . just like rocks.
And hitting yourself in the head with them.

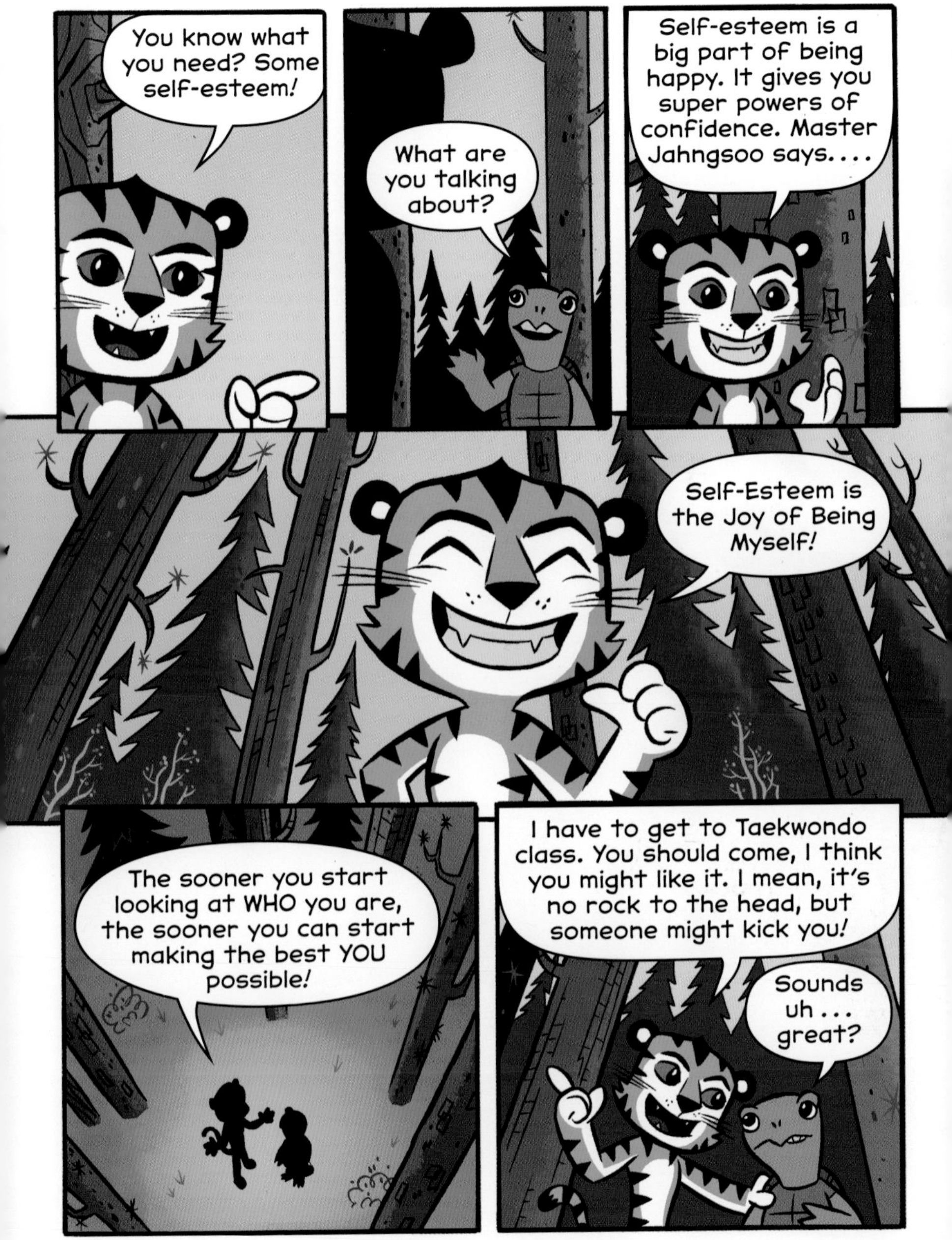
You know what you need? Some self-esteem!
What are you talking about?
Self-esteem is a big part of being happy. It gives you super powers of confidence. Master Jahngsoo says. . . .
Self-Esteem is the Joy of Being Myself!
The sooner you start looking at WHO you are, the sooner you can start making the best YOU possible!
I have to get to Taekwondo class. You should come, I think you might like it. I mean, it's no rock to the head, but someone might kick you!
Sounds uh . . . great?

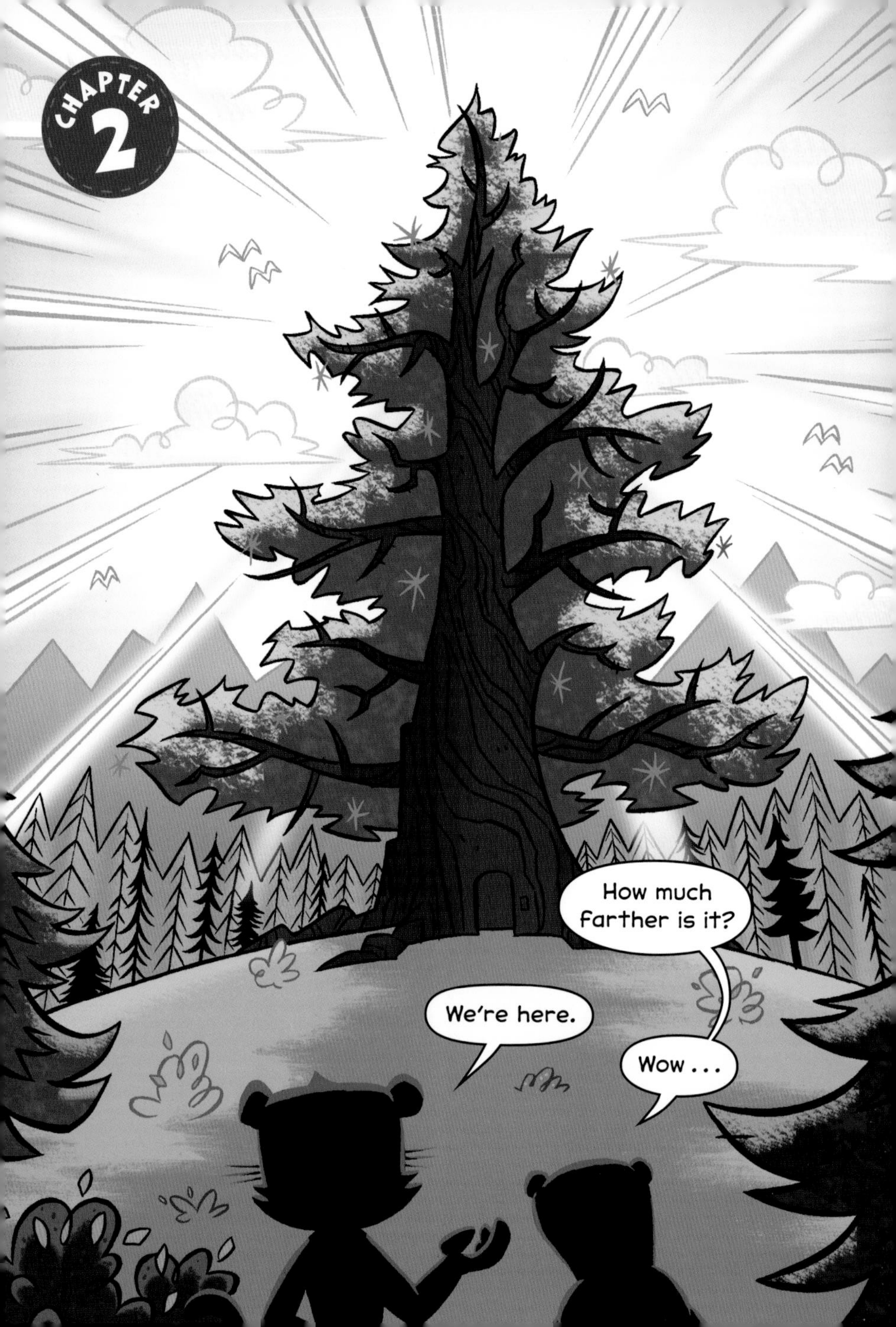
CHAPTER 2
How much farther is it?
We're here.
Wow . . .

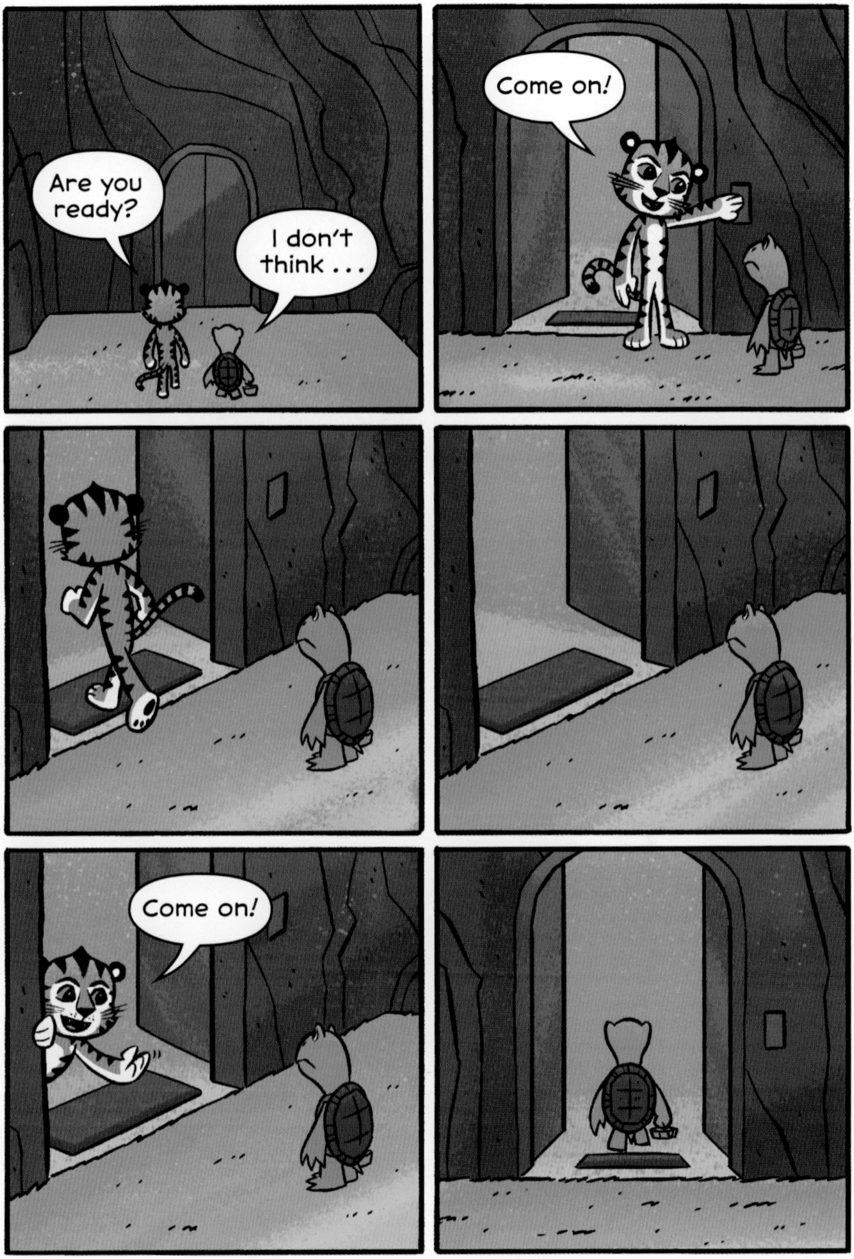
Are you ready?
I don't think . . .
Come on!
Come on!

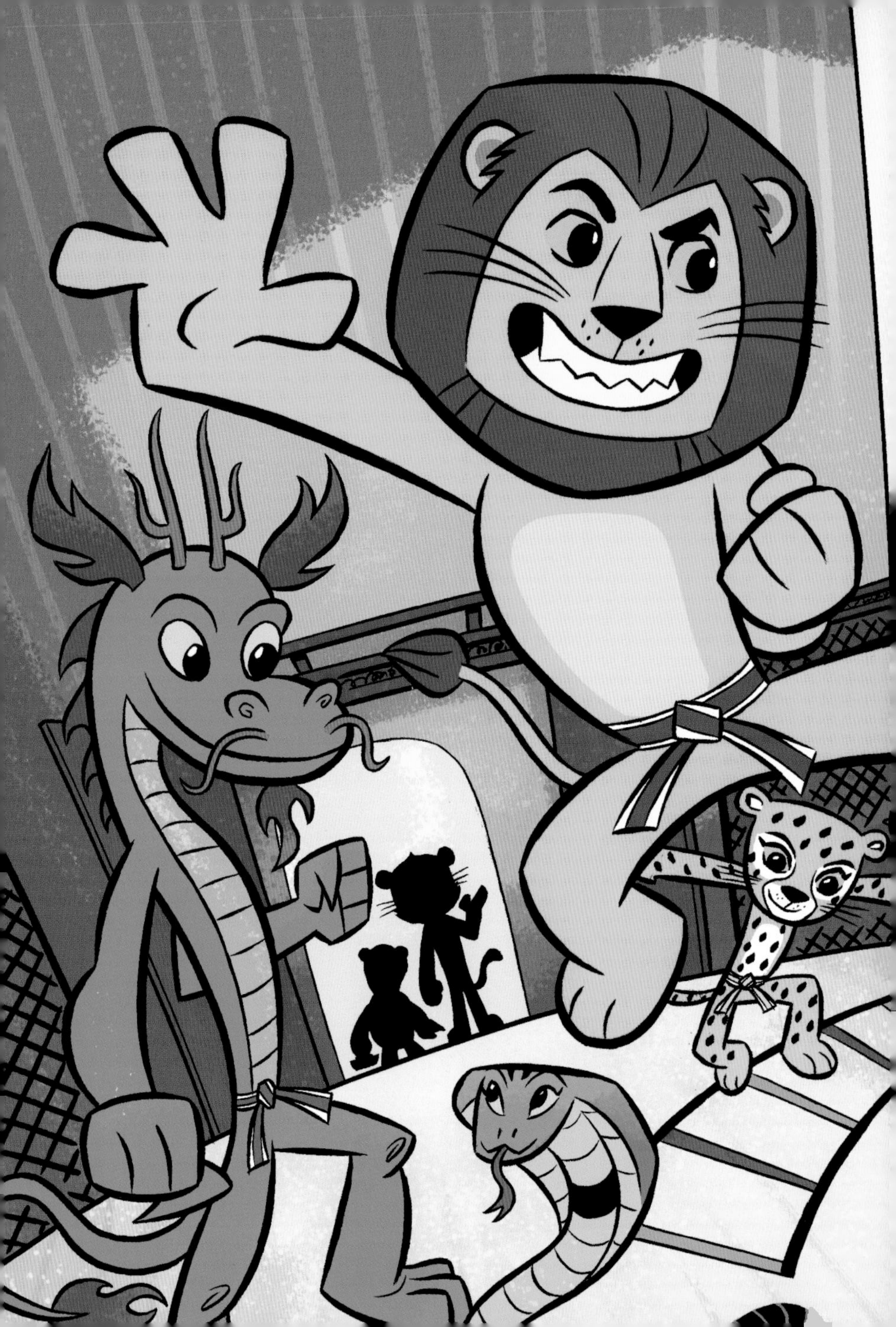

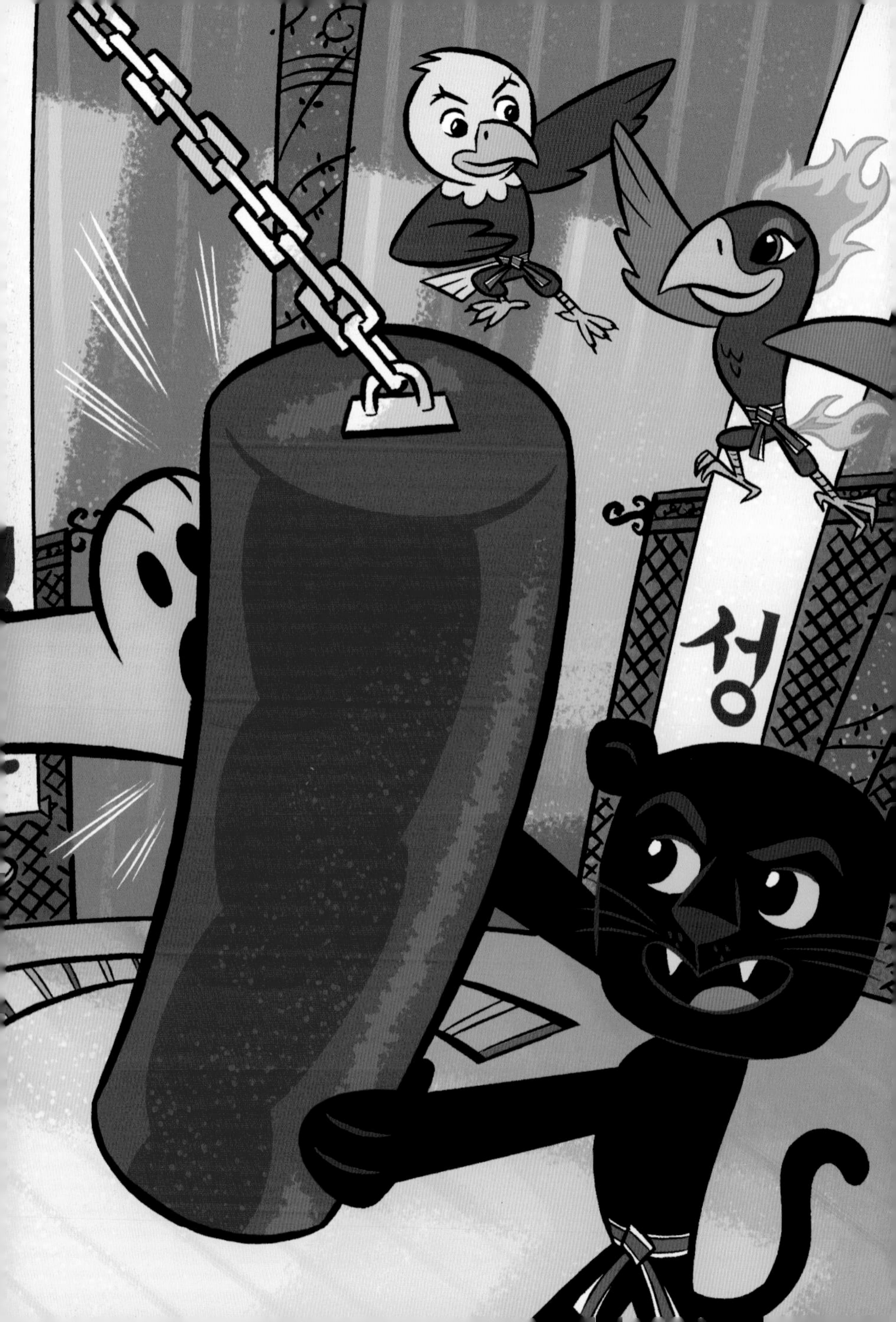
성

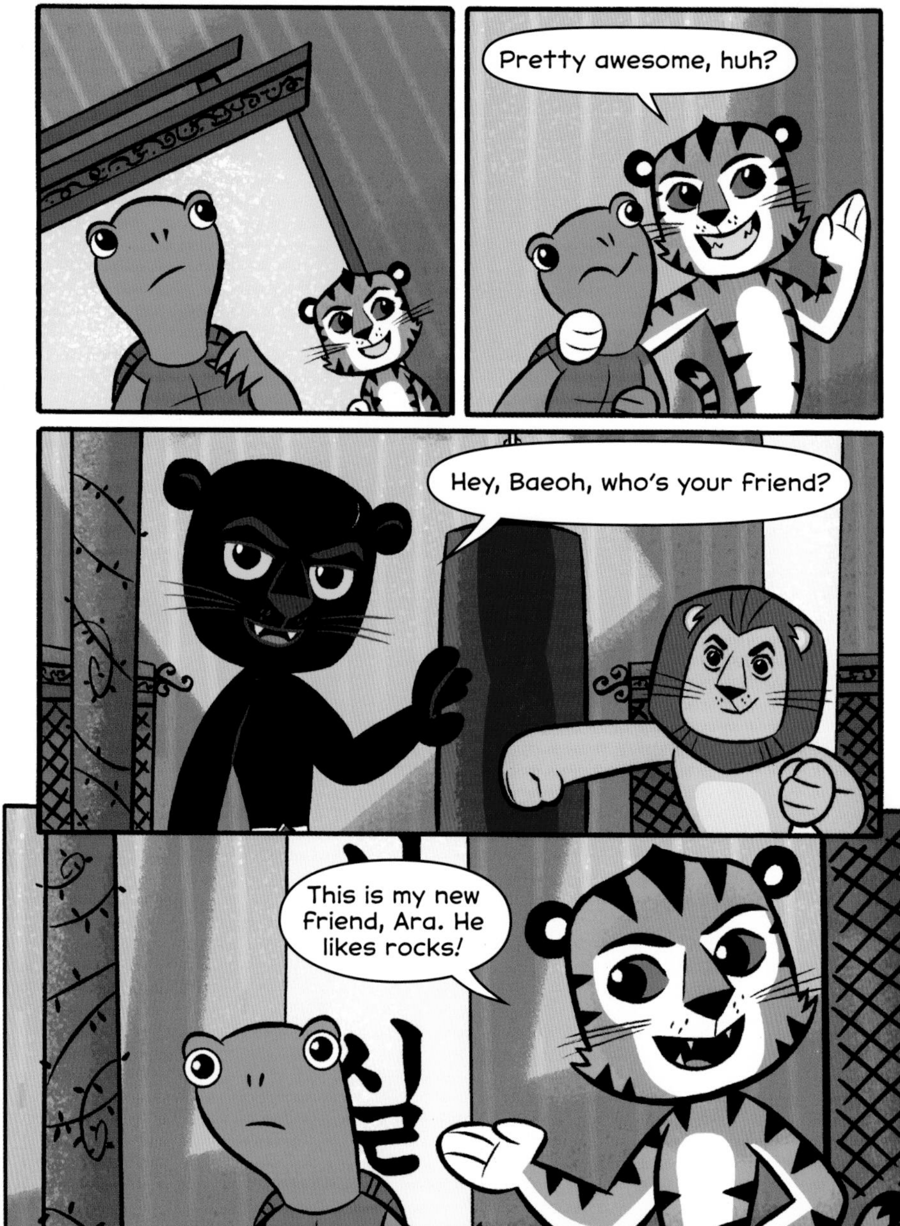
Pretty awesome, huh?
Hey, Baeoh, who's your friend?
This is my new friend, Ara. He likes rocks!

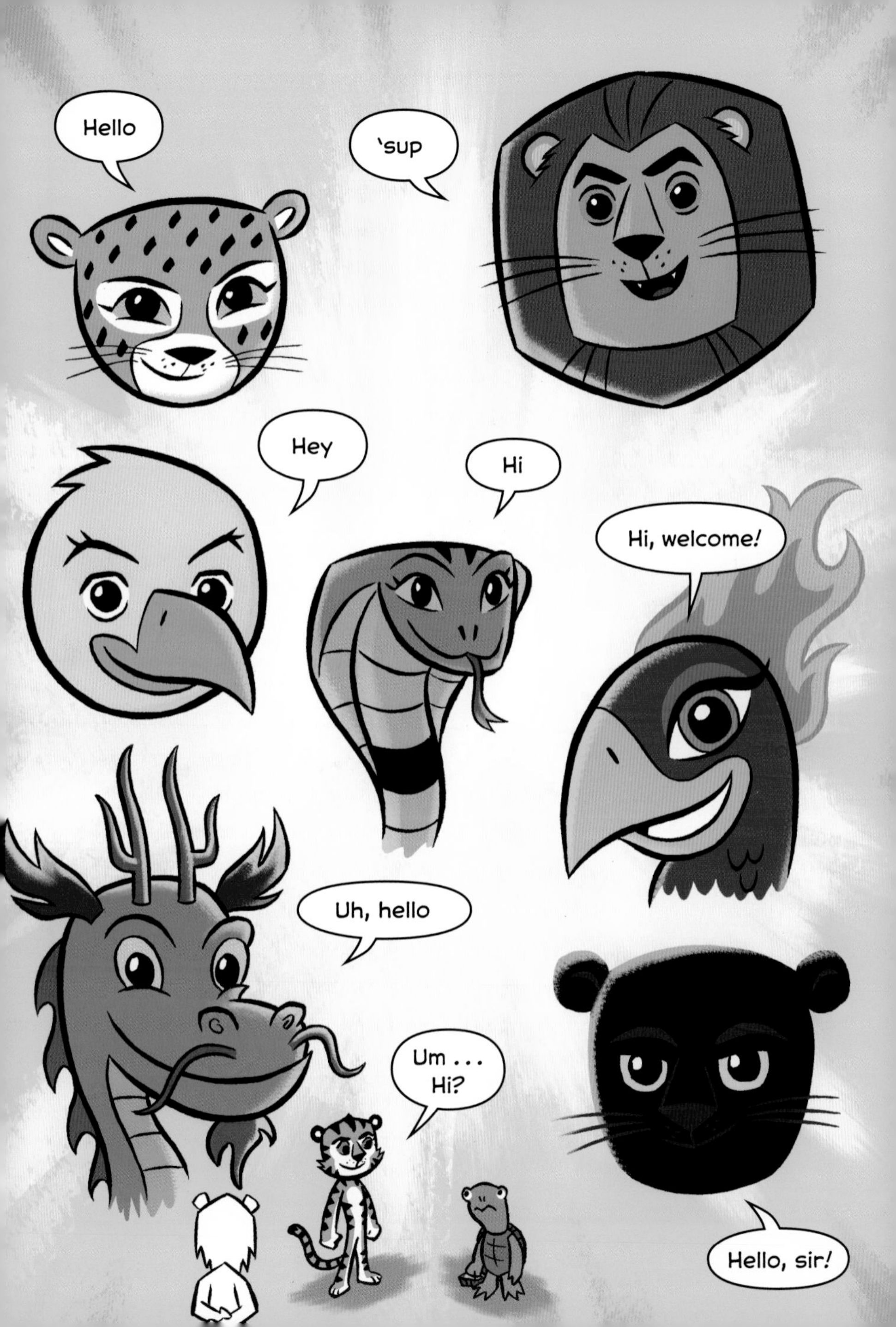
Hello
'sup
Hey
Hi
Hi, welcome!
Uh, hello
Um . . . Hi?
Hello, sir!

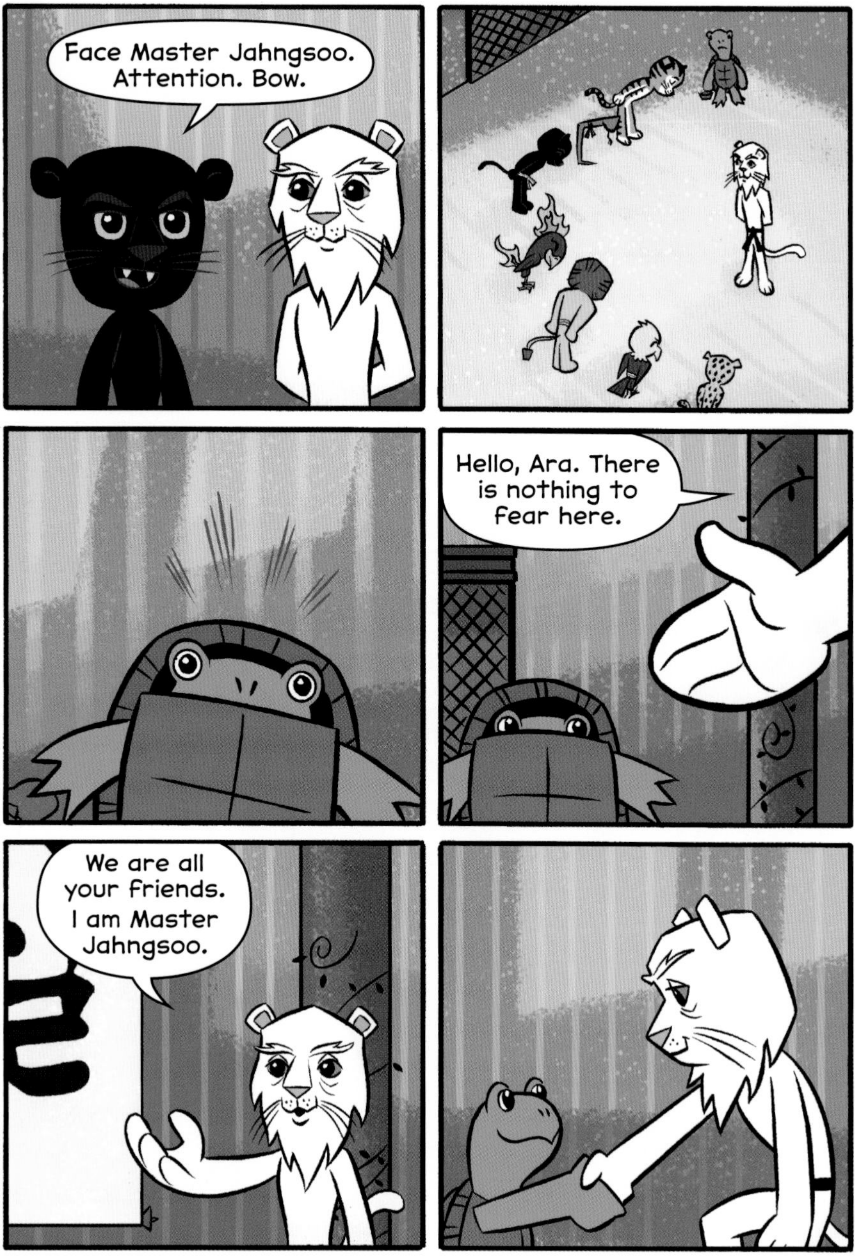
Face Master Jahngsoo. Attention. Bow.
Hello, Ara. There is nothing to fear here.
We are all your friends. I am Master Jahngsoo.

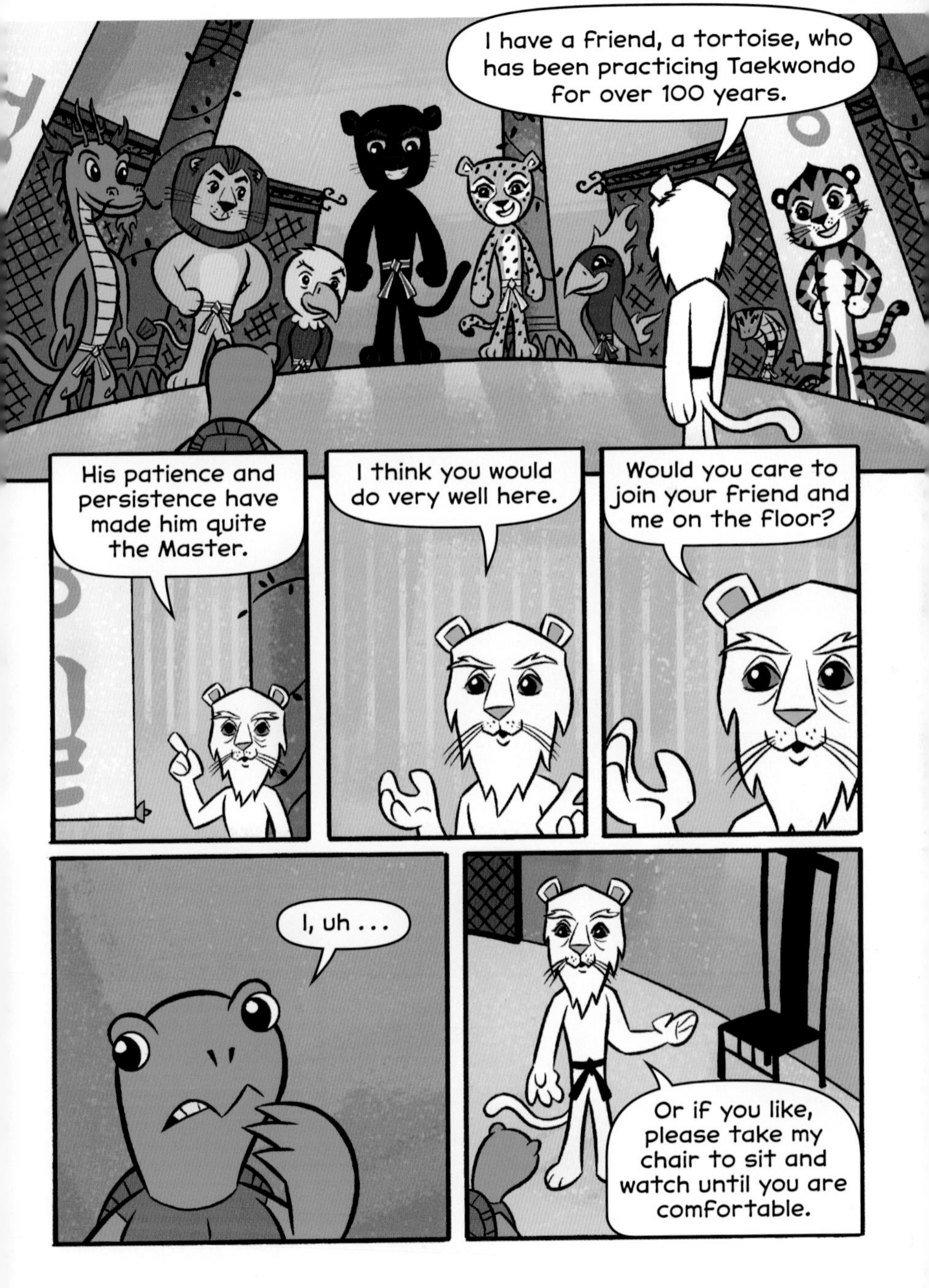
I have a friend, a tortoise, who has been practicing Taekwondo for over 100 years.
His patience and persistence have made him quite the Master.
I think you would do very well here.
Would you care to join your friend and me on the floor?
I, uh . . .
Or if you like, please take my chair to sit and watch until you are comfortable.

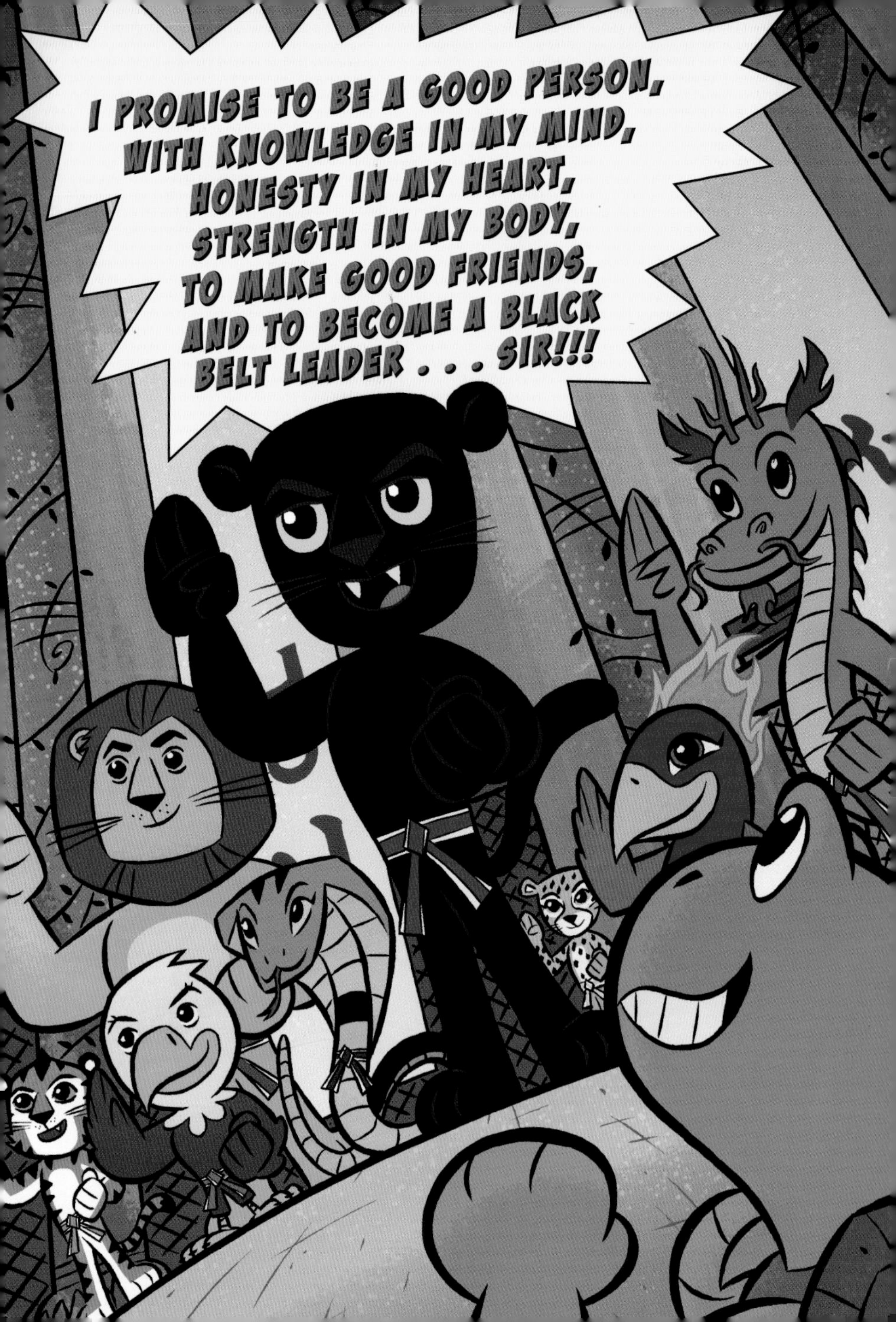
I PROMISE TO BE A GOOD PERSON, WITH KNOWLEDGE IN MY MIND, HONESTY IN MY HEART, STRENGTH IN MY BODY, TO MAKE GOOD FRIENDS, AND TO BECOME A BLACK BELT LEADER . . . SIR!!!

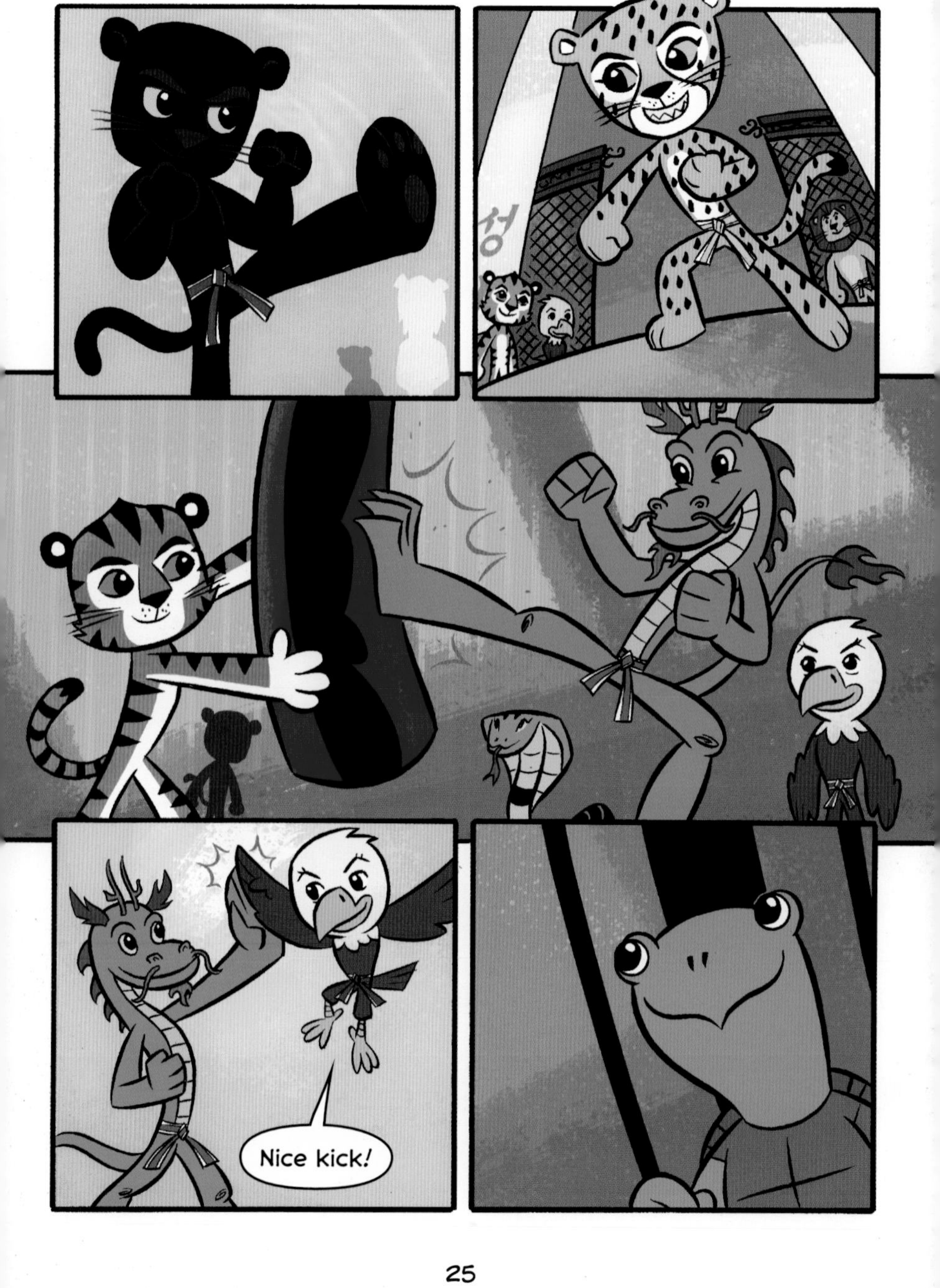
성
Nice kick!

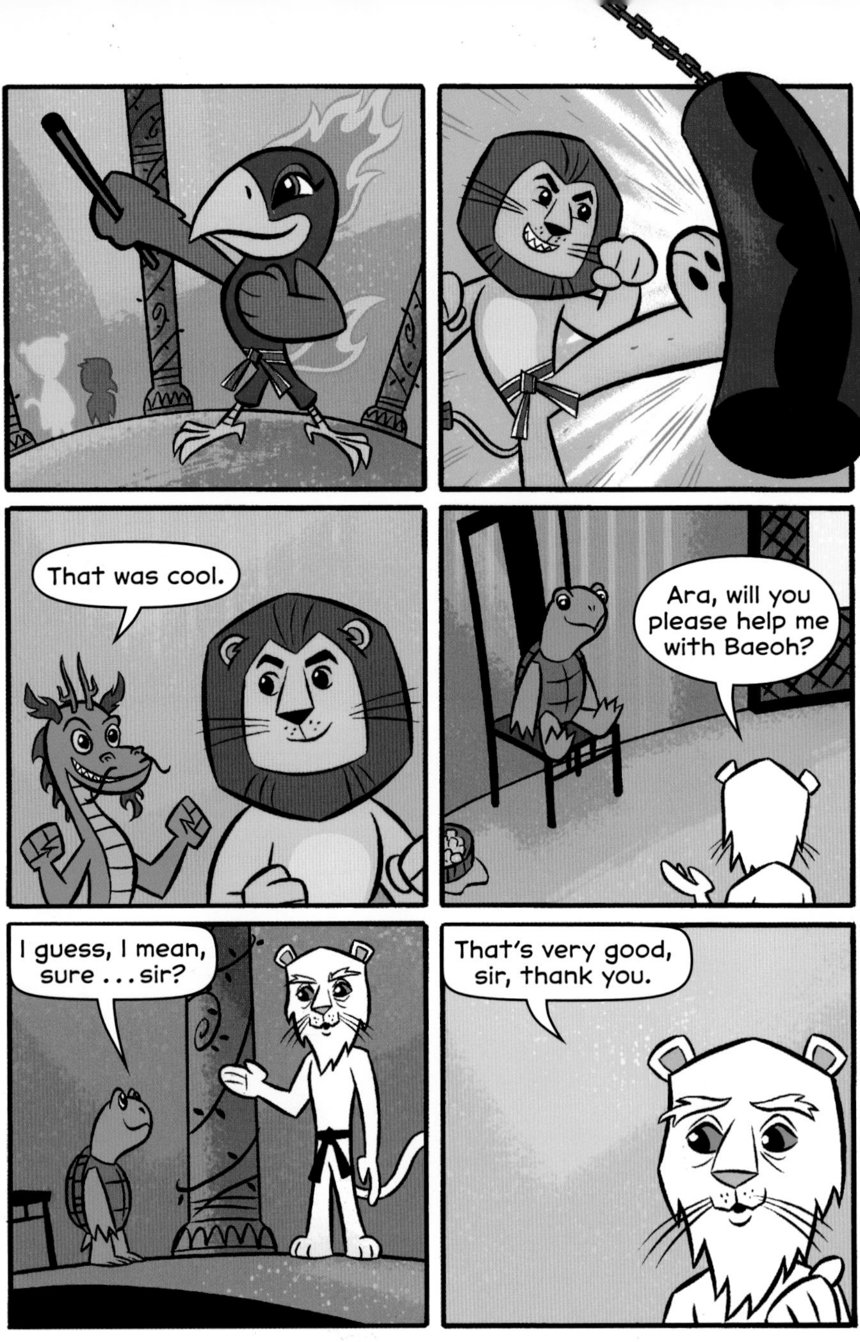
That was cool.
Ara, will you please help me with Baeoh?
I guess, I mean, sure . . . sir?
That's very good, sir, thank you.

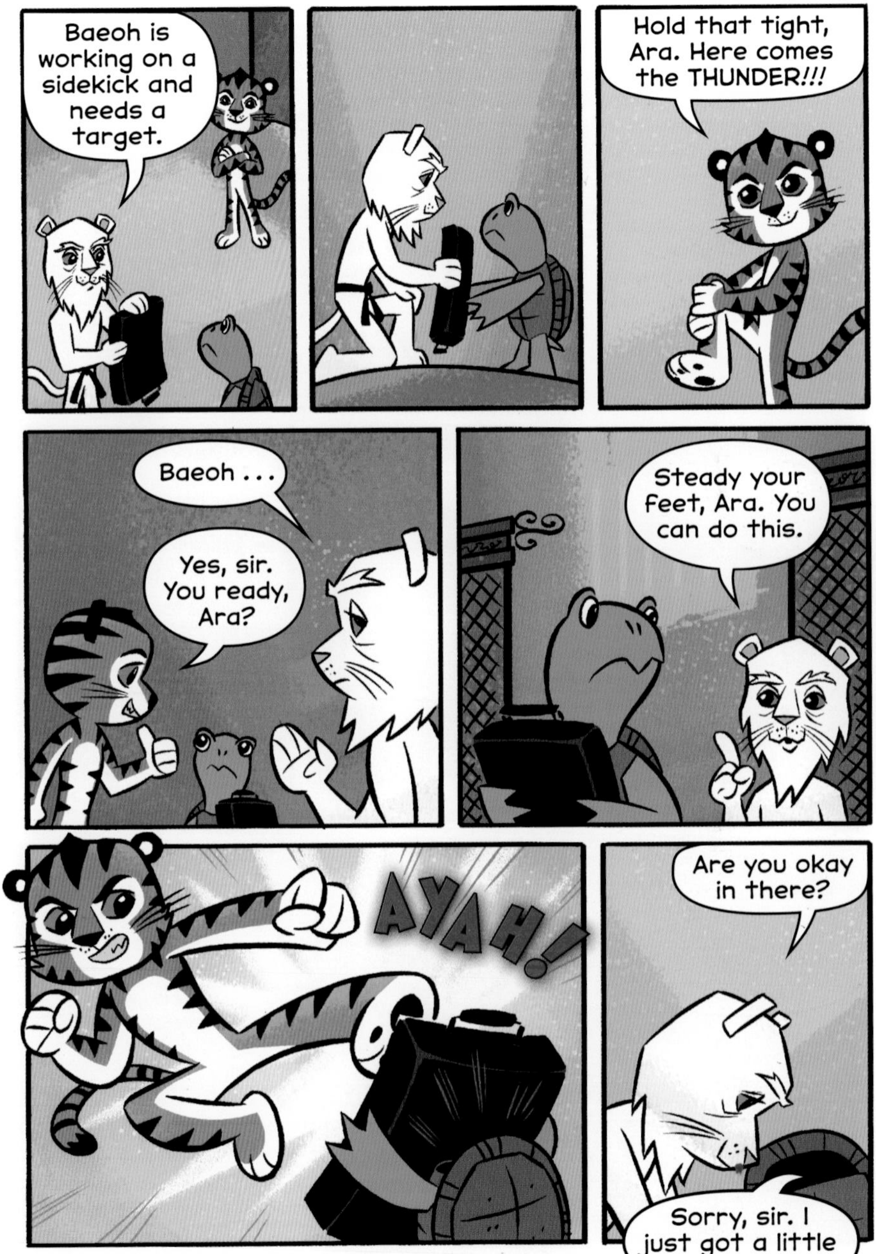
Baeoh is working on a sidekick and needs a target.
Hold that tight, Ara. Here comes the THUNDER!!!
Baeoh . . .
Yes, sir. You ready, Ara?
Steady your feet, Ara. You can do this.
AYAH!
Are you okay in there?
Sorry, sir. I just got a little scared.

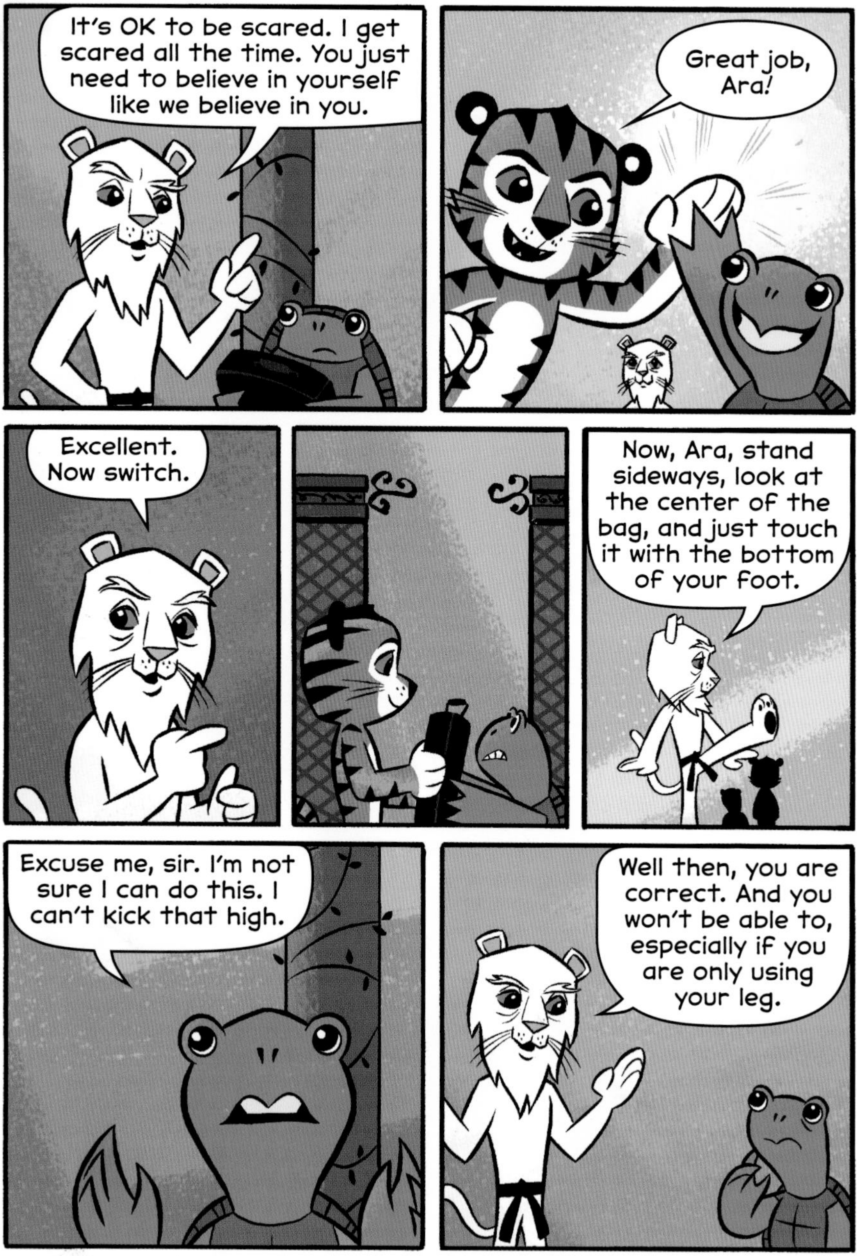
It's OK to be scared. I get scared all the time. You just need to believe in yourself like we believe in you.
Great job, Ara!
Excellent. Now switch.
Now, Ara, stand sideways, look at the center of the bag, and just touch it with the bottom of your foot.
Excuse me, sir. I'm not sure I can do this. I can't kick that high.
Well then, you are correct. And you won't be able to, especially if you are only using your leg.

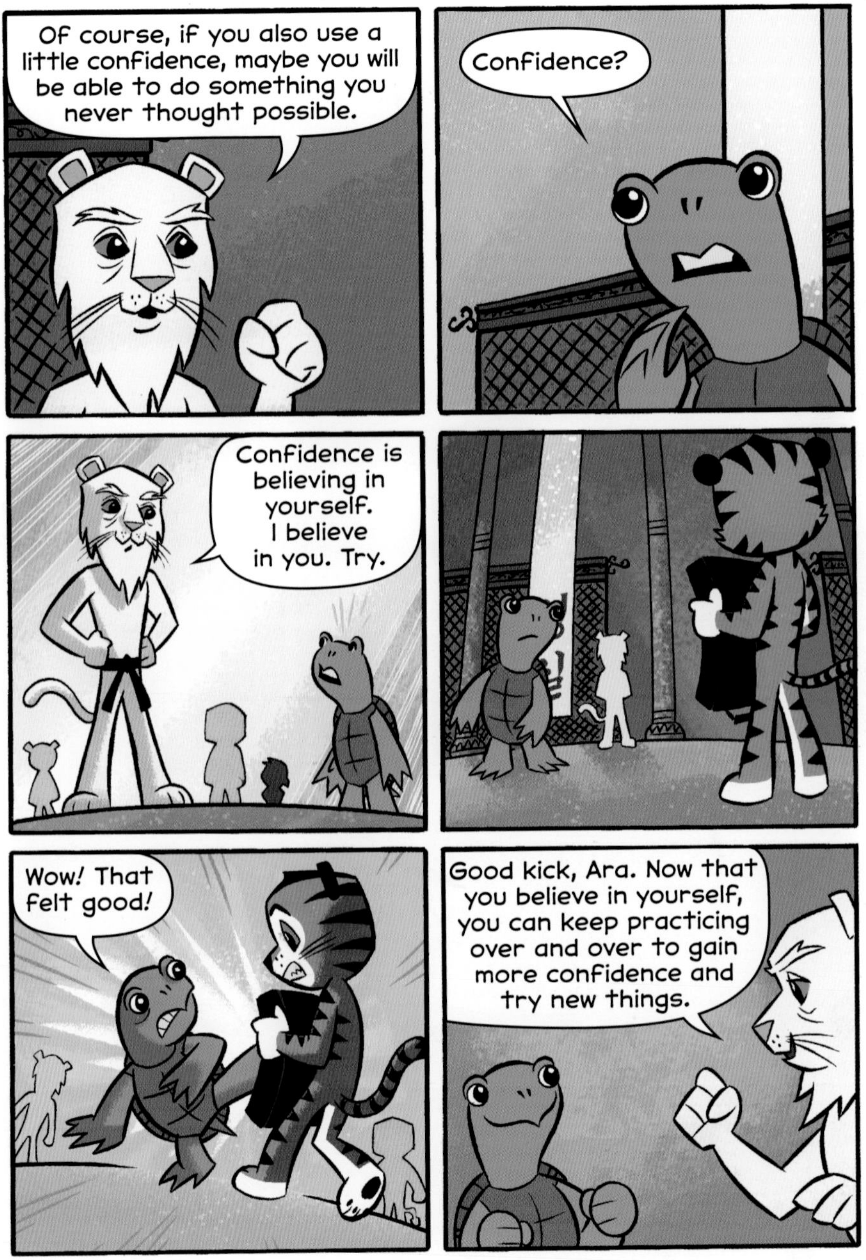
Of course, if you also use a little confidence, maybe you will be able to do something you never thought possible.
Confidence?
Confidence is believing in yourself. I believe in you. Try.
Wow! That felt good!
Good kick, Ara. Now that you believe in yourself, you can keep practicing over and over to gain more confidence and try new things.

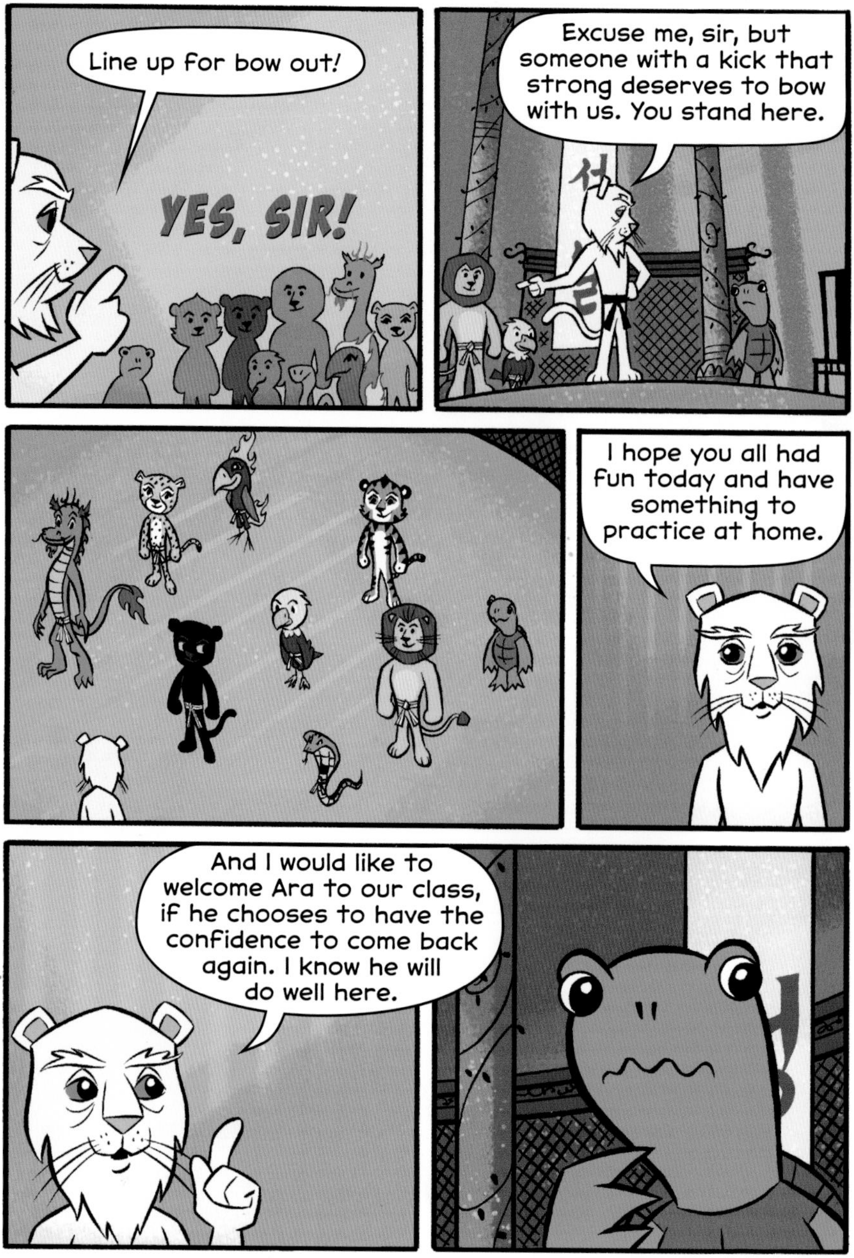
Line up for bow out!
YES, SIR!
Excuse me, sir, but someone with a kick that strong deserves to bow with us. You stand here.
I hope you all had fun today and have something to practice at home.
And I would like to welcome Ara to our class, if he chooses to have the confidence to come back again. I know he will do well here.

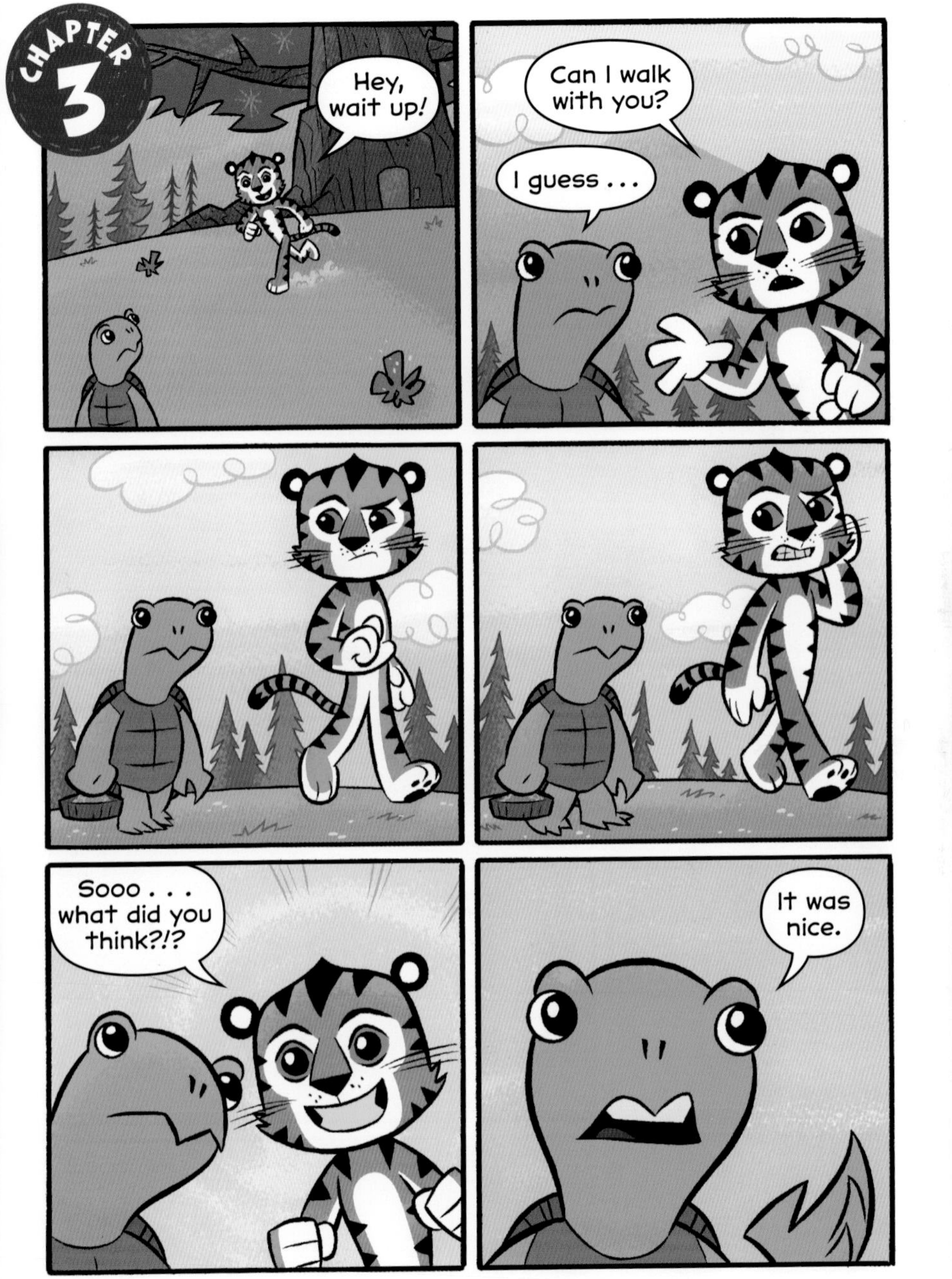
CHAPTER 3
Hey, wait up!
Can I walk with you?
I guess . . .
Sooo . . . what did you think?!?
It was nice.

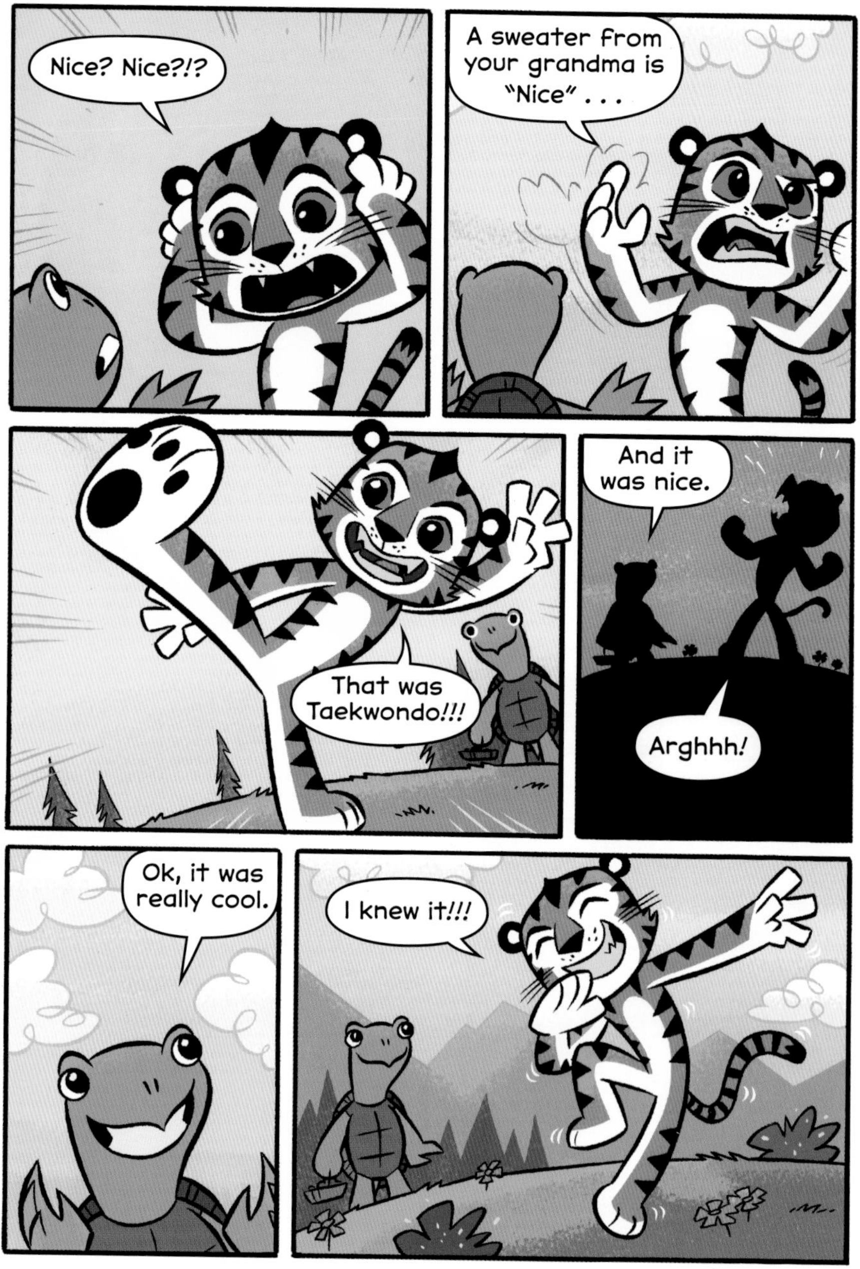
Nice? Nice?!?
A sweater from your grandma is "Nice" . . .
That was Taekwondo!!!
And it was nice.
Arghhh!
Ok, it was really cool.
I knew it!!!

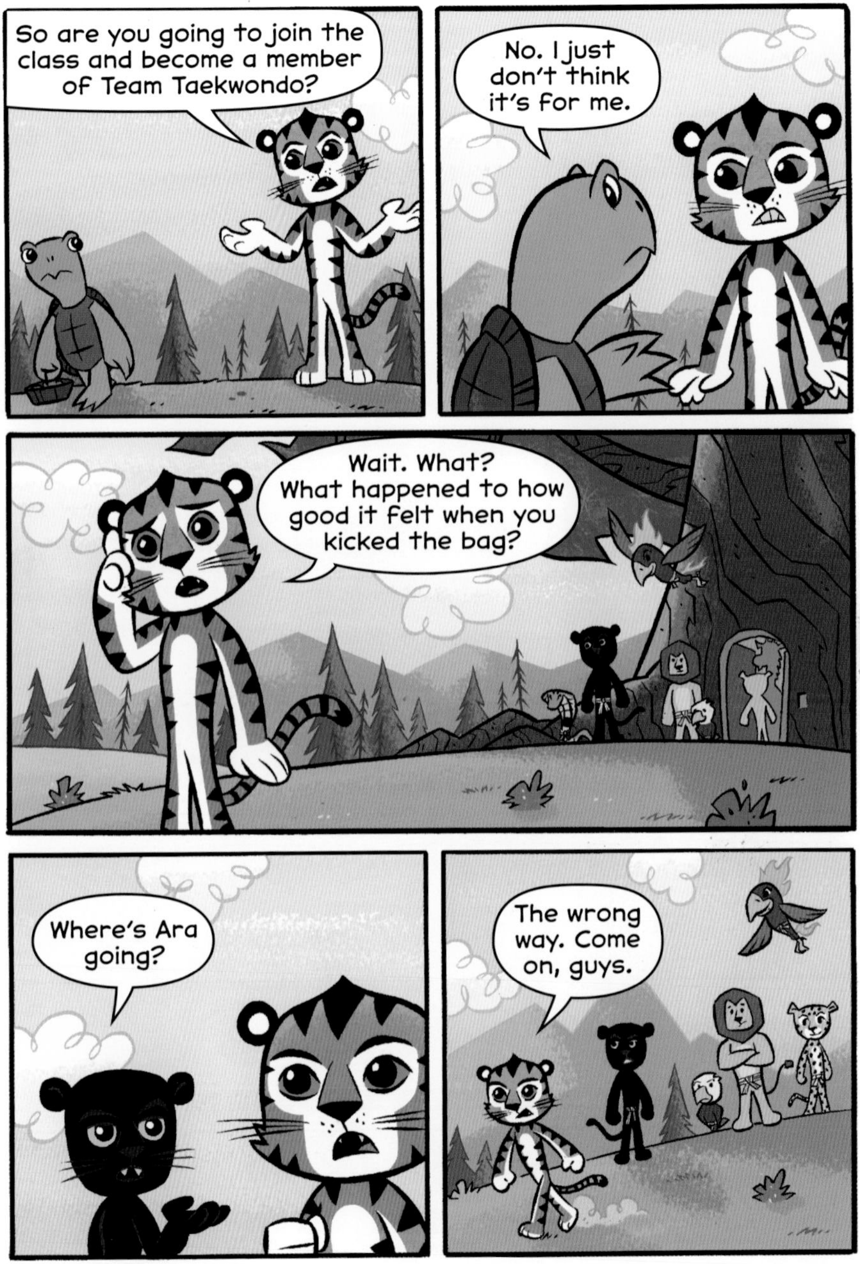
So are you going to join the class and become a member of Team Taekwondo?
No. I just don't think it's for me.
Wait. What? What happened to how good it felt when you kicked the bag?
Where's Ara going?
The wrong way. Come on, guys.

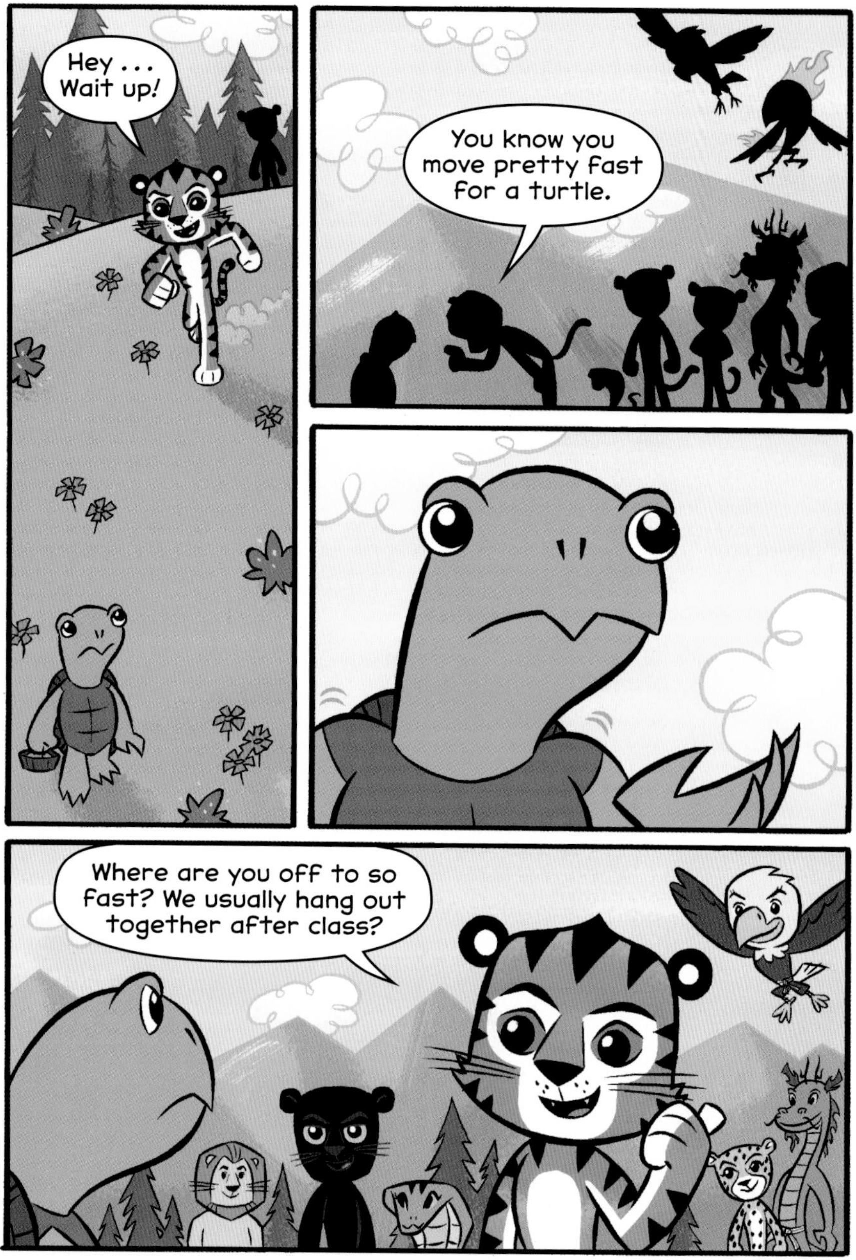
Hey . . . Wait up!
You know you move pretty fast for a turtle.
Where are you off to so fast? We usually hang out together after class?

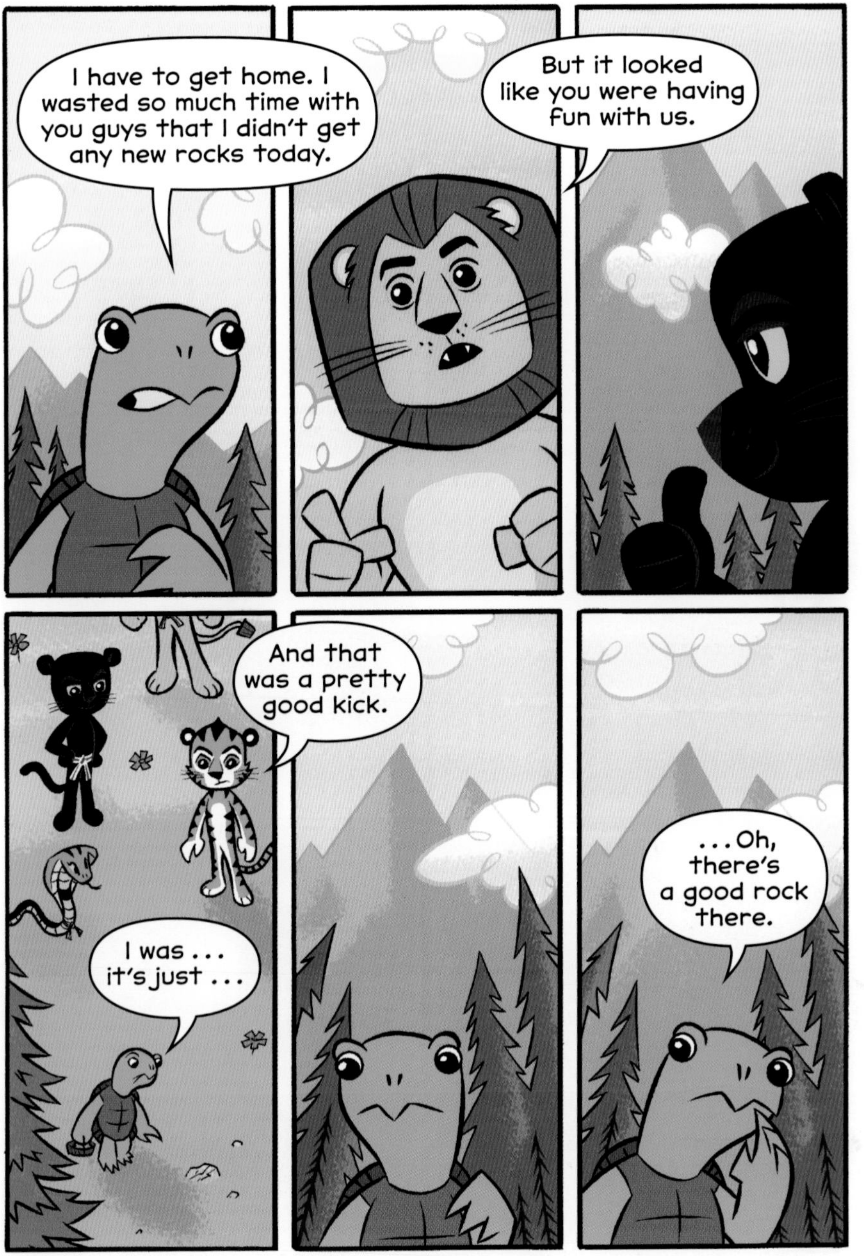
I have to get home. I wasted so much time with you guys that I didn't get any new rocks today.
But it looked like you were having fun with us.
And that was a pretty good kick.
I was . . . it's just . . .
. . . Oh, there's a good rock there.

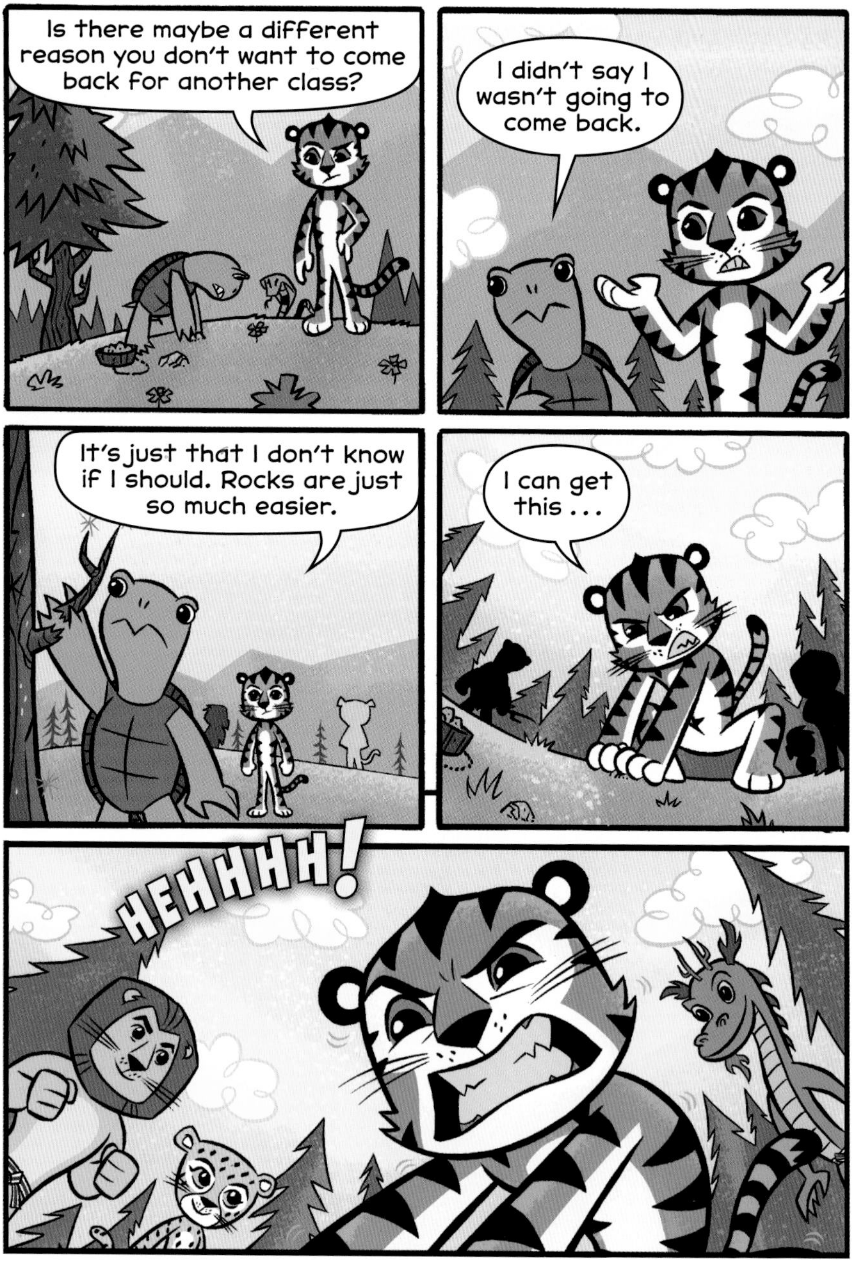
Is there maybe a different reason you don't want to come back for another class?
I didn't say I wasn't going to come back.
It's just that I don't know if I should. Rocks are just so much easier.
I can get this . . .
HEHHHHH!

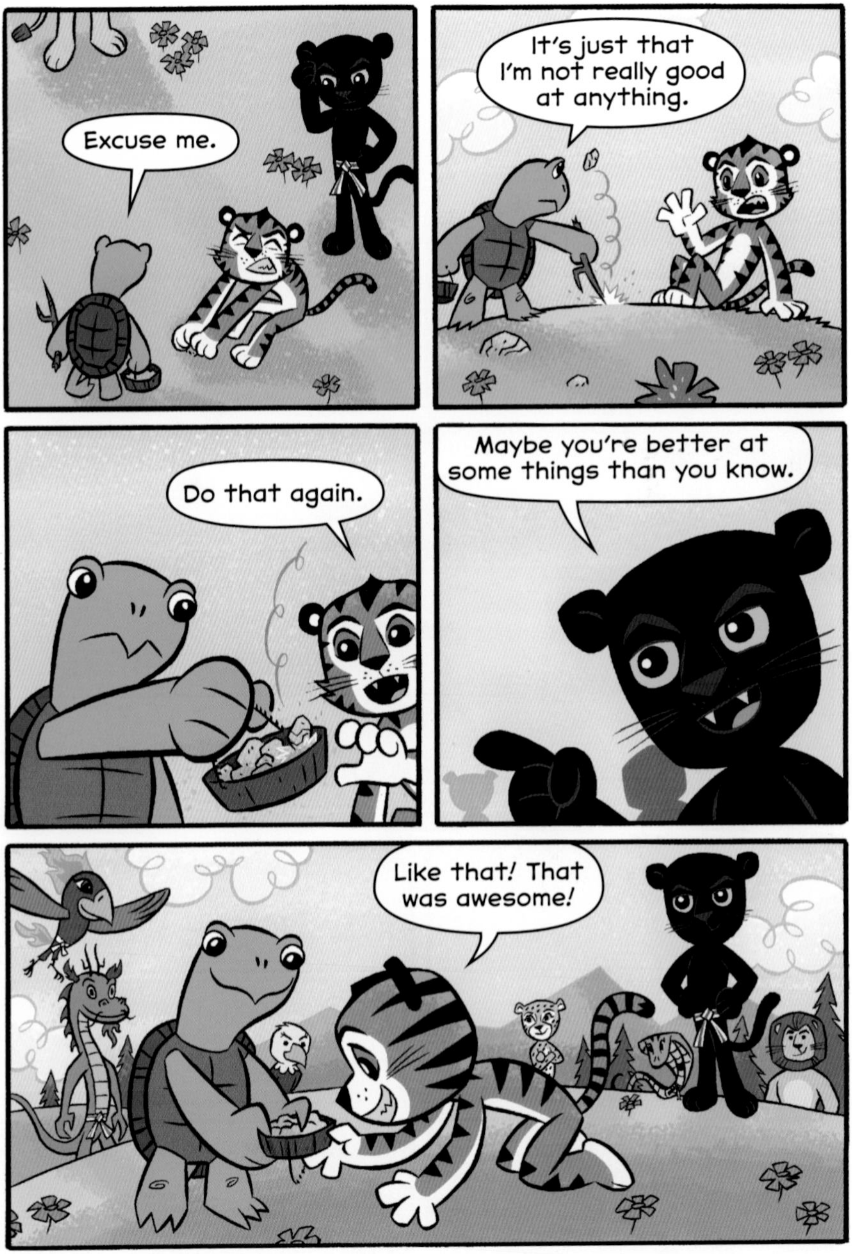
Excuse me.
It's just that I'm not really good at anything.
Do that again.
Maybe you're better at some things than you know.
Like that! That was awesome!

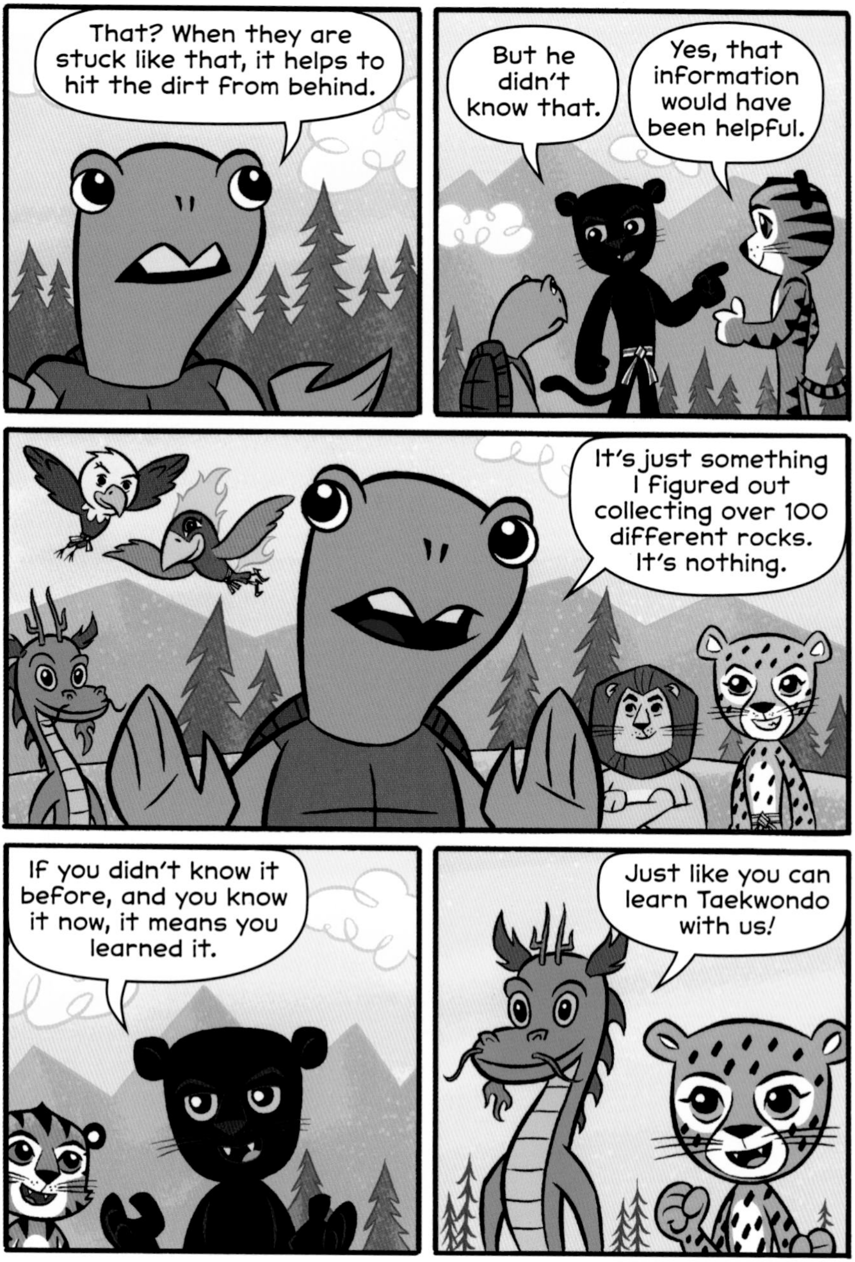
That? When they are stuck like that, it helps to hit the dirt from behind.
But he didn't know that.
Yes, that information would have been helpful.
It's just something I figured out collecting over 100 different rocks. It's nothing.
If you didn't know it before, and you know it now, it means you learned it.
Just like you can learn Taekwondo with us!

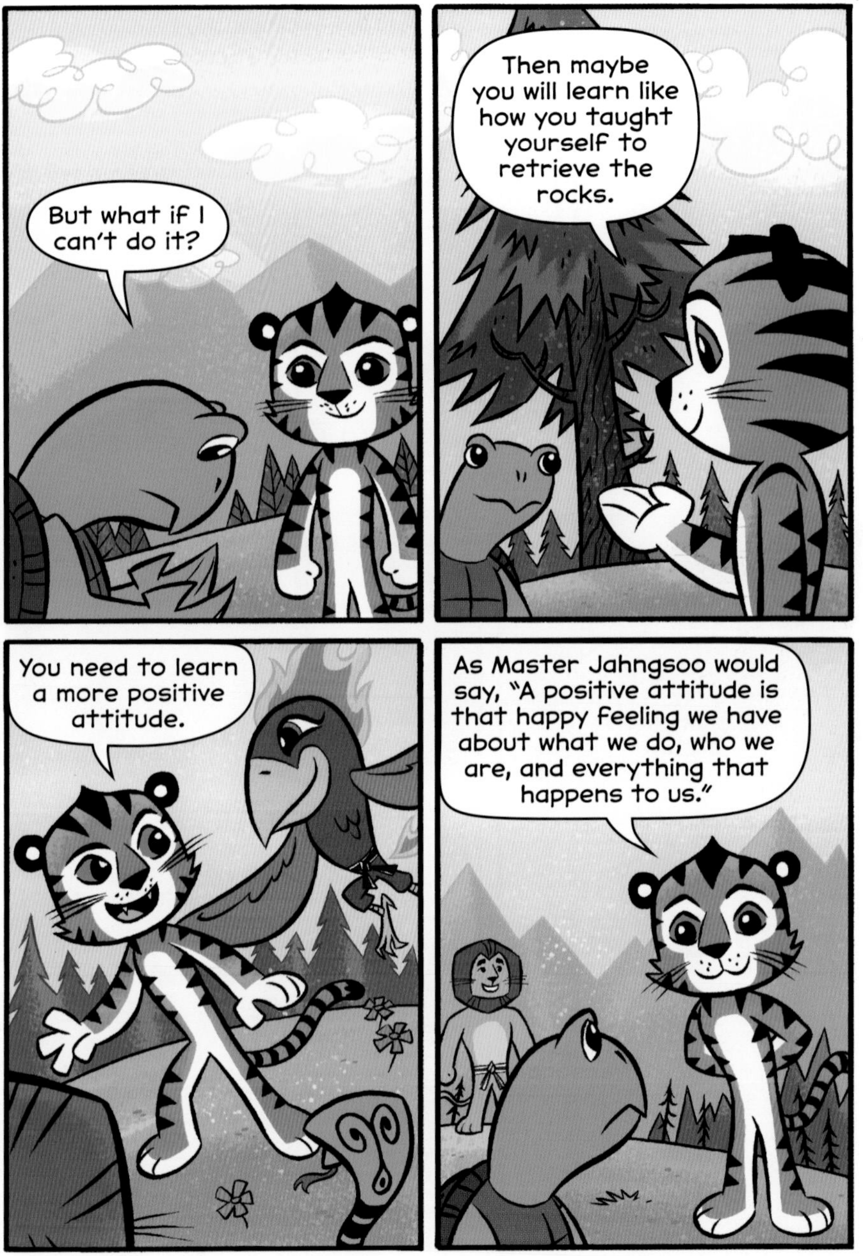
But what if I can't do it?
Then maybe you will learn like how you taught yourself to retrieve the rocks.
You need to learn a more positive attitude.
As Master Jahngsoo would say, "A positive attitude is that happy feeling we have about what we do, who we are, and everything that happens to us."

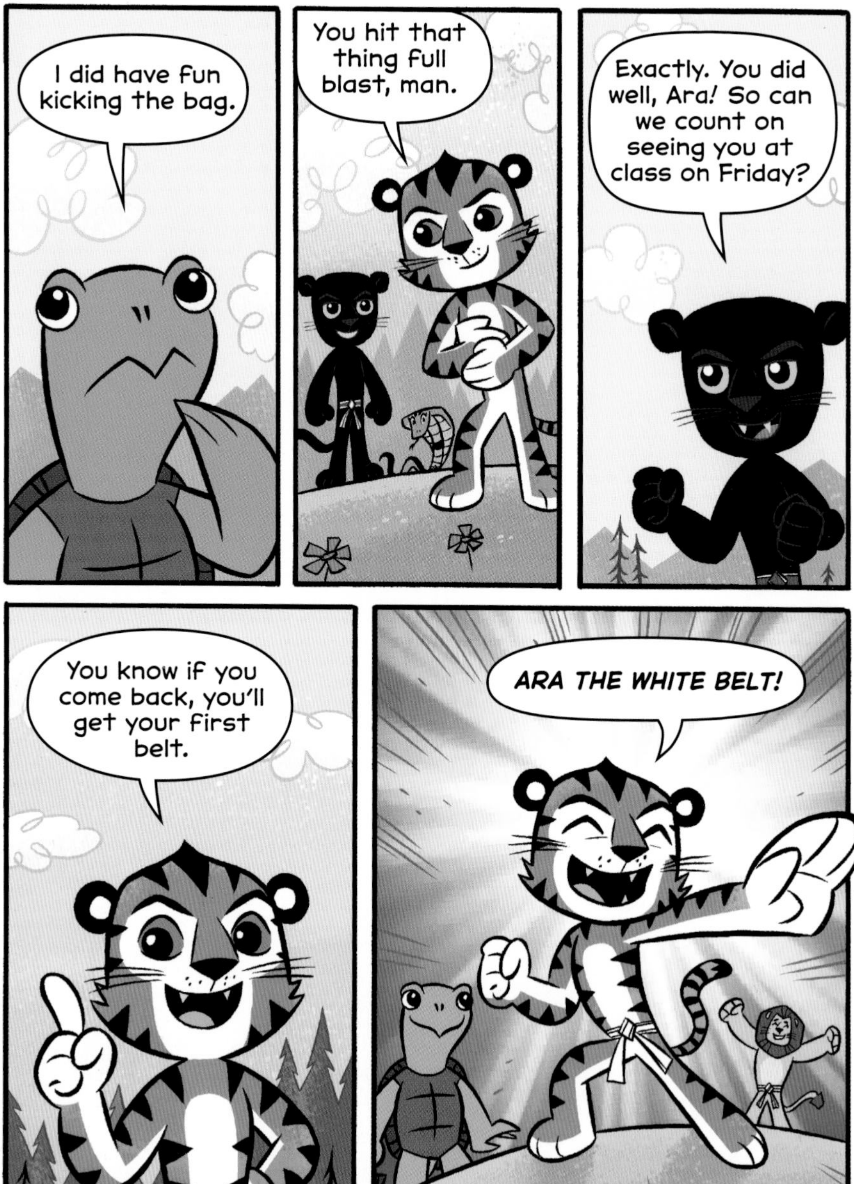
I did have fun kicking the bag.
You hit that thing full blast, man.
Exactly. You did well, Ara! So can we count on seeing you at class on Friday?
You know if you come back, you'll get your first belt.
ARA THE WHITE BELT!

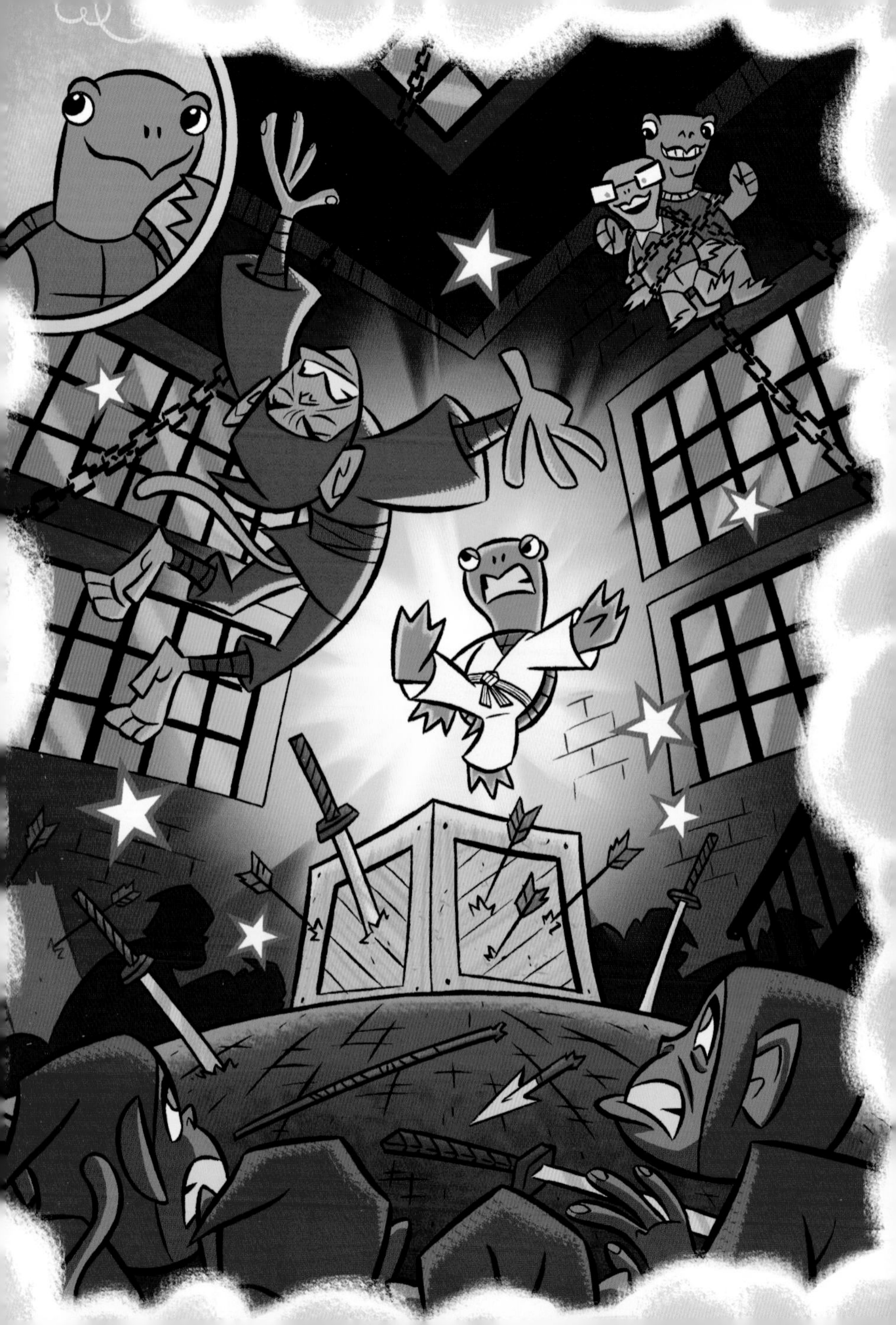

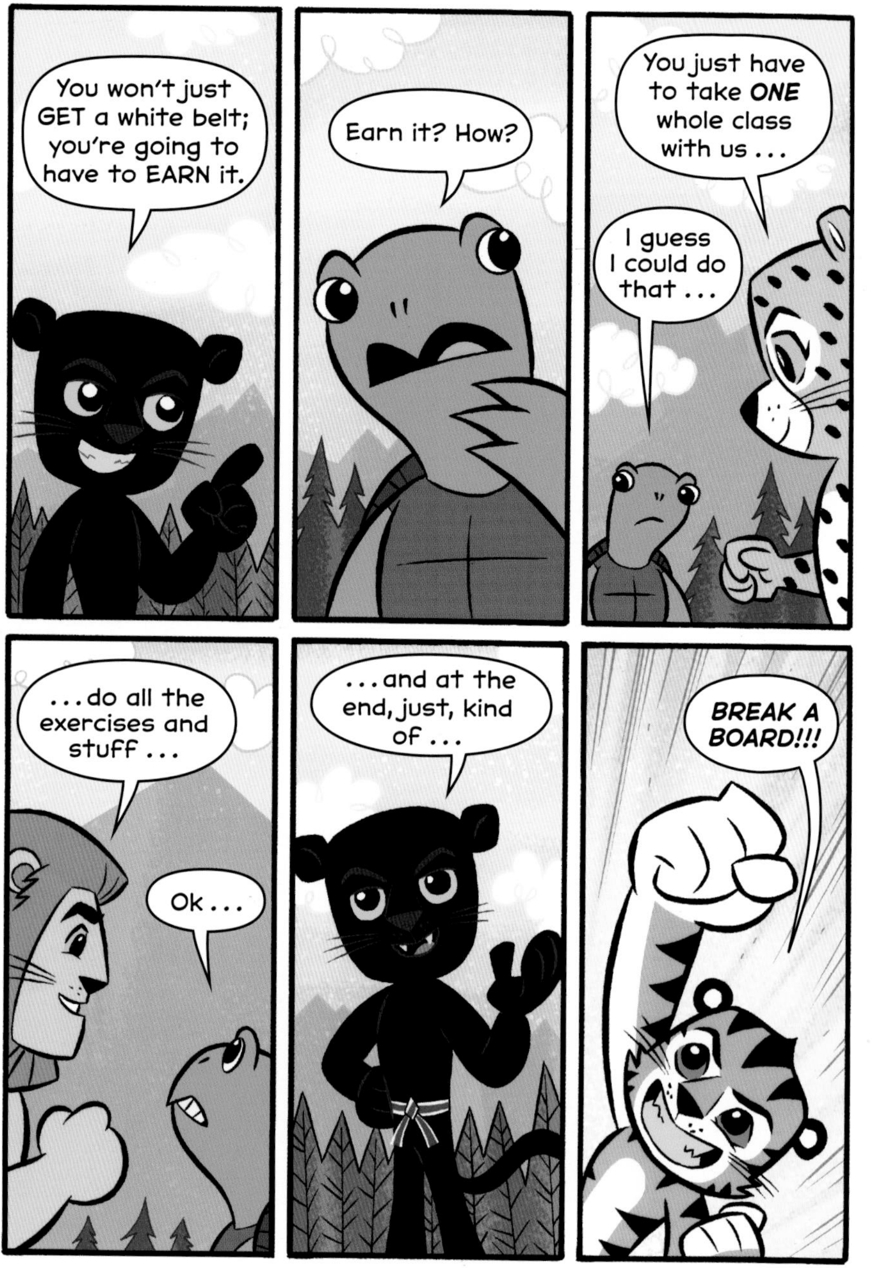
You won't just GET a white belt; you're going to have to EARN it.
Earn it? How?
You just have to take ONE whole class with us . . .
I guess I could do that . . .
. . . do all the exercises and stuff . . .
Ok . . .
. . . and at the end, just, kind of . . .
BREAK A BOARD!!!

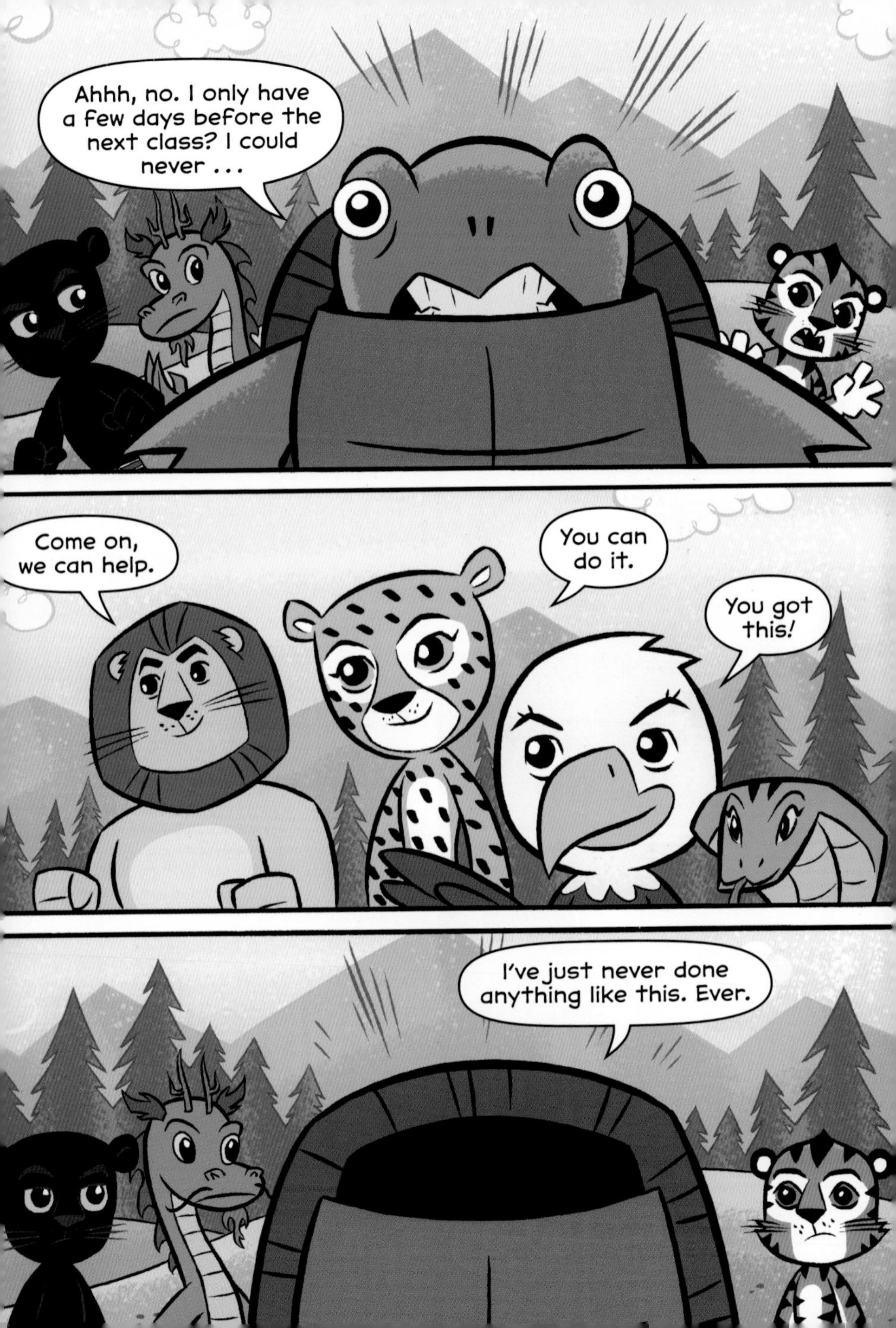
Ahhh, no. I only have a few days before the next class? I could never . . .
Come on, we can help.
You can do it.
You got this!
I've just never done anything like this. Ever.

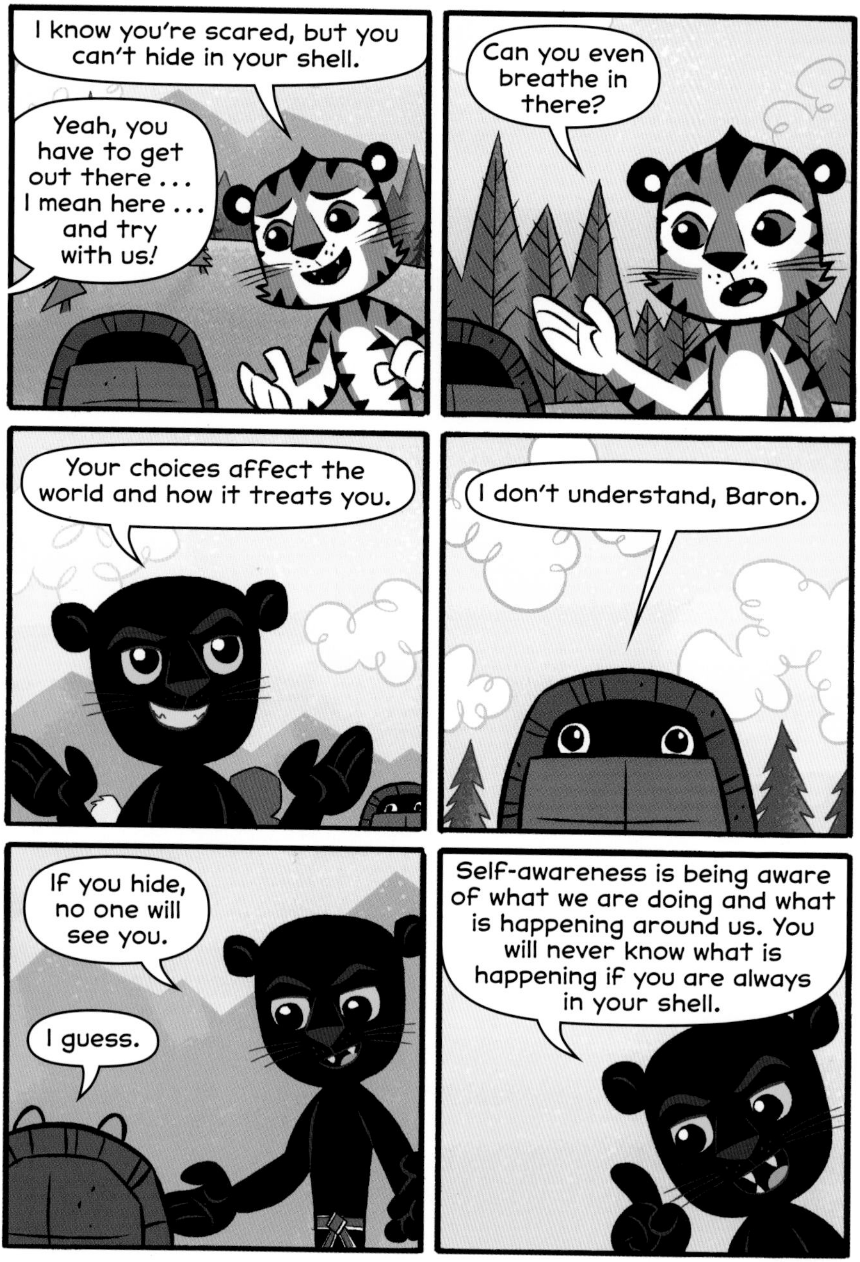
I know you're scared, but you can't hide in your shell.
Yeah, you have to get out there . . . I mean here . . . and try with us!
Can you even breathe in there?
Your choices affect the world and how it treats you.
I don't understand, Baron.
If you hide, no one will see you.
I guess.
Self-awareness is being aware of what we are doing and what is happening around us. You will never know what is happening if you are always in your shell.

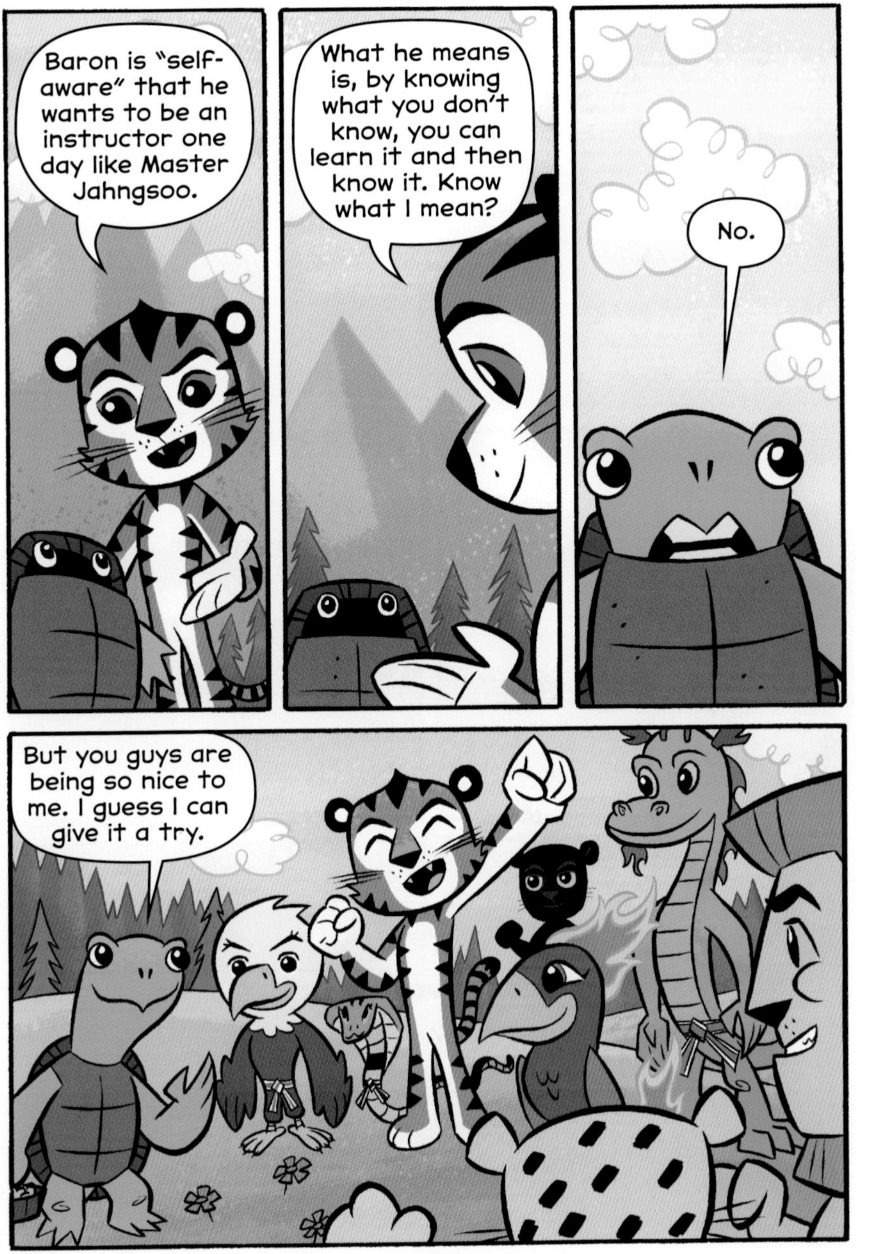
Baron is "self-aware" that he wants to be an instructor one day like Master Jahngsoo.
What he means is, by knowing what you don't know, you can learn it and then know it. Know what I mean?
No.
But you guys are being so nice to me. I guess I can give it a try.

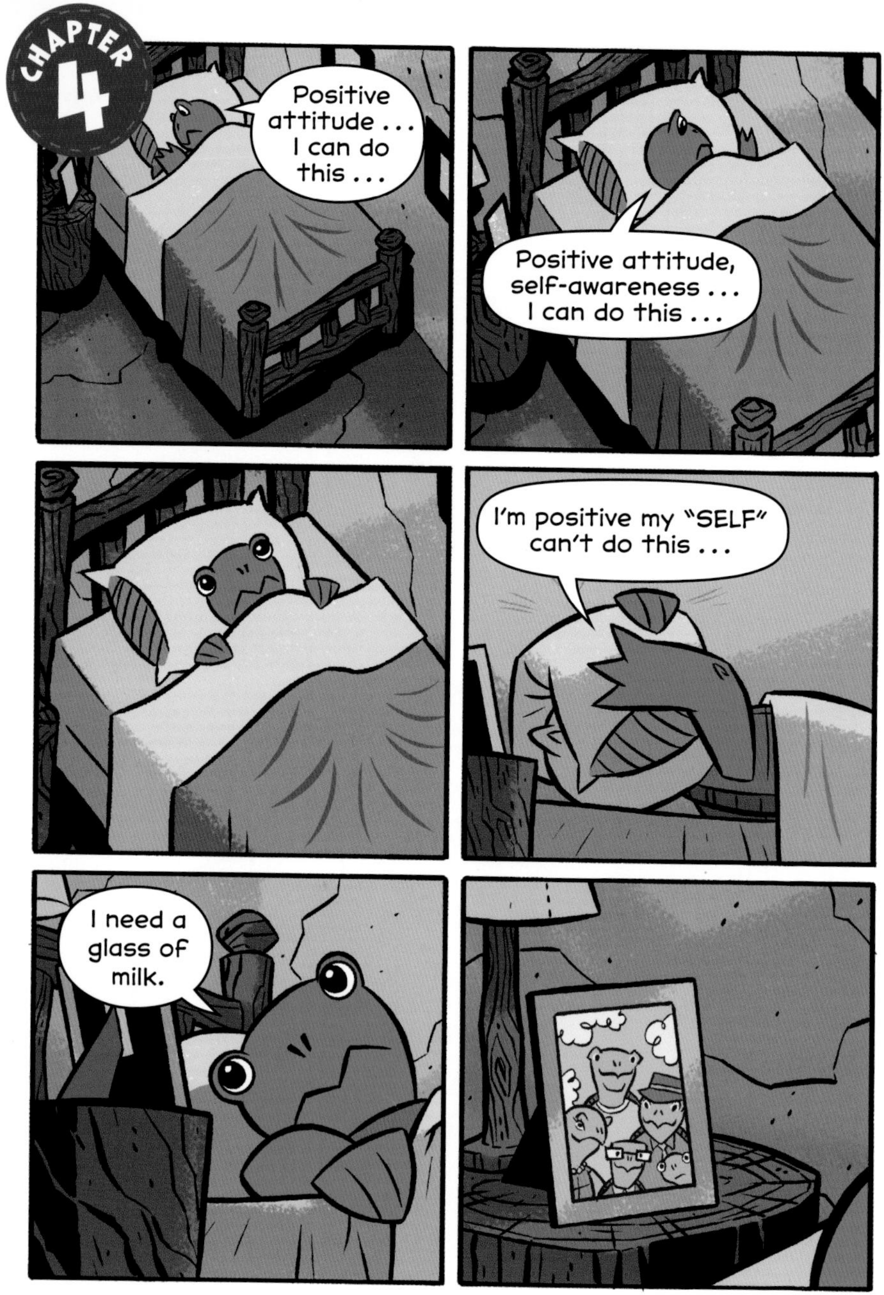
CHAPTER 4
Positive attitude . . . I can do this . . .
Positive attitude, self-awareness . . . I can do this . . .
I'm positive my "SELF" can't do this . . .
I need a glass of milk.

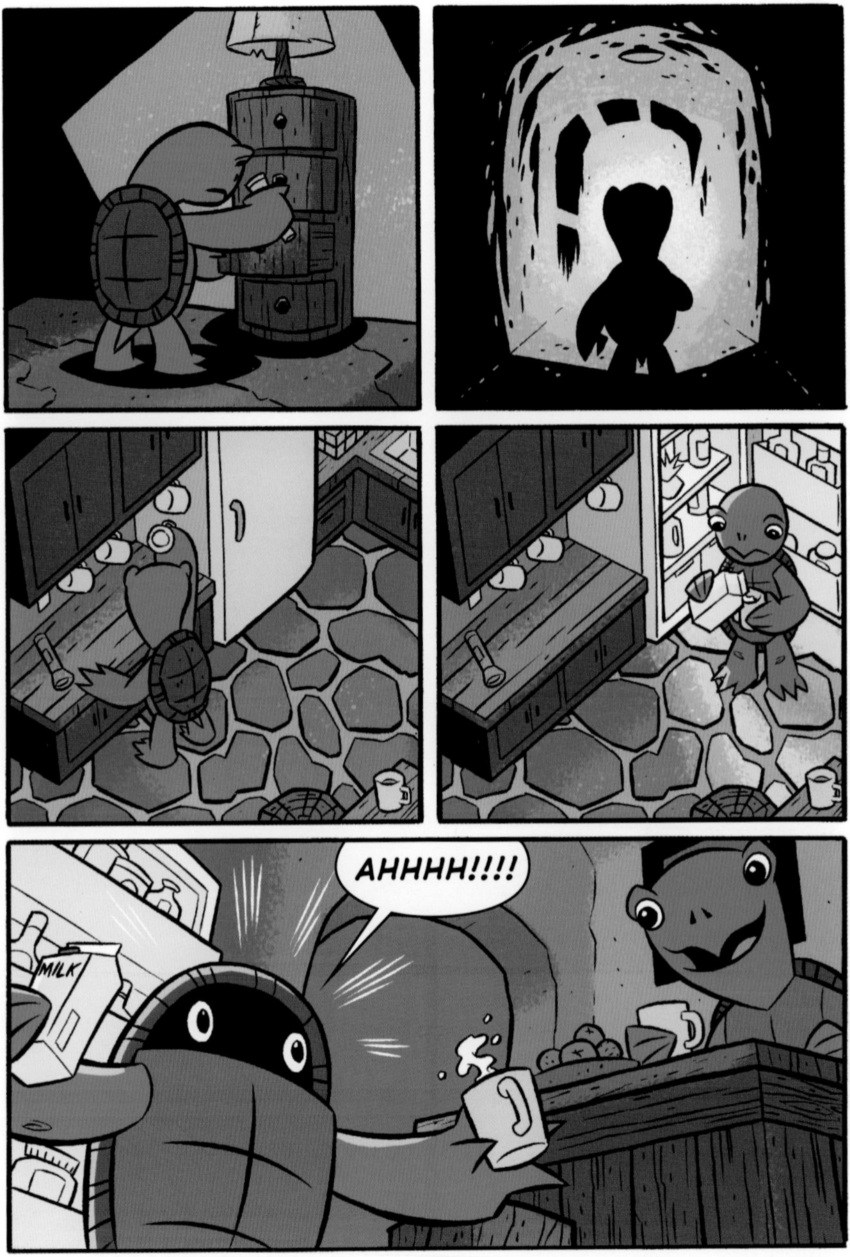
AHHHH!!!!!
MILK

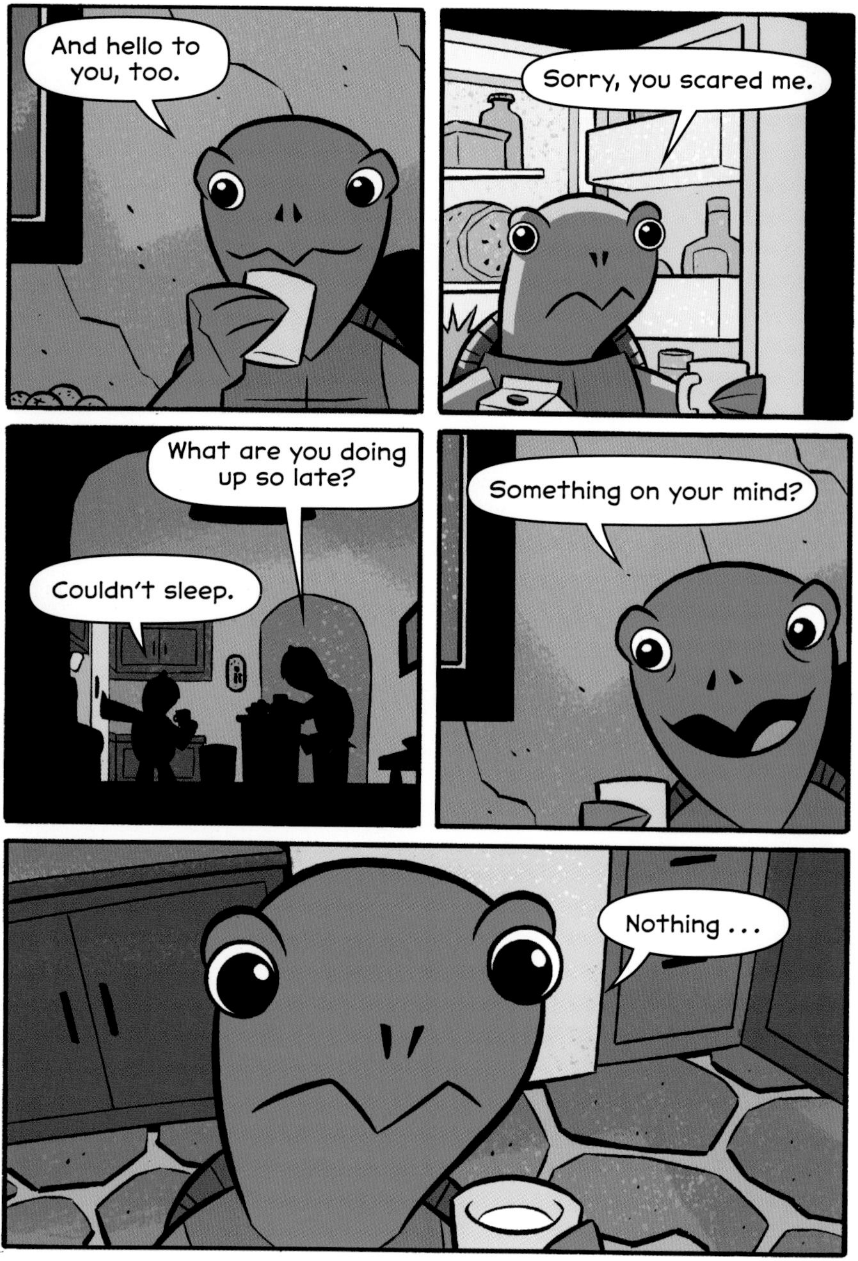
And hello to you, too.
Sorry, you scared me.
What are you doing up so late?
Couldn't sleep.
Something on your mind?
Nothing . . .

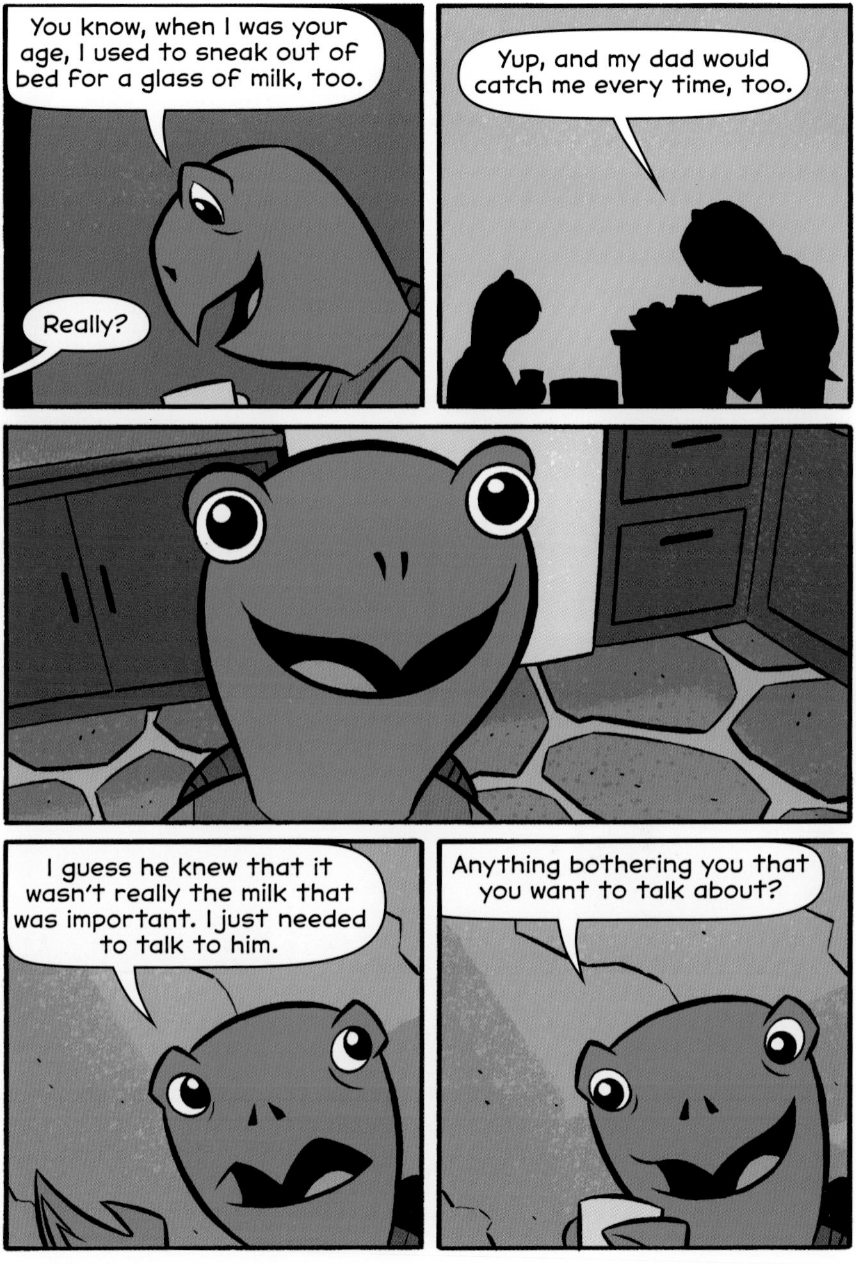
You know, when I was your age, I used to sneak out of bed for a glass of milk, too.
Really?
Yup, and my dad would catch me every time, too.
I guess he knew that it wasn't really the milk that was important. I just needed to talk to him.
Anything bothering you that you want to talk about?

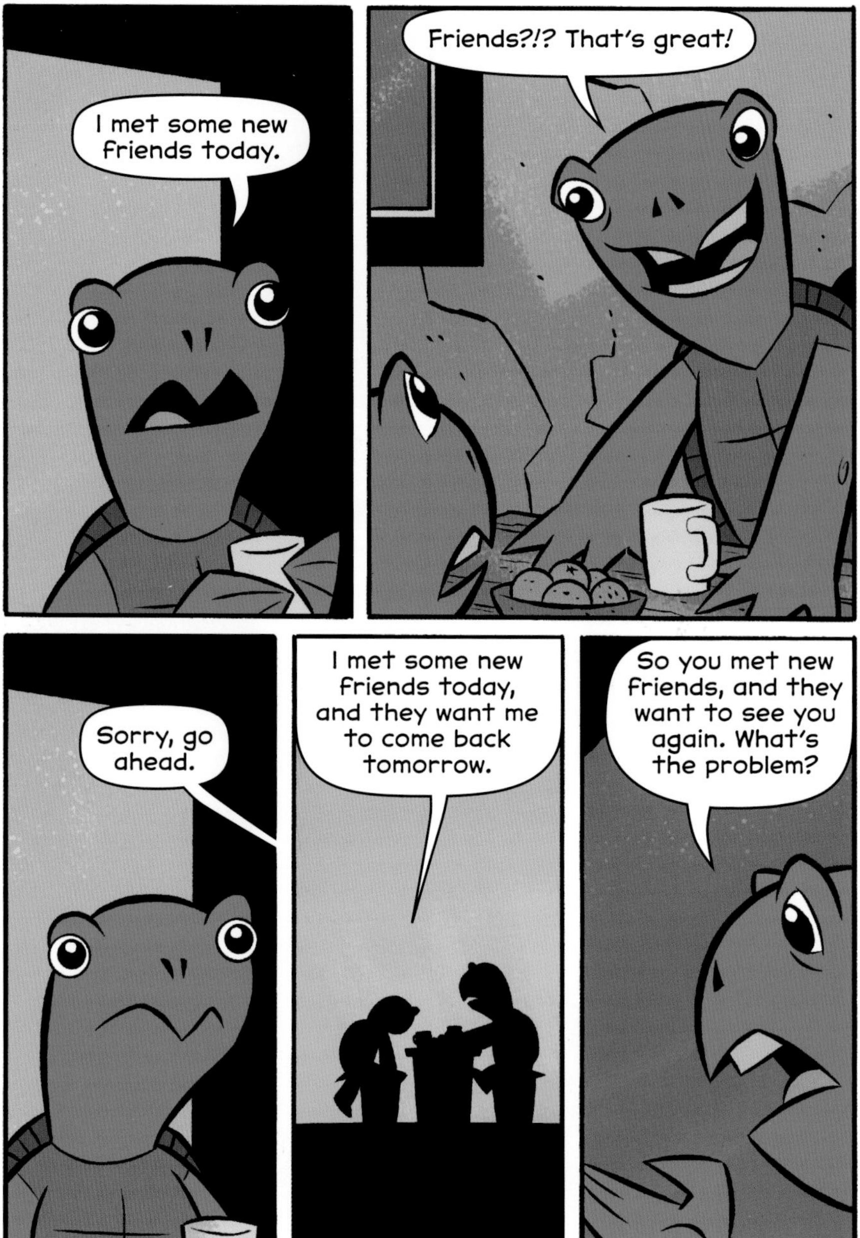
I met some new friends today.
Friends?!? That's great!
Sorry, go ahead.
I met some new friends today, and they want me to come back tomorrow.
So you met new friends, and they want to see you again. What's the problem?

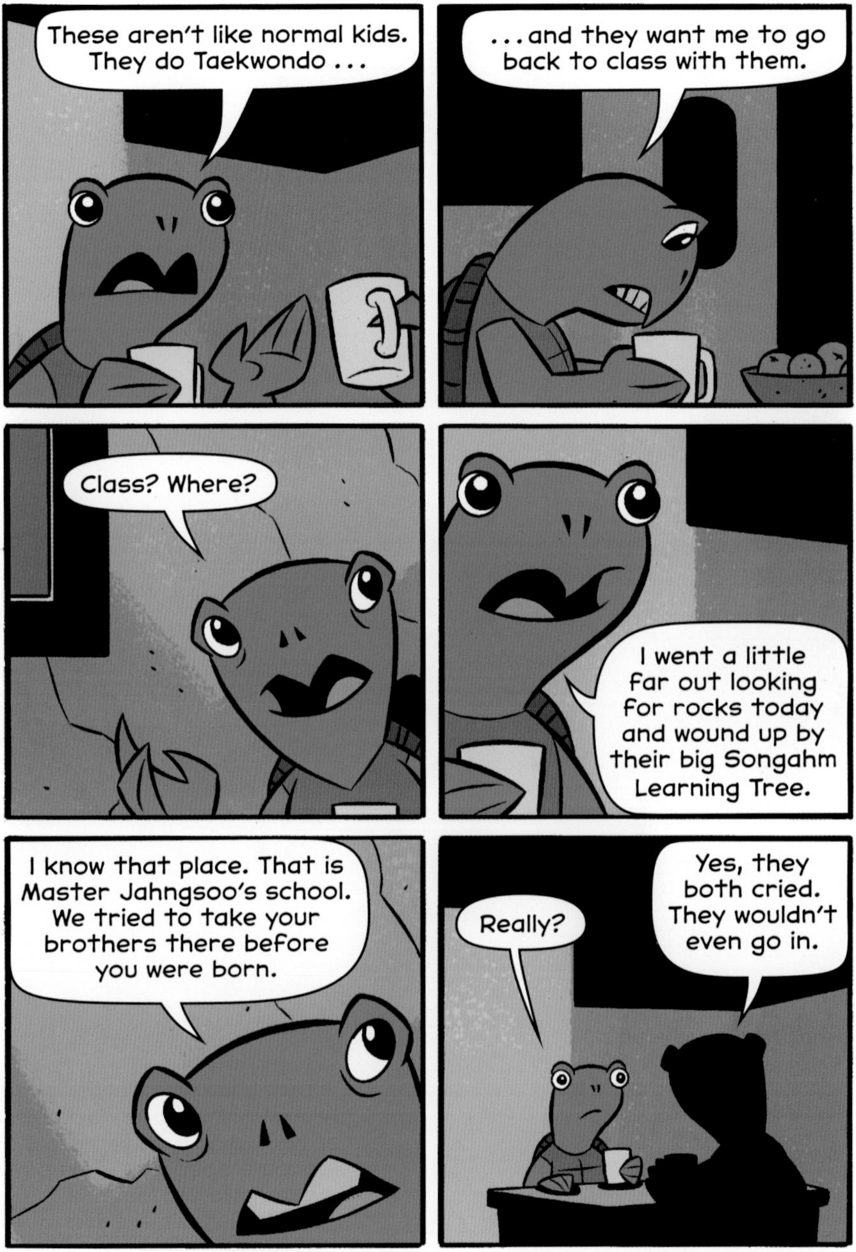
These aren't like normal kids. They do Taekwondo . . .
. . . and they want me to go back to class with them.
Class? Where?
I went a little far out looking for rocks today and wound up by their big Songahm Learning Tree.
I know that place. That is Master Jahngsoo's school. We tried to take your brothers there before you were born.
Really?
Yes, they both cried. They wouldn't even go in.

Well, I went in, and now they want me to come back and try to earn a white belt.

How do you do that?

That's the problem. I don't think I can. The team said they would help me get ready and practice with me.

That's nice of them. They sound like good friends.

They are, especially this really funny tiger named Baeoh. I told them I would come back. I just don't think I want to.

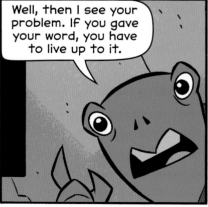

Well, then I see your problem. If you gave your word, you have to live up to it.

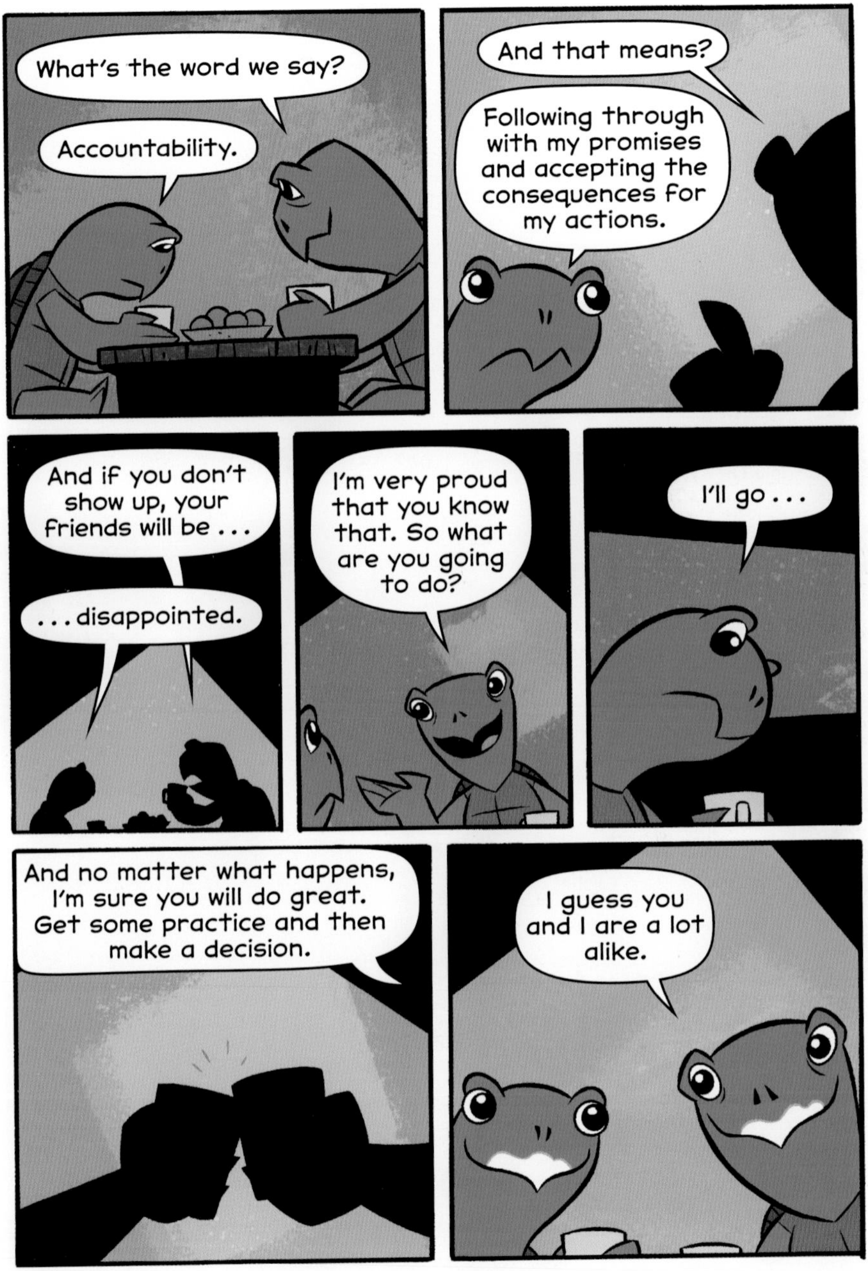
What's the word we say?
Accountability.
And that means?
Following through with my promises and accepting the consequences for my actions.
And if you don't show up, your friends will be . . .
. . . disappointed.
I'm very proud that you know that. So what are you going to do?
I'll go . . .
And no matter what happens, I'm sure you will do great. Get some practice and then make a decision.
I guess you and I are a lot alike.

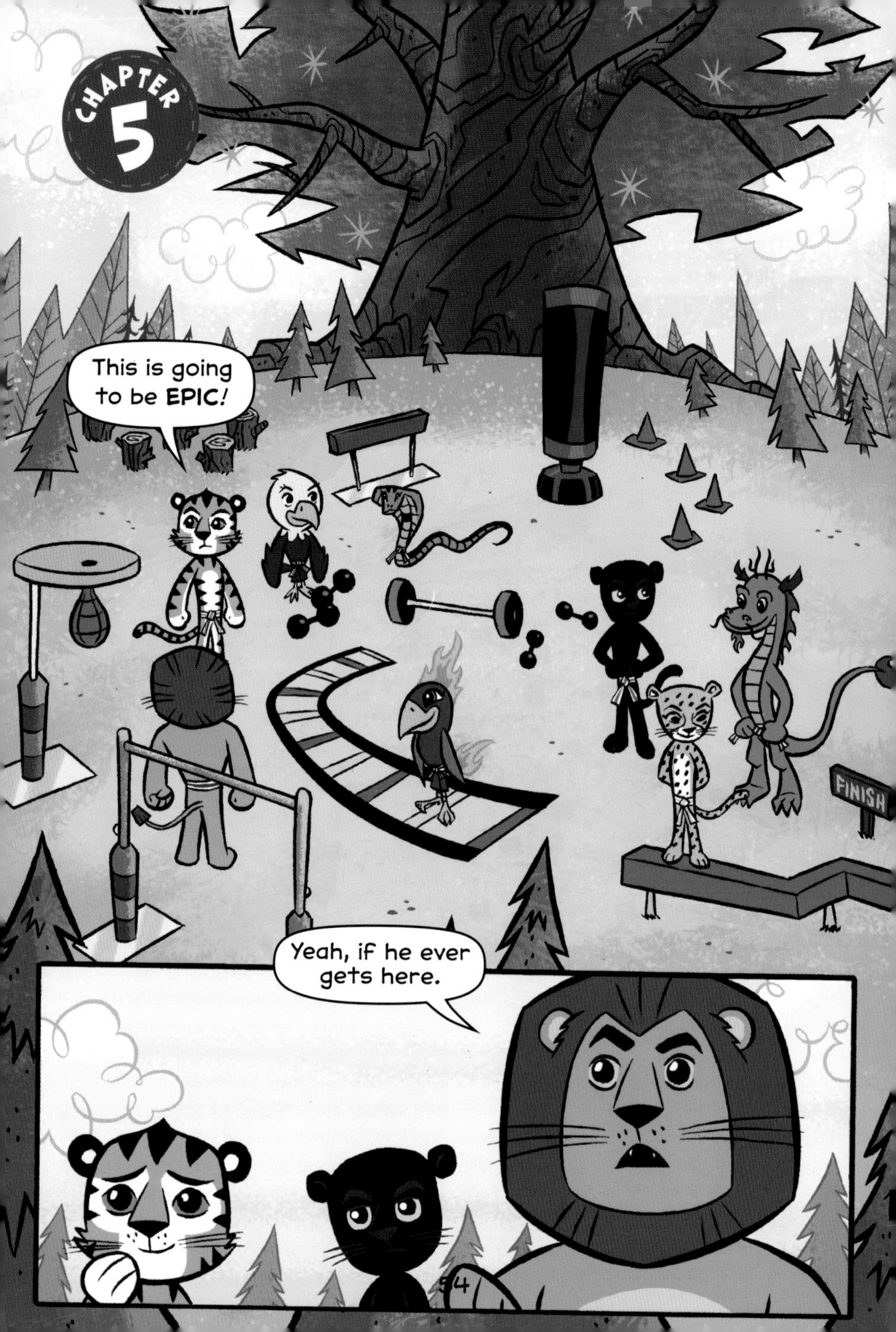
CHAPTER 5
This is going to be EPIC!
FINISH
Yeah, if he ever gets here.

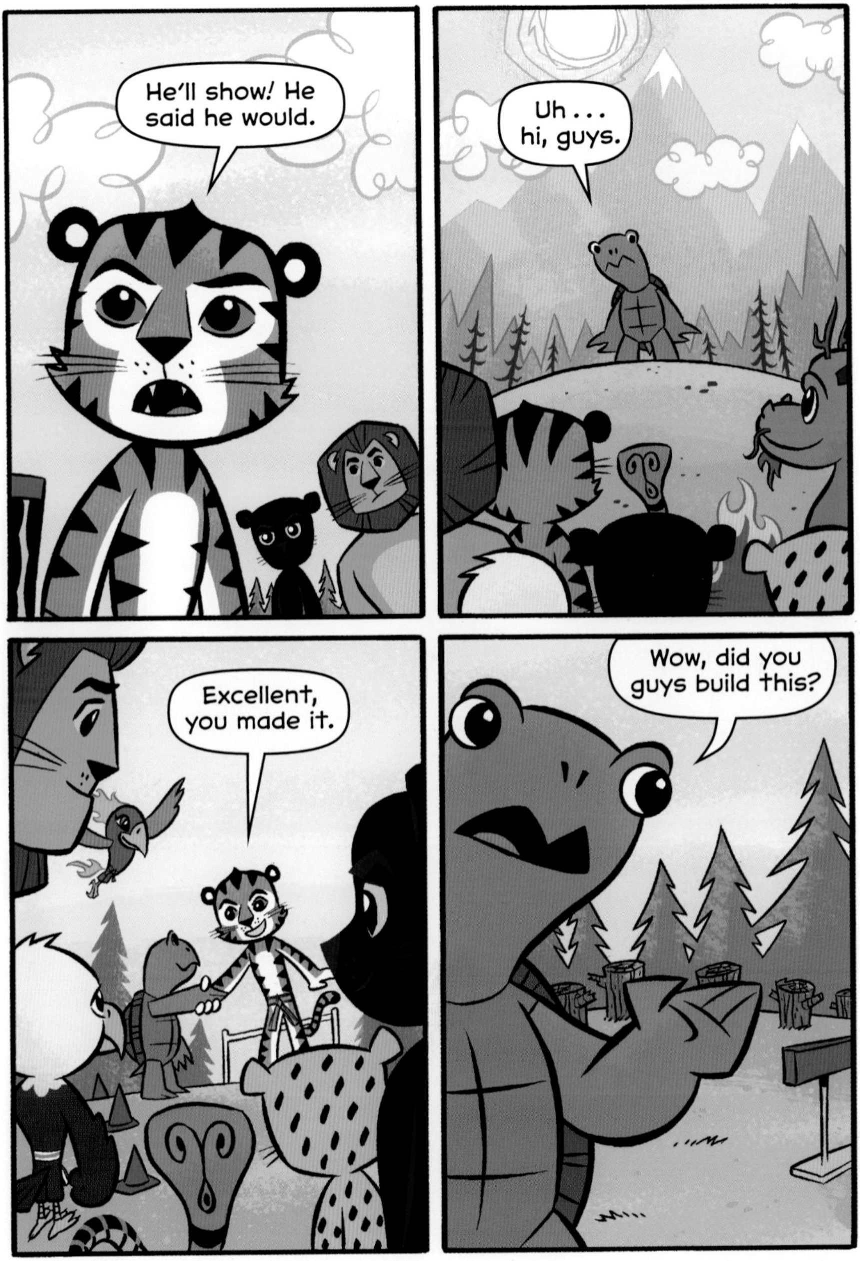
He'll show! He said he would.
Uh . . . hi, guys.
Excellent, you made it.
Wow, did you guys build this?

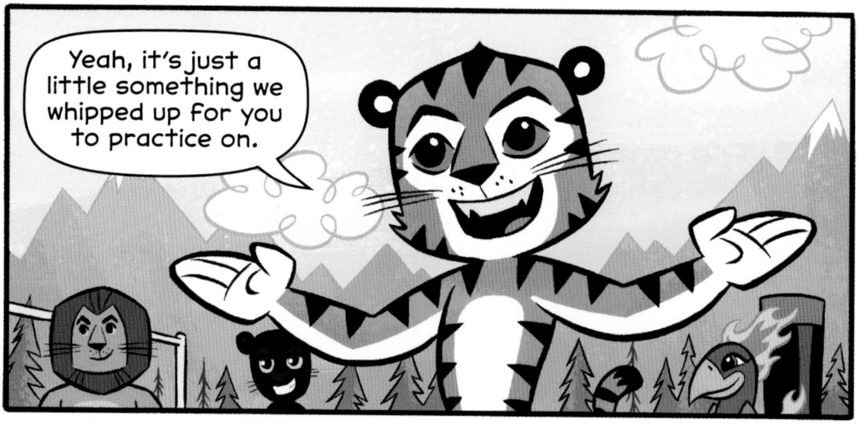
Yeah, it's just a little something we whipped up for you to practice on.

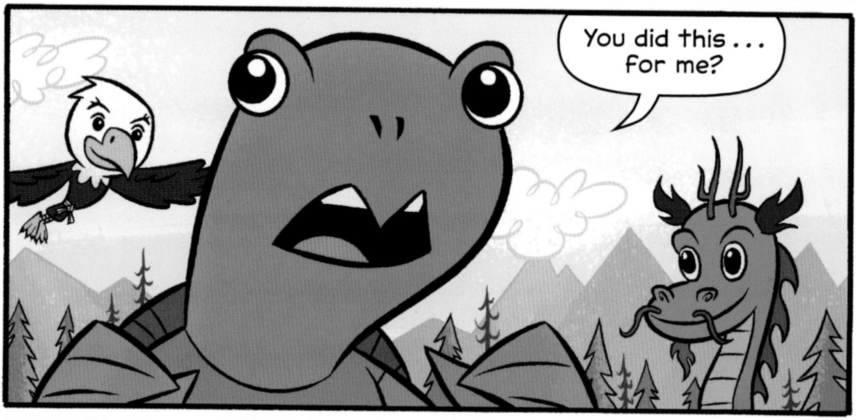
You did this . . . for me?

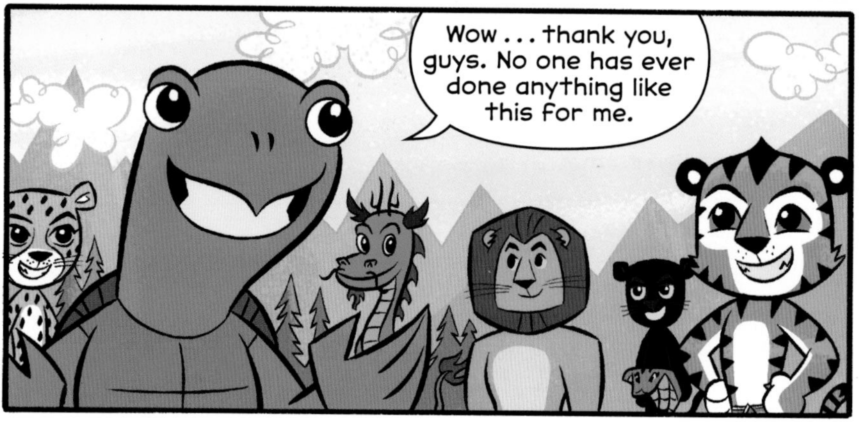
Wow . . . thank you, guys. No one has ever done anything like this for me.

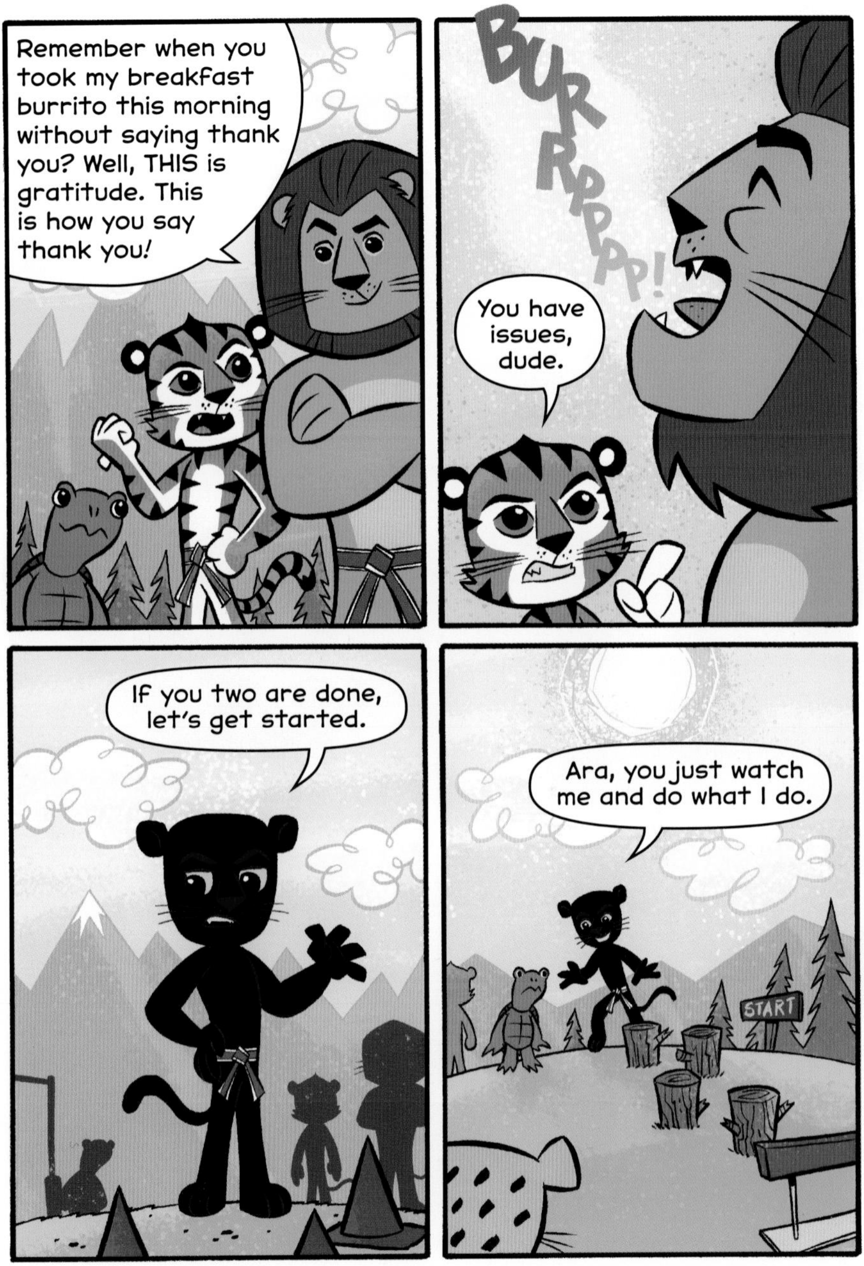
Remember when you took my breakfast burrito this morning without saying thank you? Well, THIS is gratitude. This is how you say thank you!
BURRPPPP!
You have issues, dude.
If you two are done, let's get started.
Ara, you just watch me and do what I do.
START

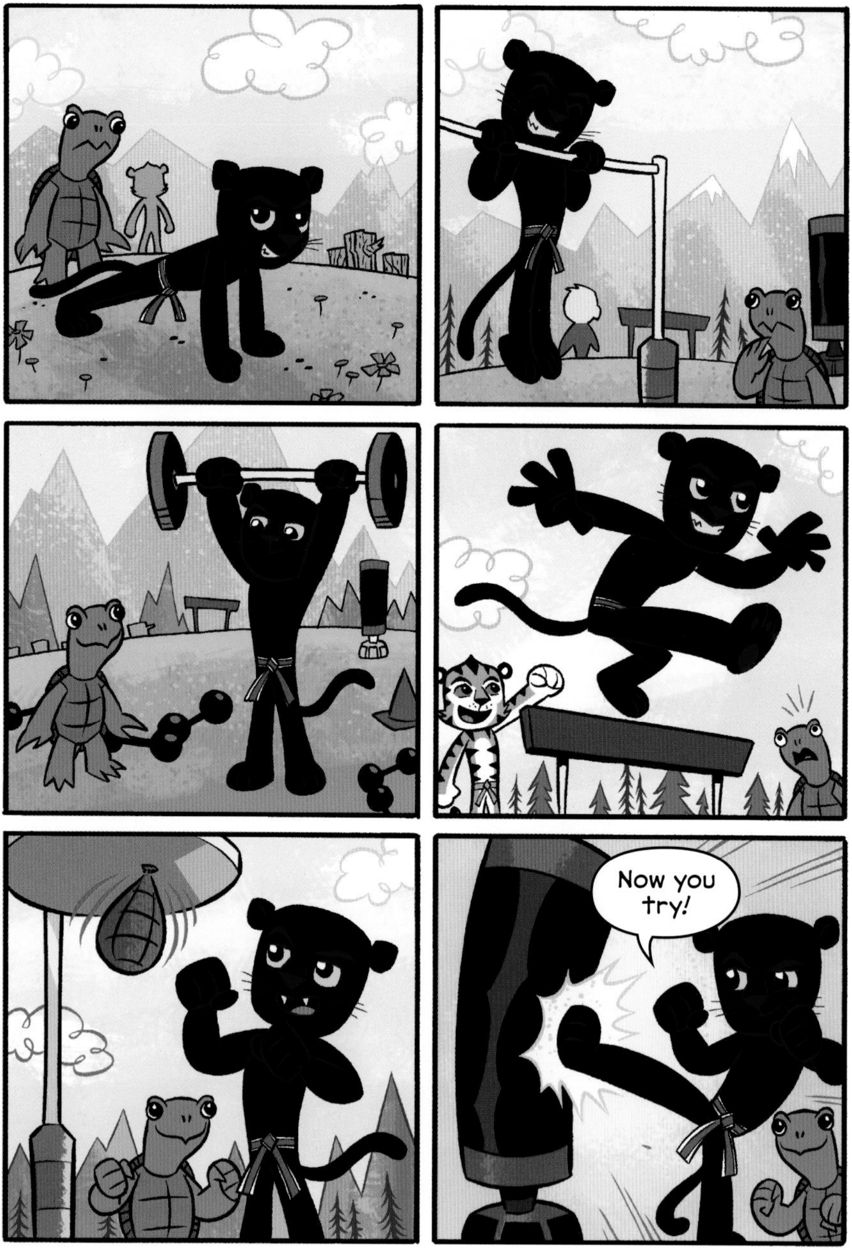
Now you try!

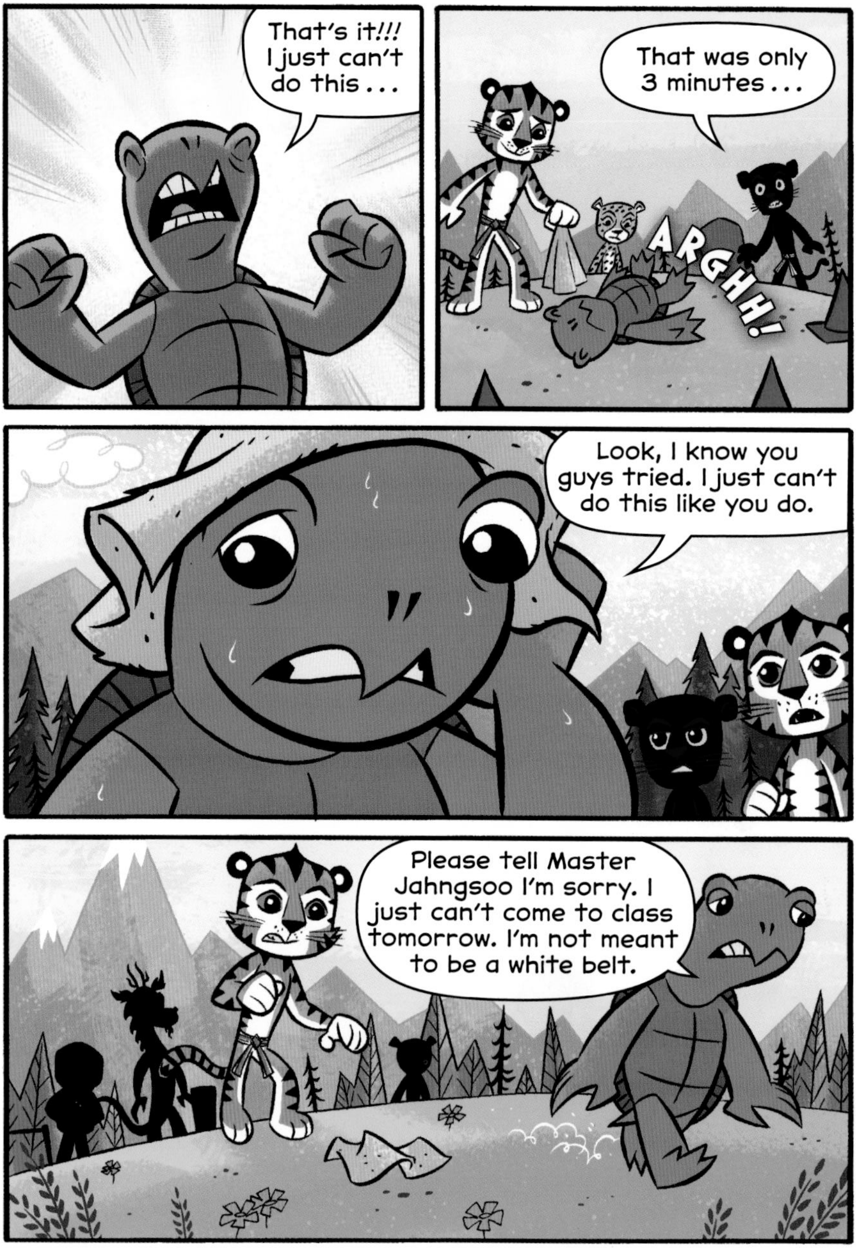
That's it!!!
I just can't
do this . . .
That was only
3 minutes . . .
ARGHH!
Look, I know you
guys tried. I just can't
do this like you do.
Please tell Master
Jahngsoo I'm sorry. I
just can't come to class
tomorrow. I'm not meant
to be a white belt.

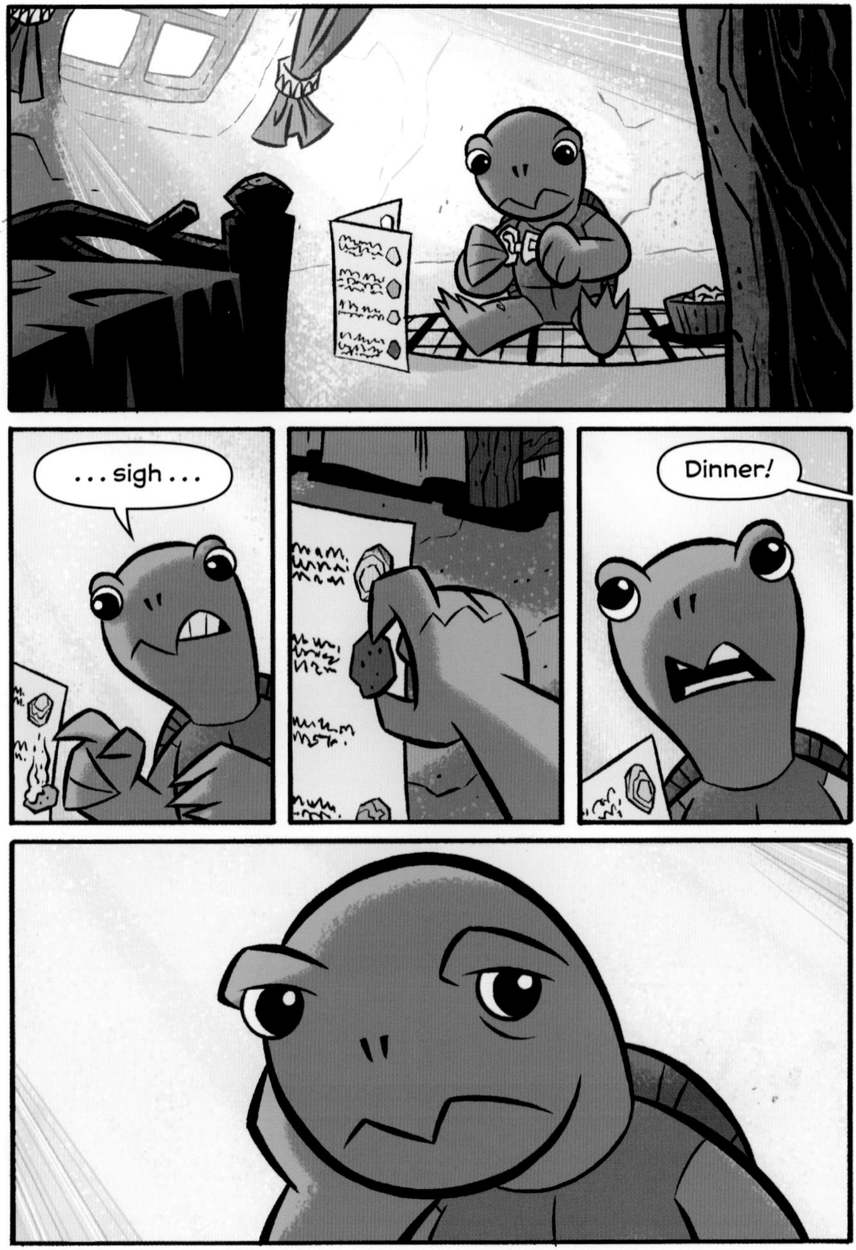
. . . sigh . . .
Dinner!

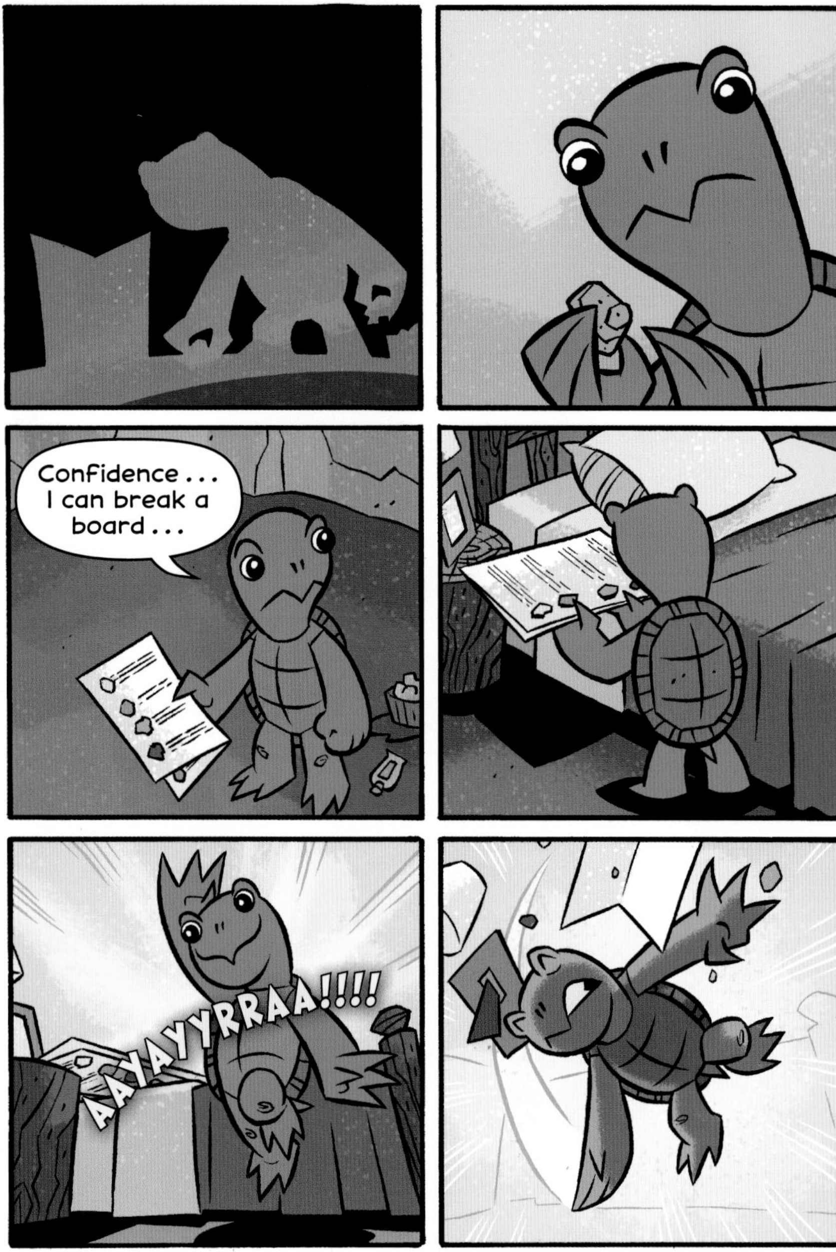
Confidence . . .
I can break a
board . . .
AAYAYYRRAA!!!!

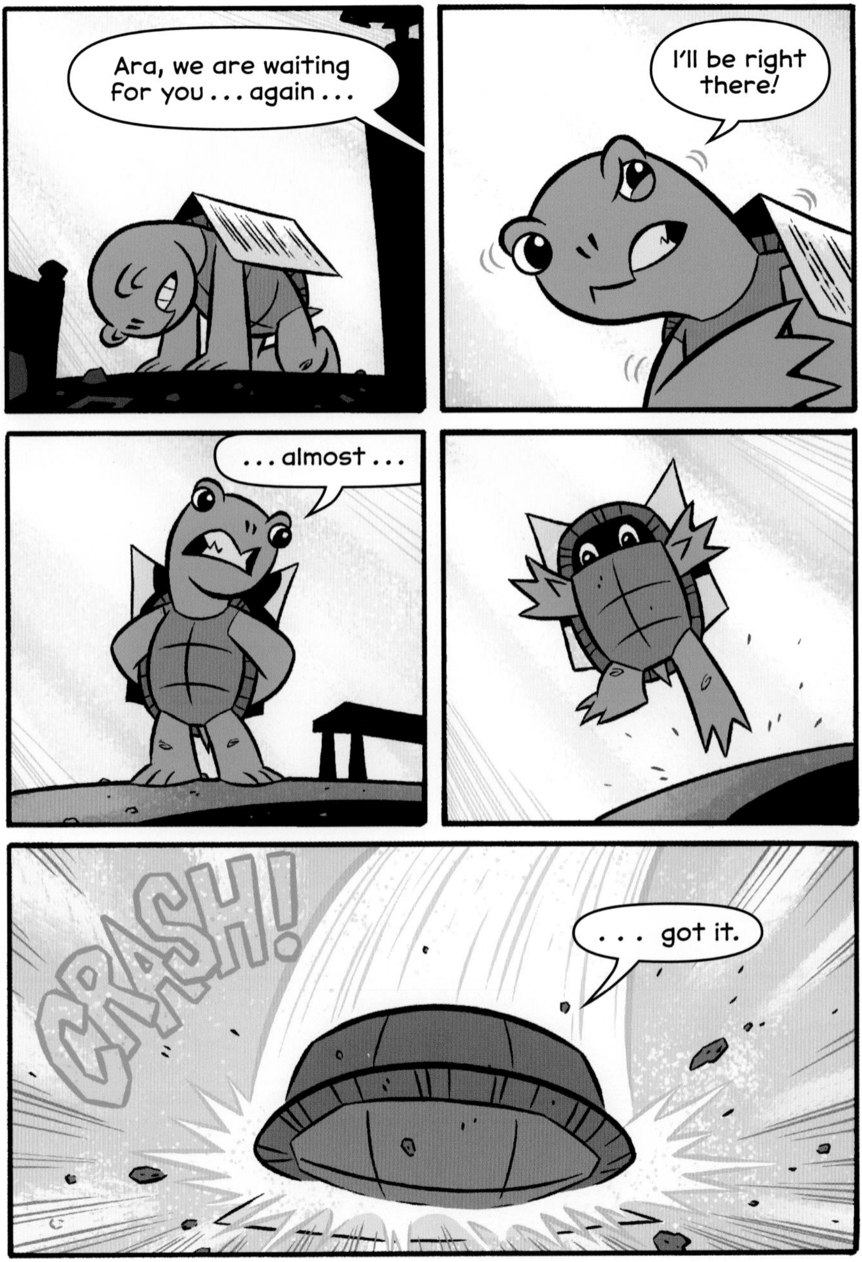

Ara, we are waiting for you . . . again . . .
I'll be right there!
. . . almost . . .
CRASH!
. . . got it.

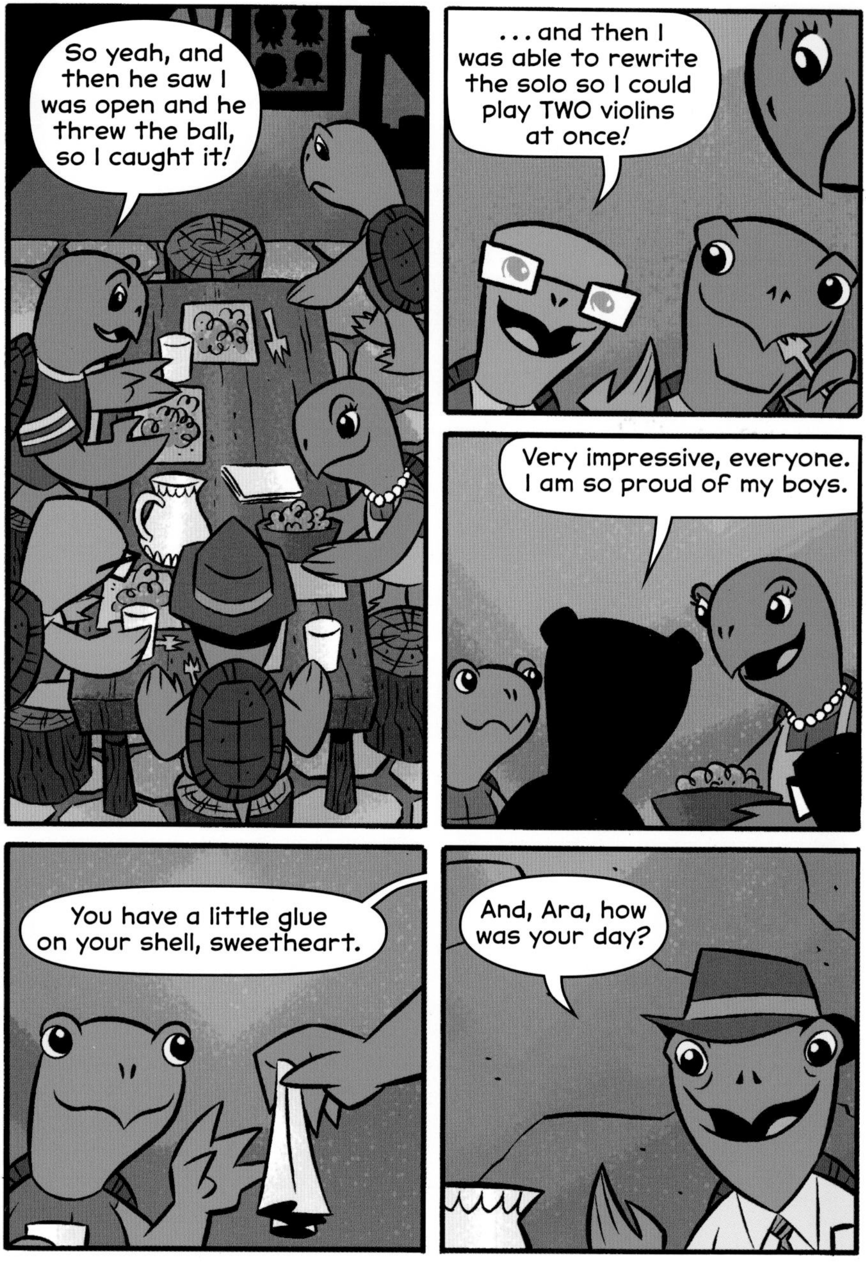
So yeah, and then he saw I was open and he threw the ball, so I caught it!
...and then I was able to rewrite the solo so I could play TWO violins at once!
Very impressive, everyone. I am so proud of my boys.
You have a little glue on your shell, sweetheart.
And, Ara, how was your day?

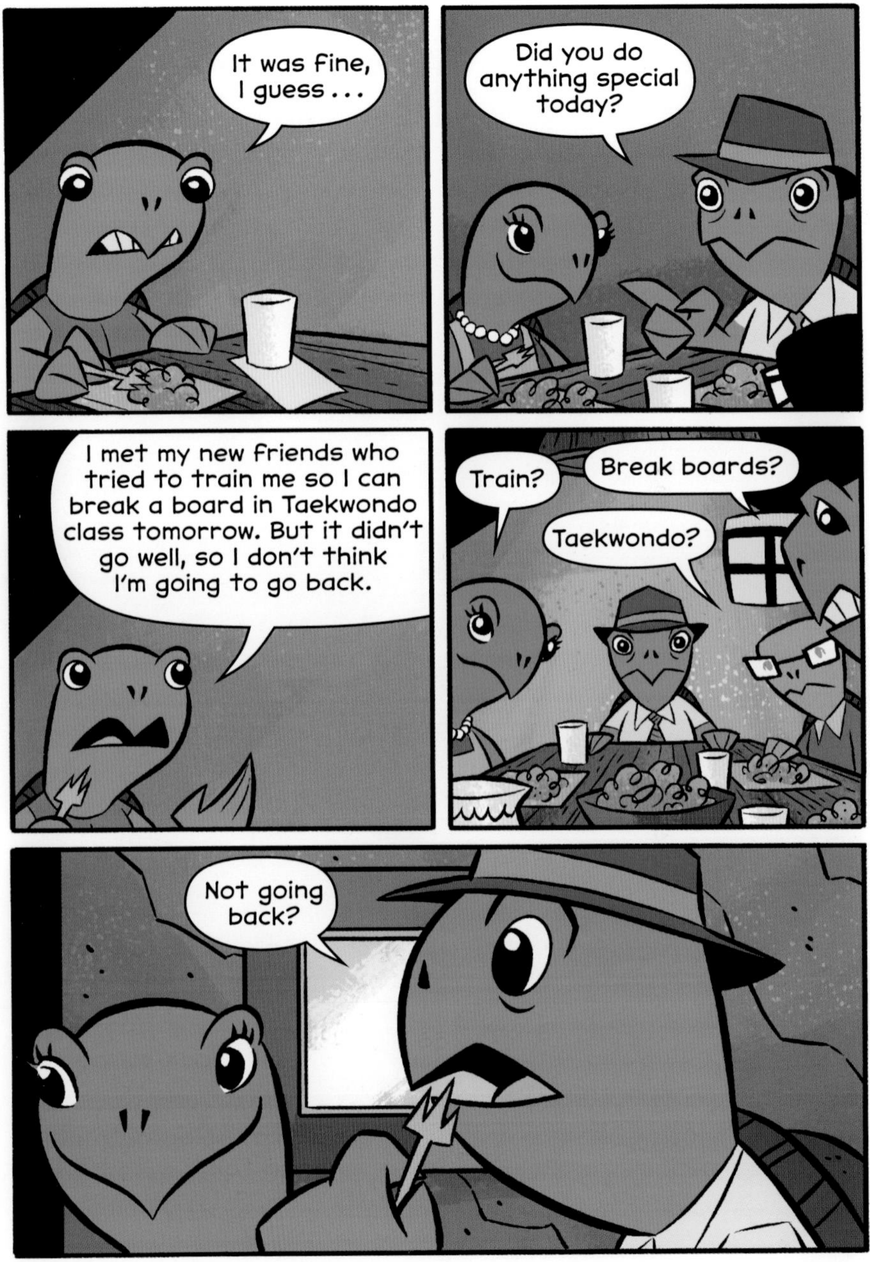
It was fine, I guess . . .
Did you do anything special today?
I met my new friends who tried to train me so I can break a board in Taekwondo class tomorrow. But it didn't go well, so I don't think I'm going to go back.
Train?
Break boards?
Taekwondo?
Not going back?

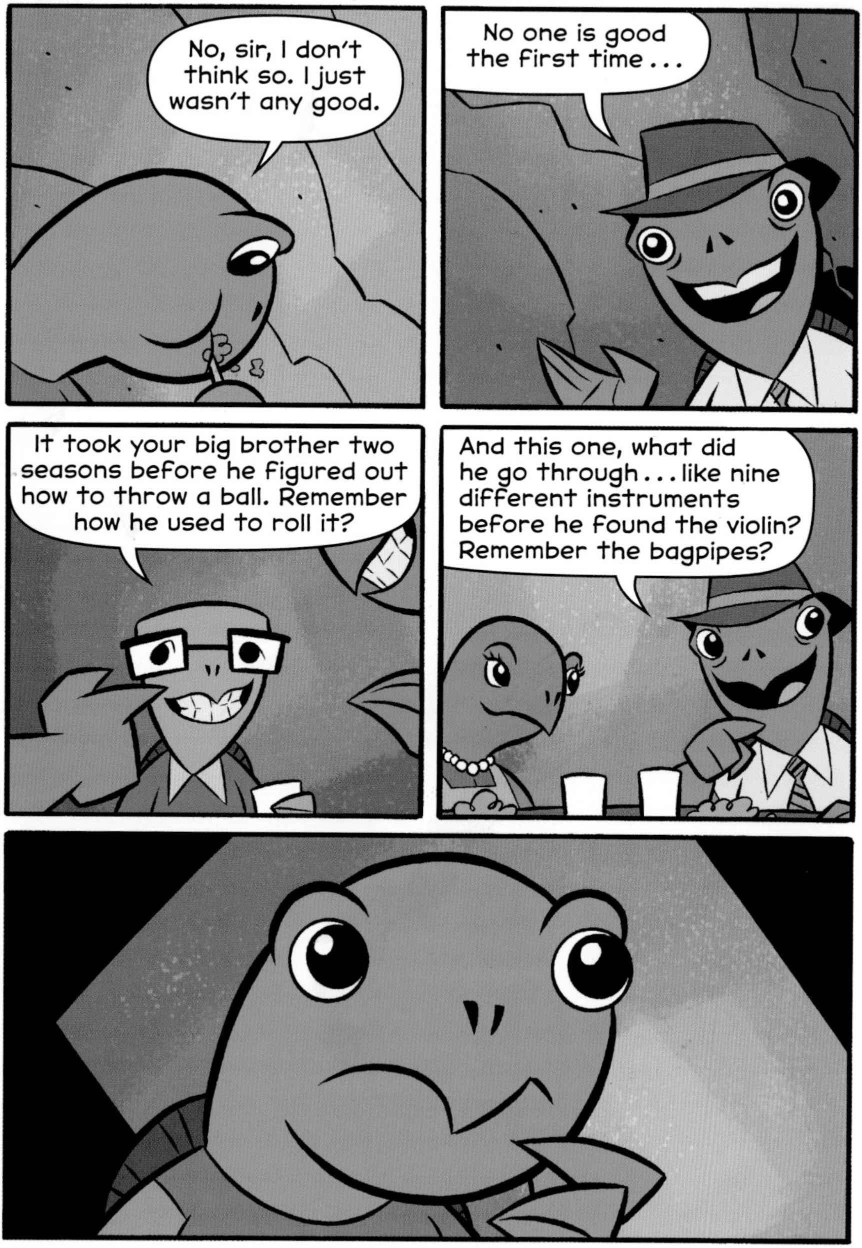
No, sir, I don't think so. I just wasn't any good.
No one is good the first time . . .
It took your big brother two seasons before he figured out how to throw a ball. Remember how he used to roll it?
And this one, what did he go through . . . like nine different instruments before he found the violin? Remember the bagpipes?

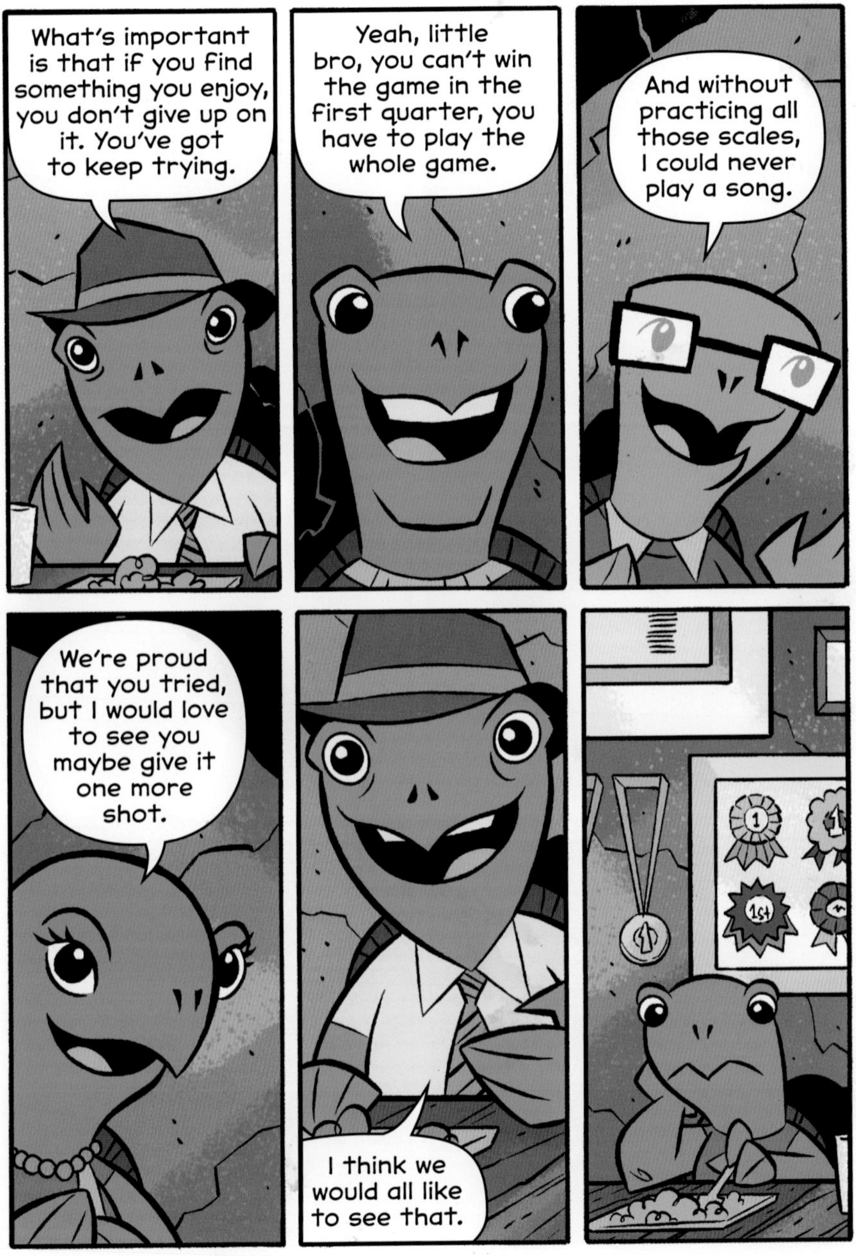
What's important is that if you find something you enjoy, you don't give up on it. You've got to keep trying.
Yeah, little bro, you can't win the game in the first quarter, you have to play the whole game.
And without practicing all those scales, I could never play a song.
We're proud that you tried, but I would love to see you maybe give it one more shot.
I think we would all like to see that.
1
1st

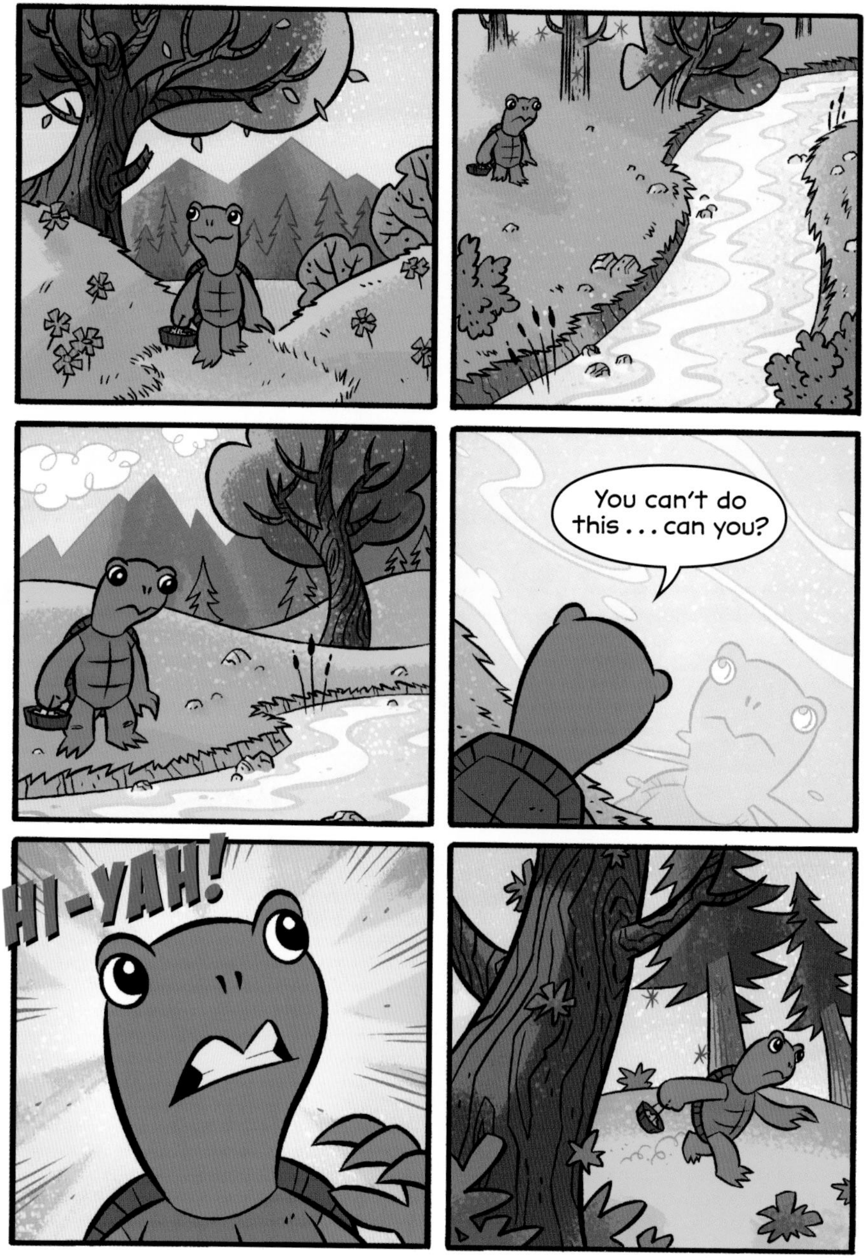
You can't do this . . . can you?
HI-YAH!

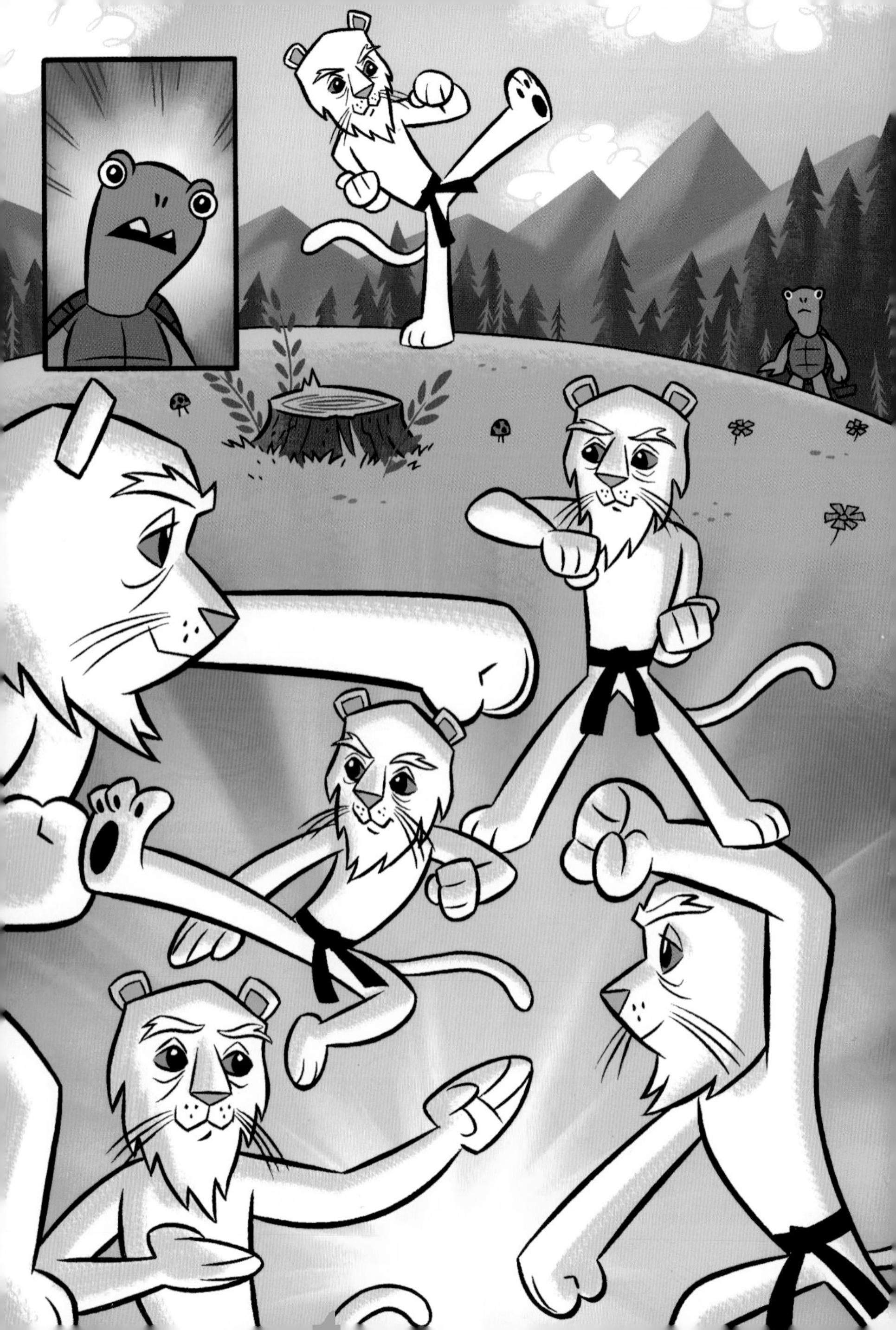

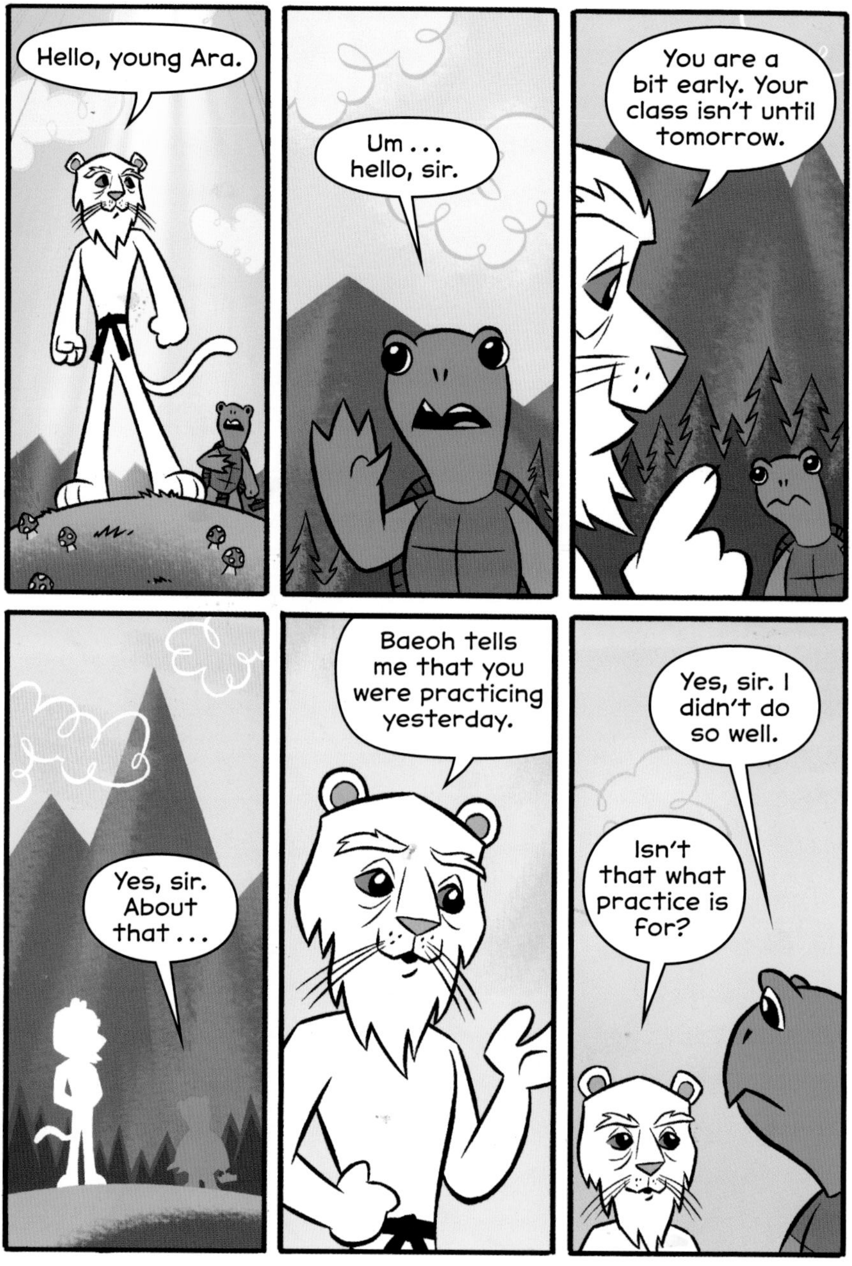
Hello, young Ara.
Um . . . hello, sir.
You are a bit early. Your class isn't until tomorrow.
Yes, sir. About that . . .
Baeoh tells me that you were practicing yesterday.
Yes, sir. I didn't do so well.
Isn't that what practice is for?

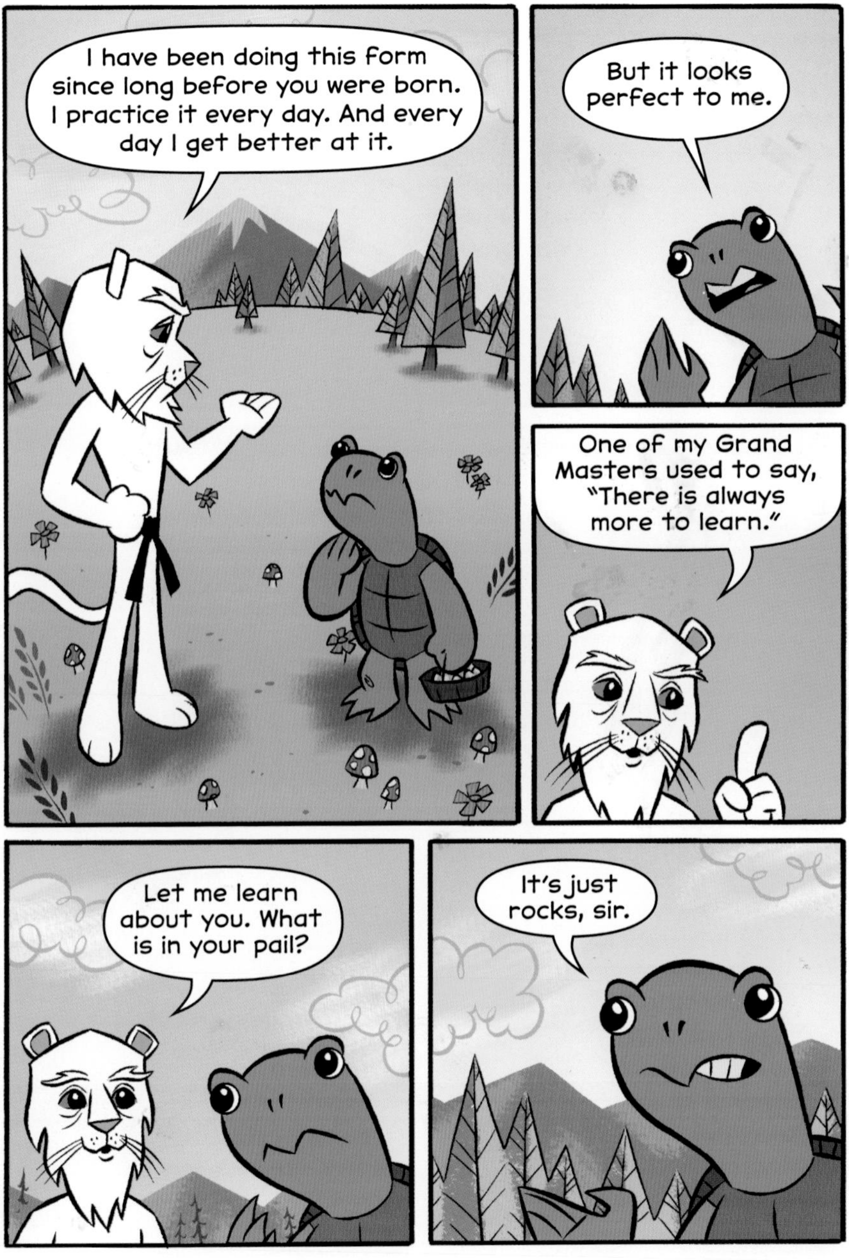
I have been doing this form since long before you were born. I practice it every day. And every day I get better at it.
But it looks perfect to me.
One of my Grand Masters used to say, "There is always more to learn."
Let me learn about you. What is in your pail?
It's just rocks, sir.

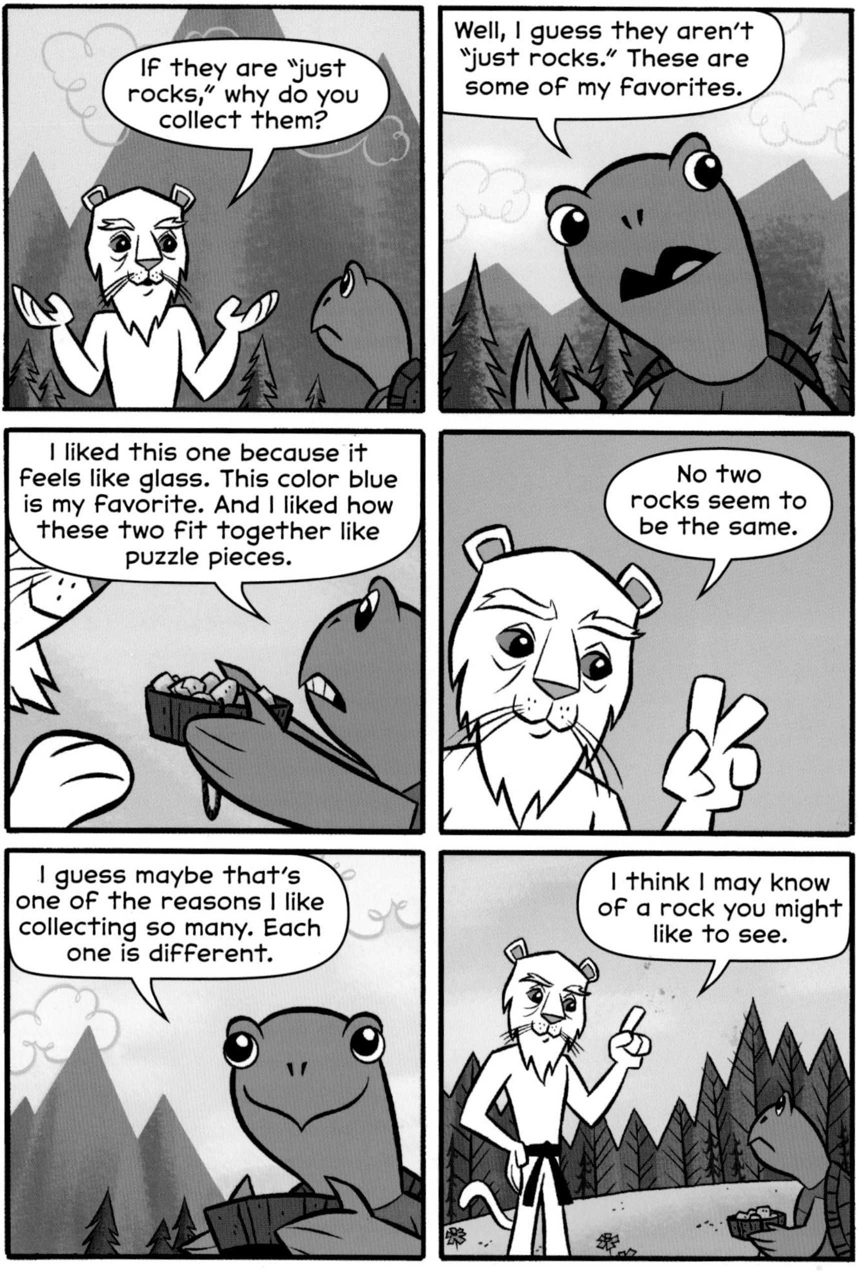
If they are "just rocks," why do you collect them?
Well, I guess they aren't "just rocks." These are some of my favorites.
I liked this one because it feels like glass. This color blue is my favorite. And I liked how these two fit together like puzzle pieces.
No two rocks seem to be the same.
I guess maybe that's one of the reasons I like collecting so many. Each one is different.
I think I may know of a rock you might like to see.

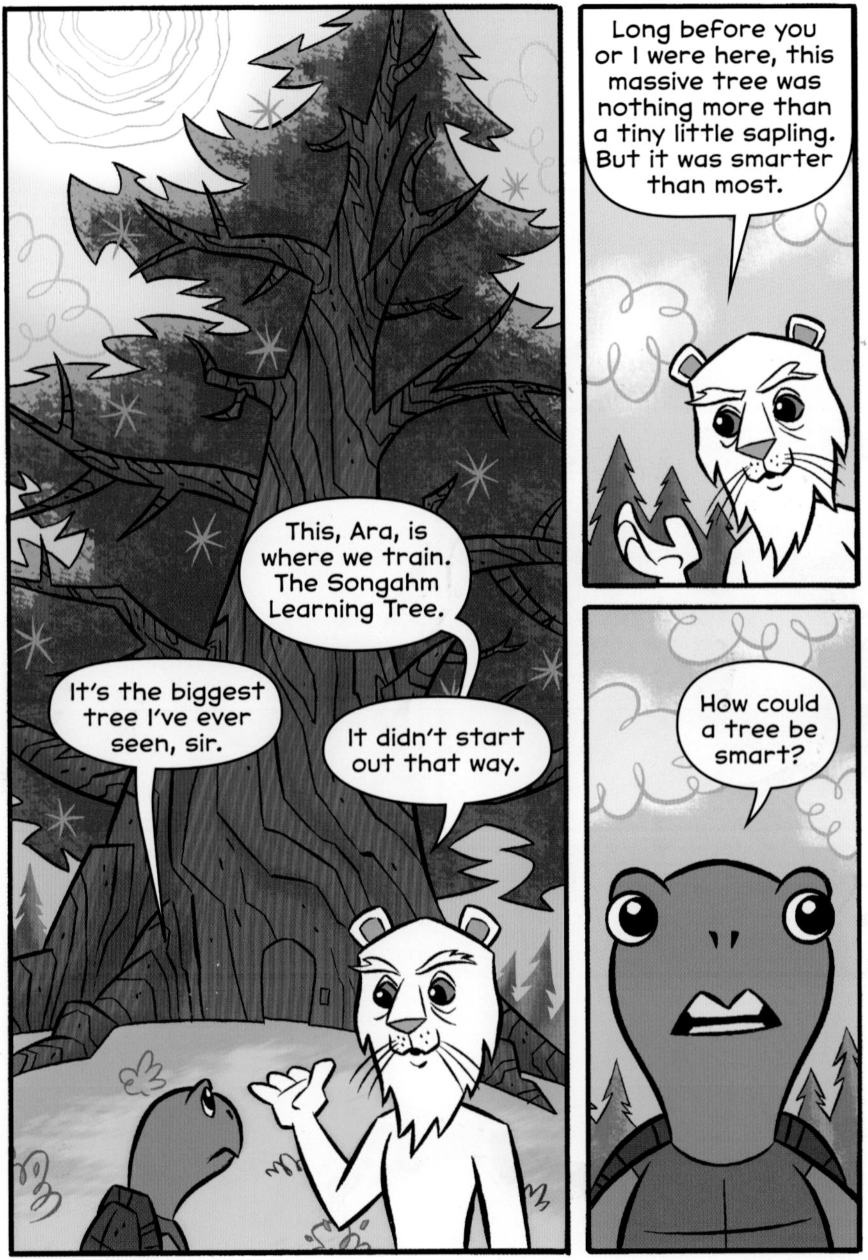
This, Ara, is where we train. The Songahm Learning Tree.
It's the biggest tree I've ever seen, sir.
It didn't start out that way.
Long before you or I were here, this massive tree was nothing more than a tiny little sapling. But it was smarter than most.
How could a tree be smart?

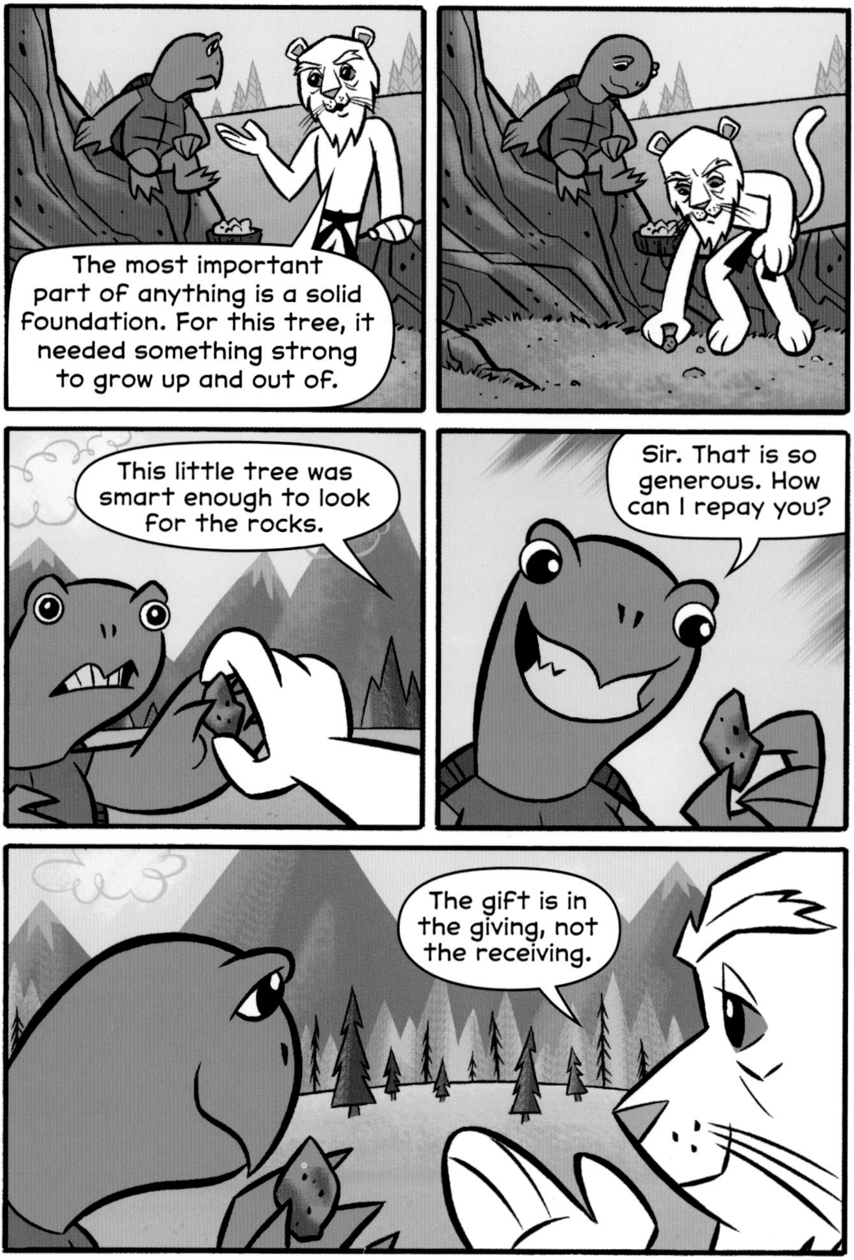
The most important part of anything is a solid foundation. For this tree, it needed something strong to grow up and out of.
This little tree was smart enough to look for the rocks.
Sir. That is so generous. How can I repay you?
The gift is in the giving, not the receiving.

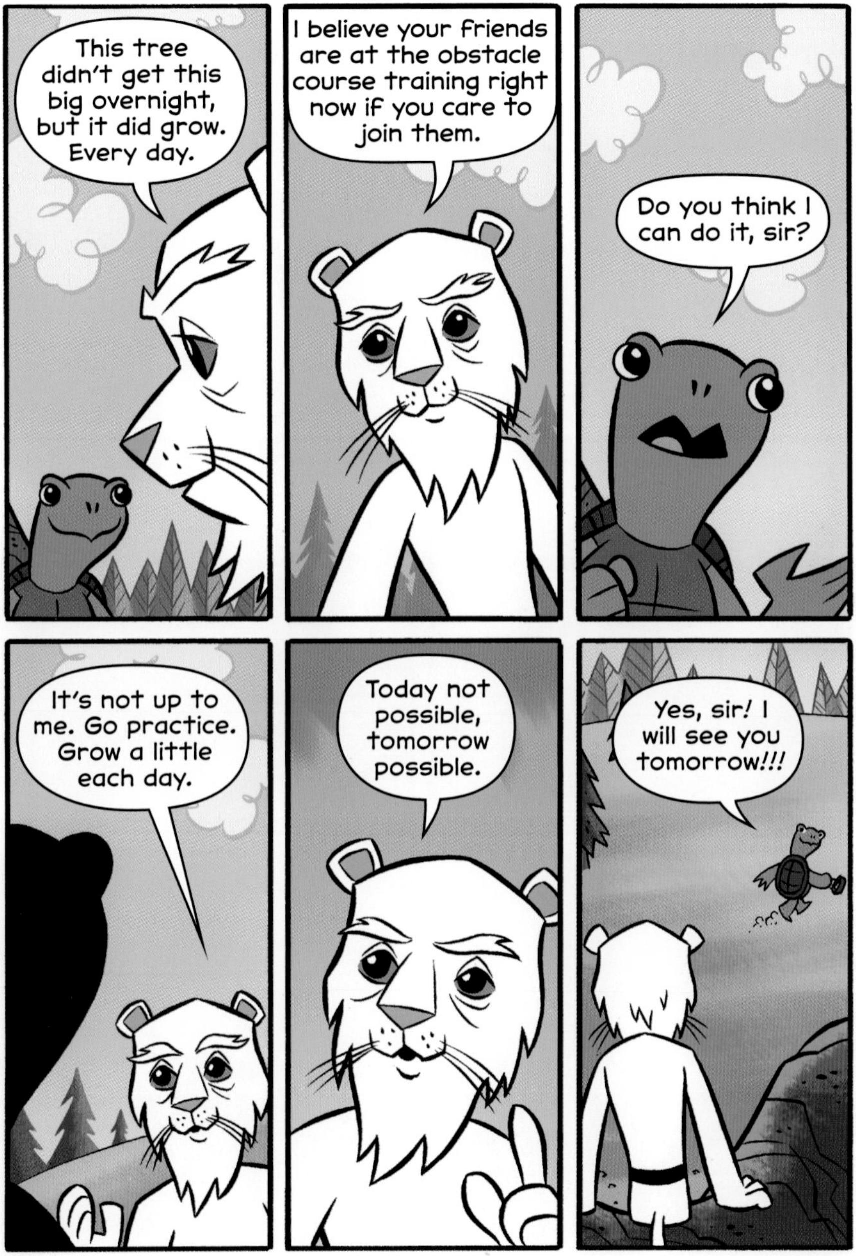
This tree didn't get this big overnight, but it did grow. Every day.
I believe your friends are at the obstacle course training right now if you care to join them.
Do you think I can do it, sir?
It's not up to me. Go practice. Grow a little each day.
Today not possible, tomorrow possible.
Yes, sir! I will see you tomorrow!!!

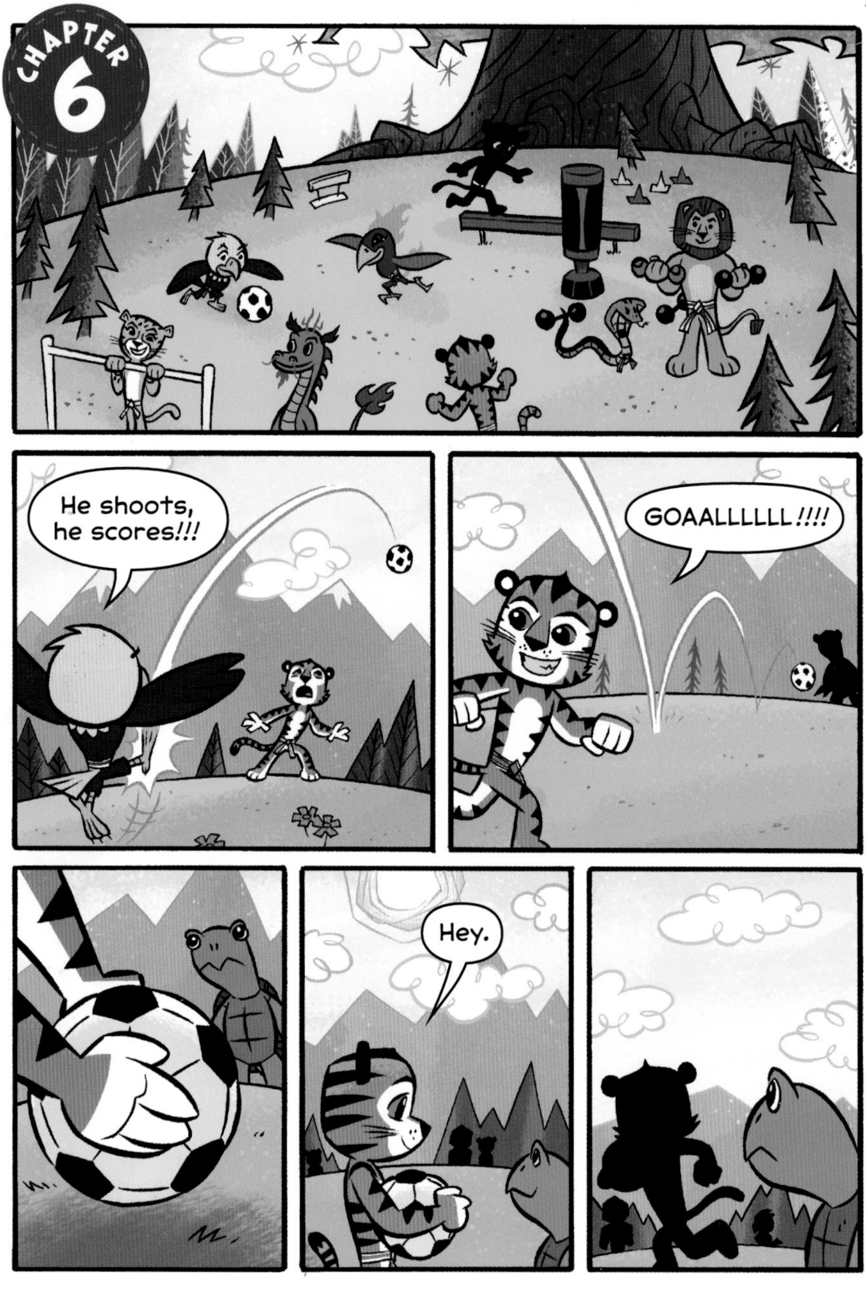
CHAPTER
6
He shoots, he scores!!!
GOAALLLLLL!!!!
Hey.

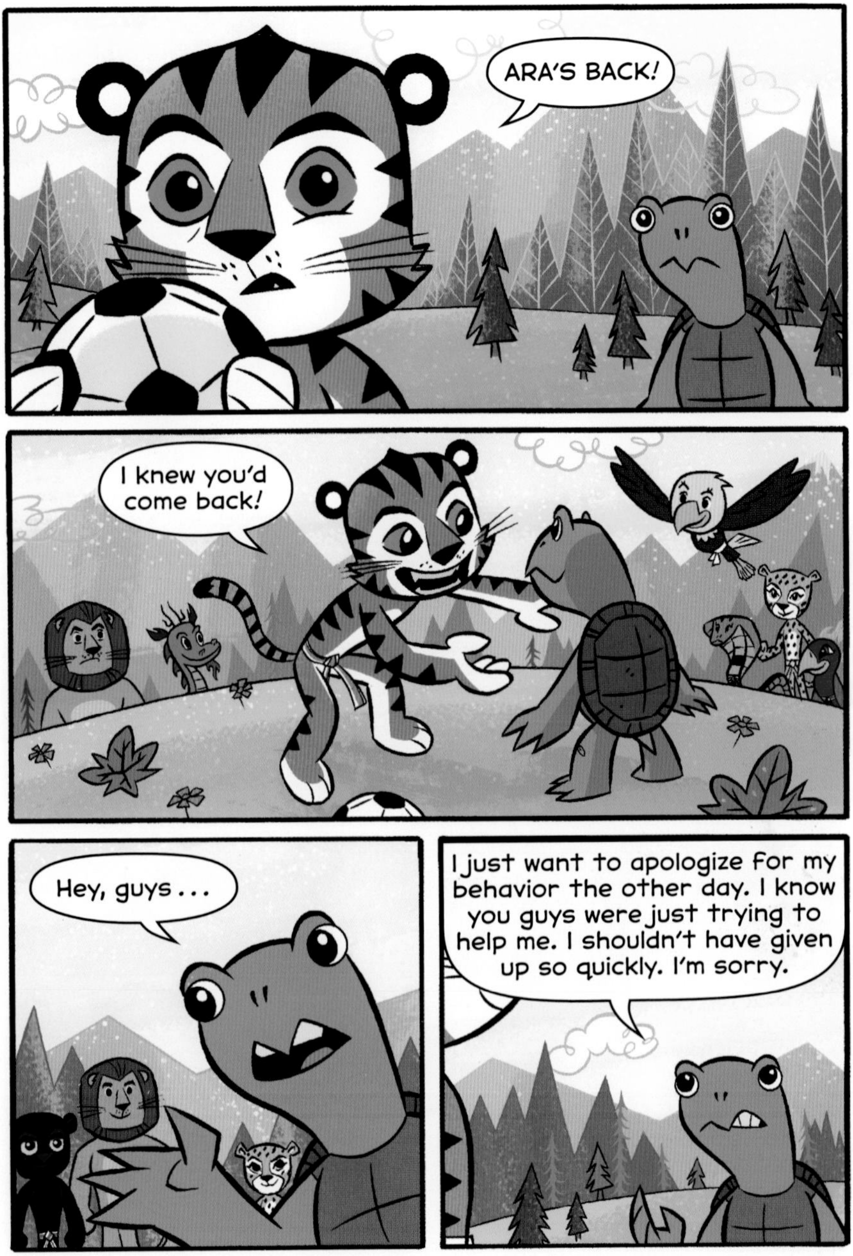
ARA'S BACK!
I knew you'd come back!
Hey, guys . . .
I just want to apologize for my behavior the other day. I know you guys were just trying to help me. I shouldn't have given up so quickly. I'm sorry.

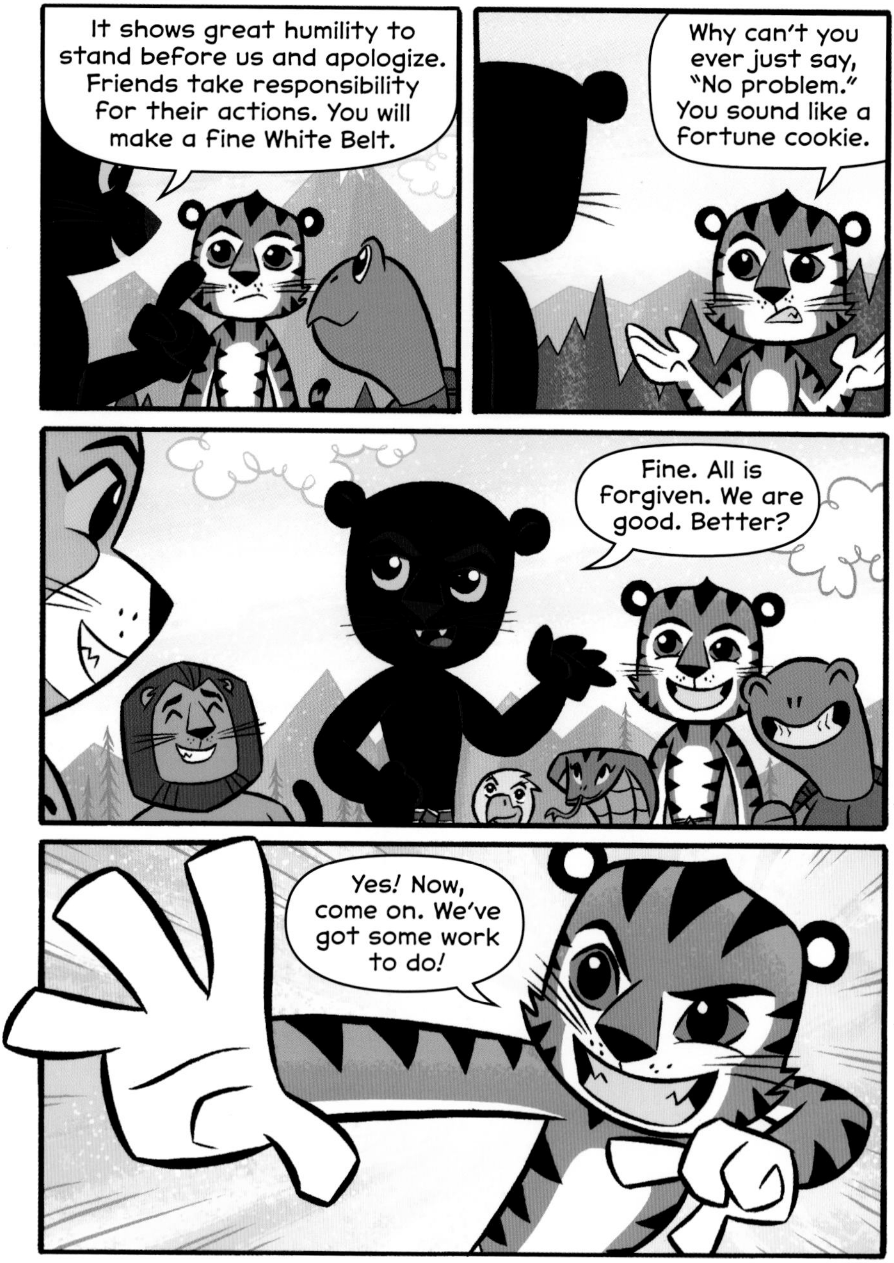
It shows great humility to stand before us and apologize. Friends take responsibility for their actions. You will make a fine White Belt.
Why can't you ever just say, "No problem." You sound like a fortune cookie.
Fine. All is forgiven. We are good. Better?
Yes! Now, come on. We've got some work to do!

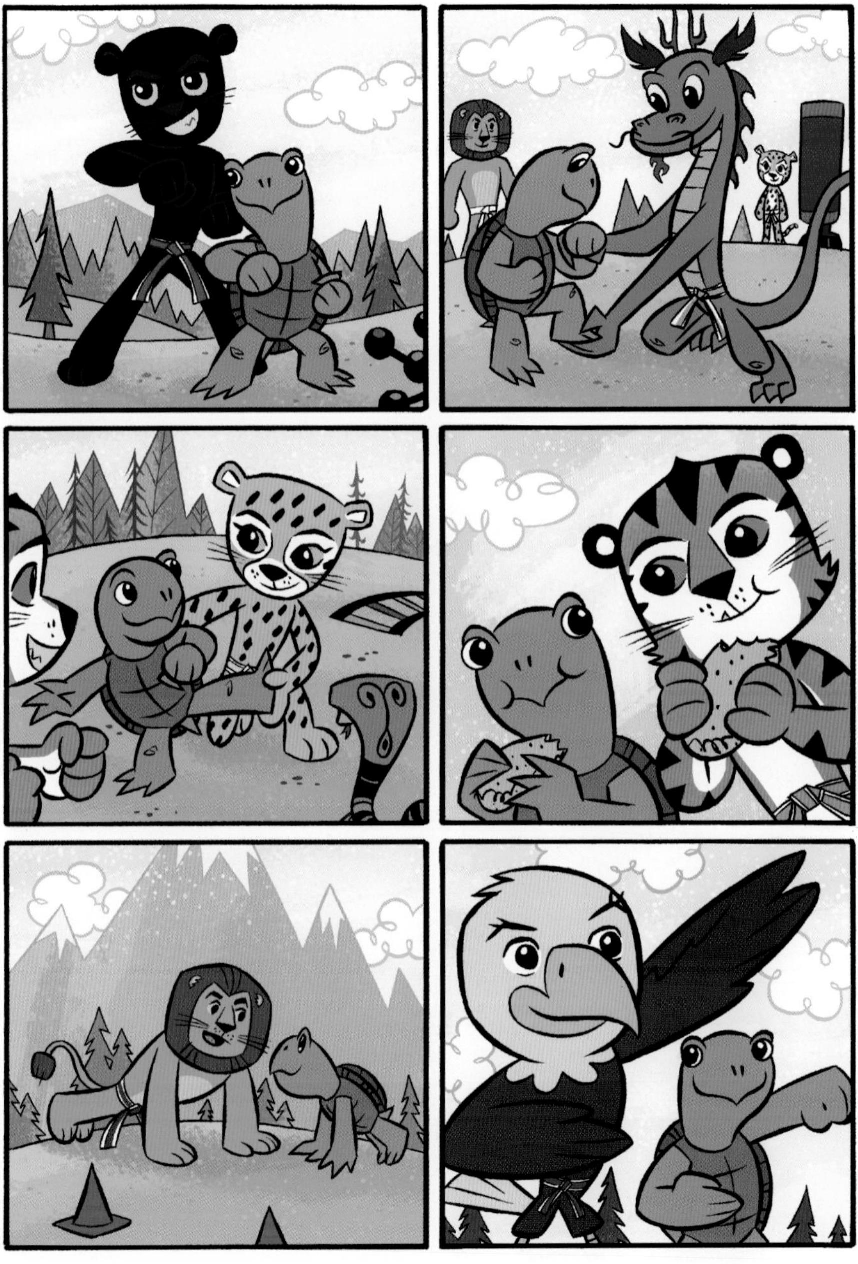

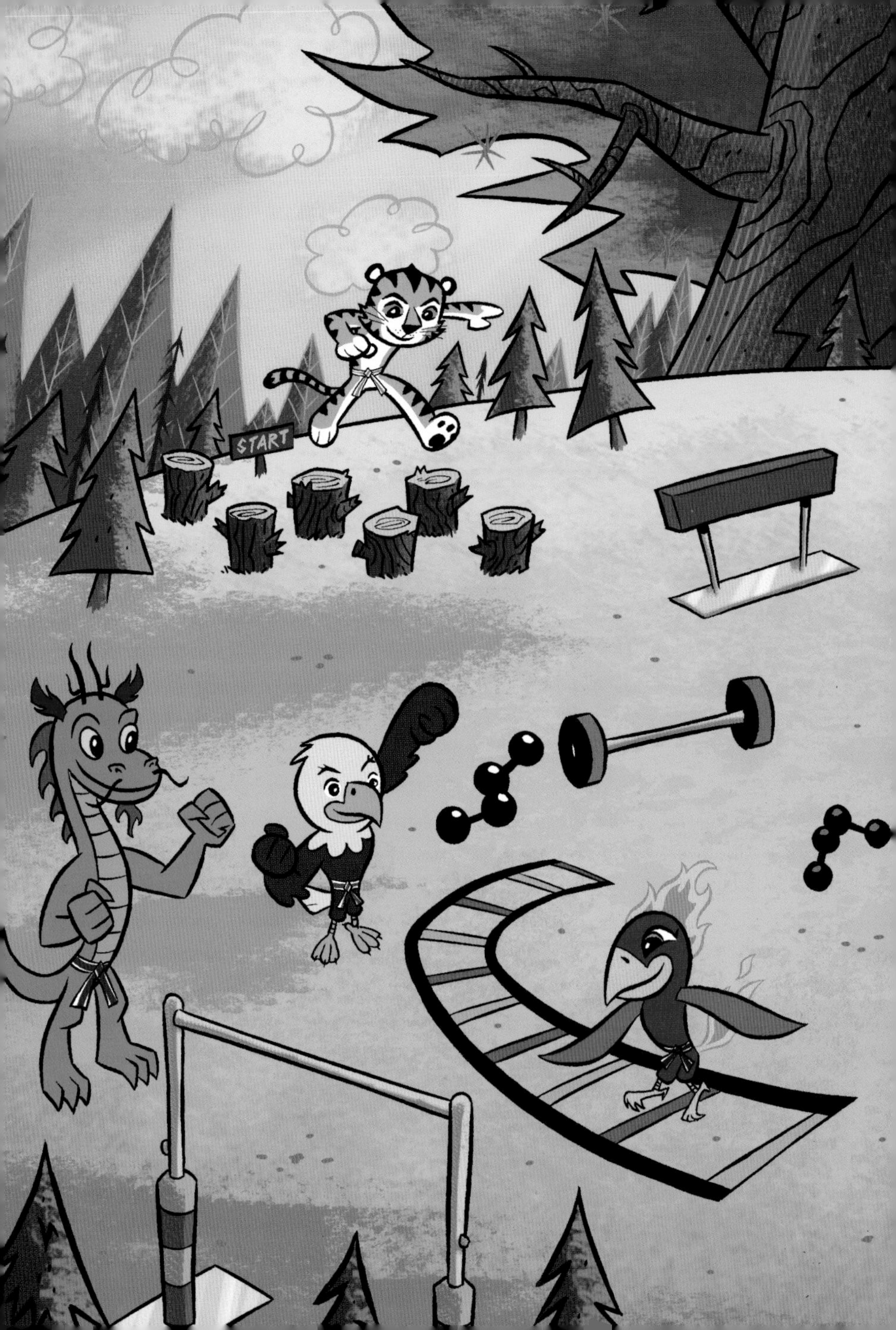
START

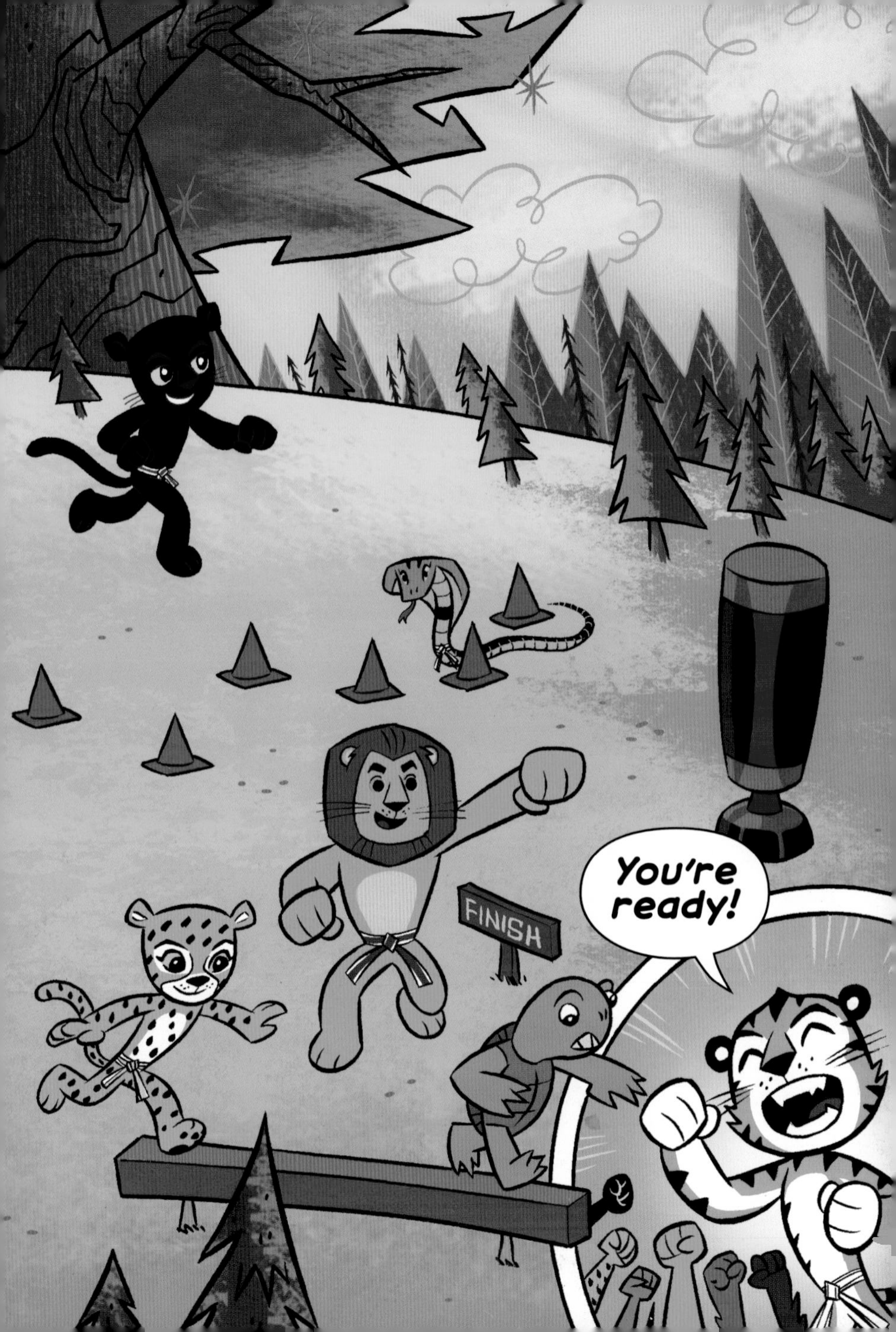

FINISH
You're ready!

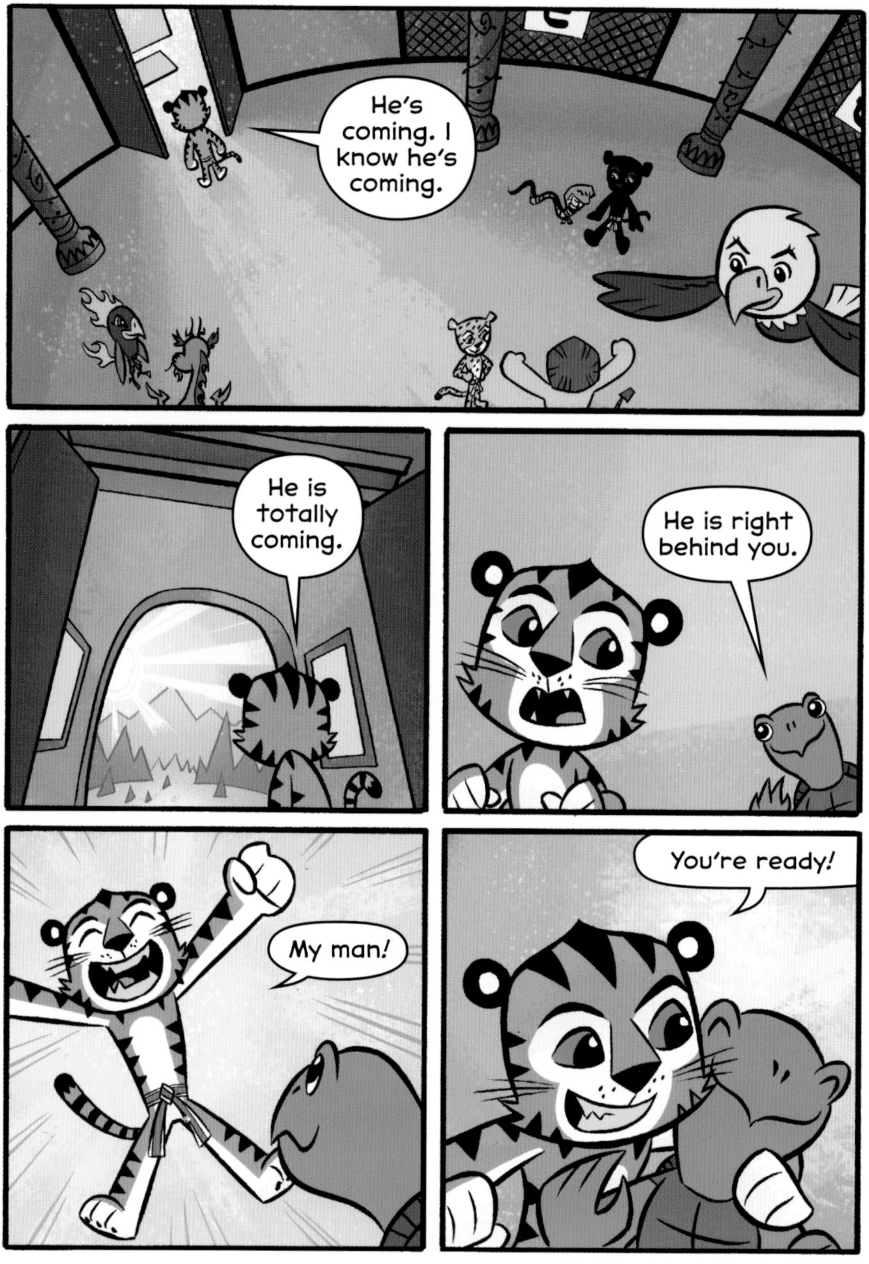
He's coming. I know he's coming.
He is totally coming.
He is right behind you.
My man!
You're ready!

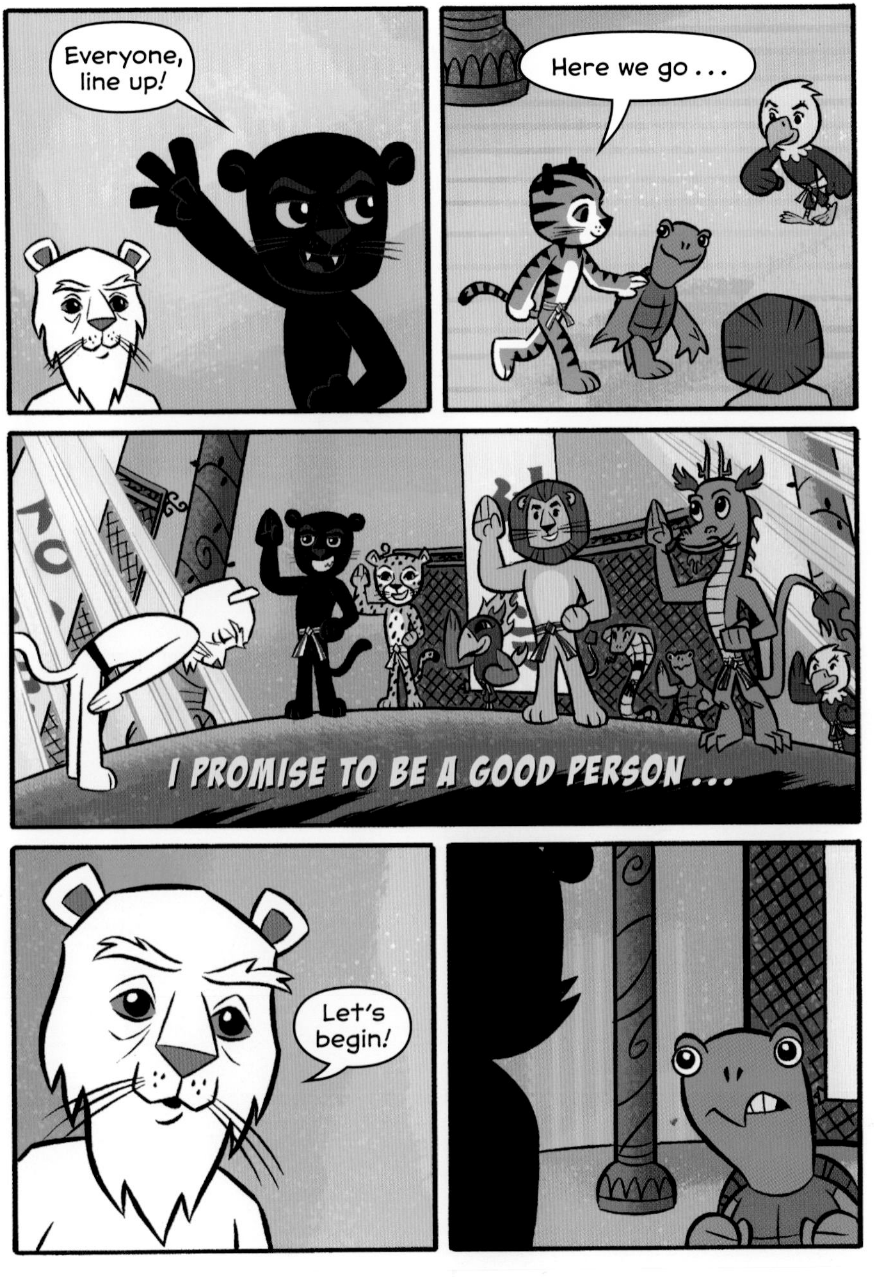
Everyone, line up!
Here we go . . .
I PROMISE TO BE A GOOD PERSON . . .
Let's begin!

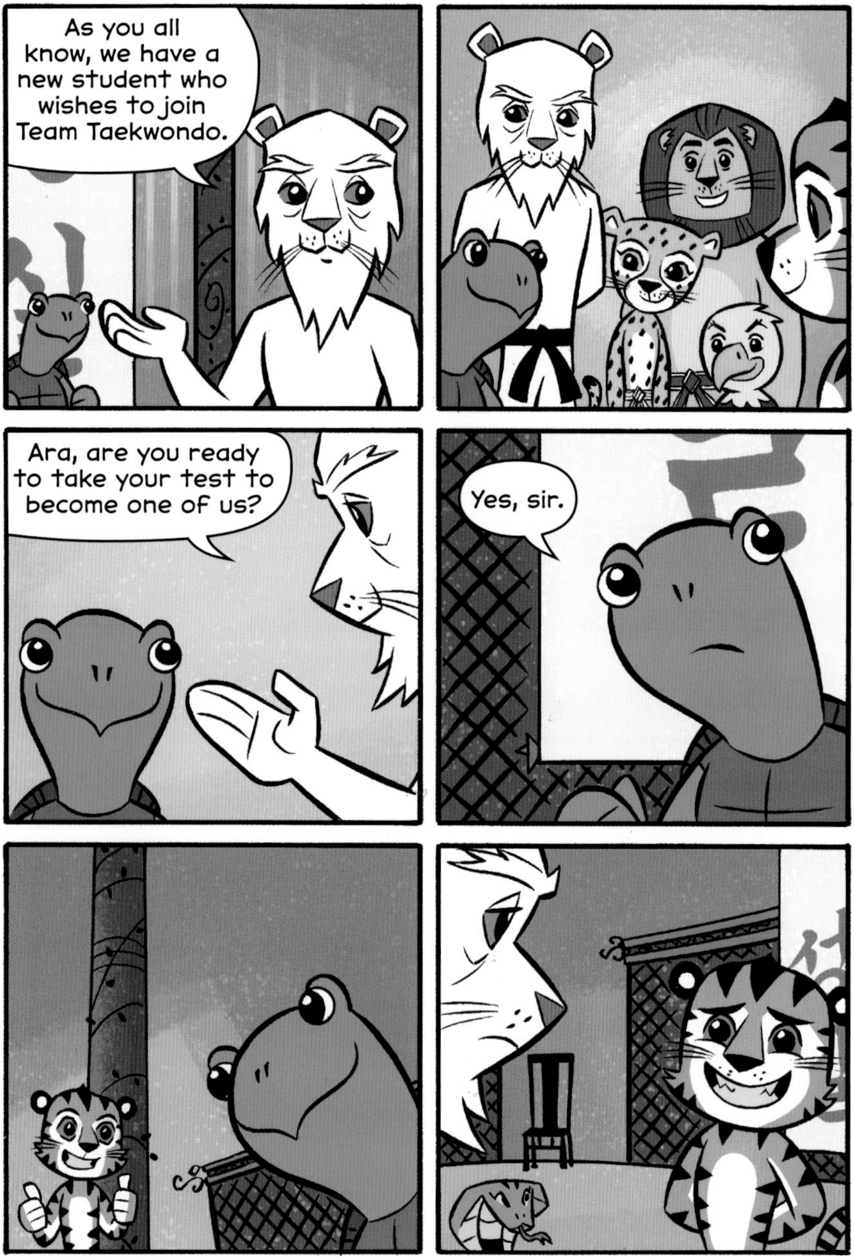
As you all know, we have a new student who wishes to join Team Taekwondo.
Ara, are you ready to take your test to become one of us?
Yes, sir.

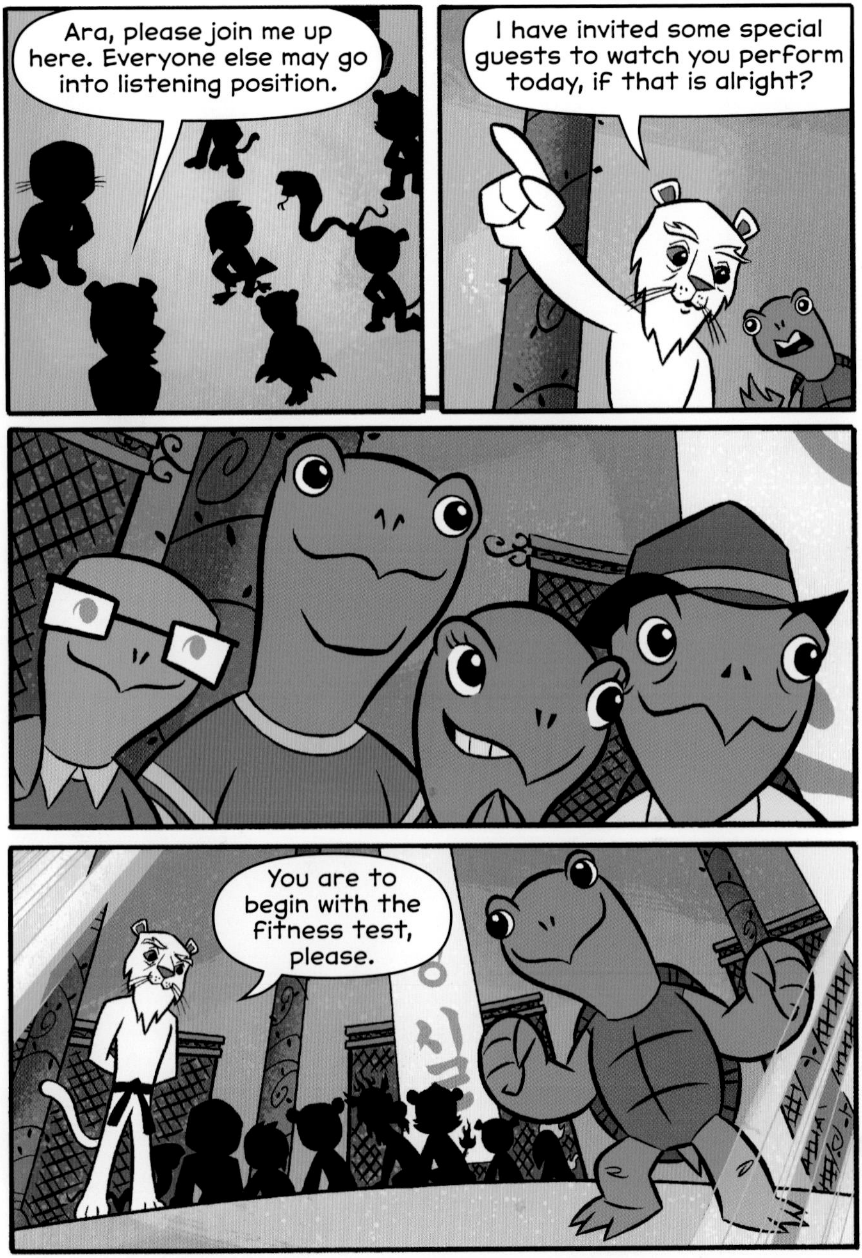
Ara, please join me up here. Everyone else may go into listening position.
I have invited some special guests to watch you perform today, if that is alright?
You are to begin with the fitness test, please.

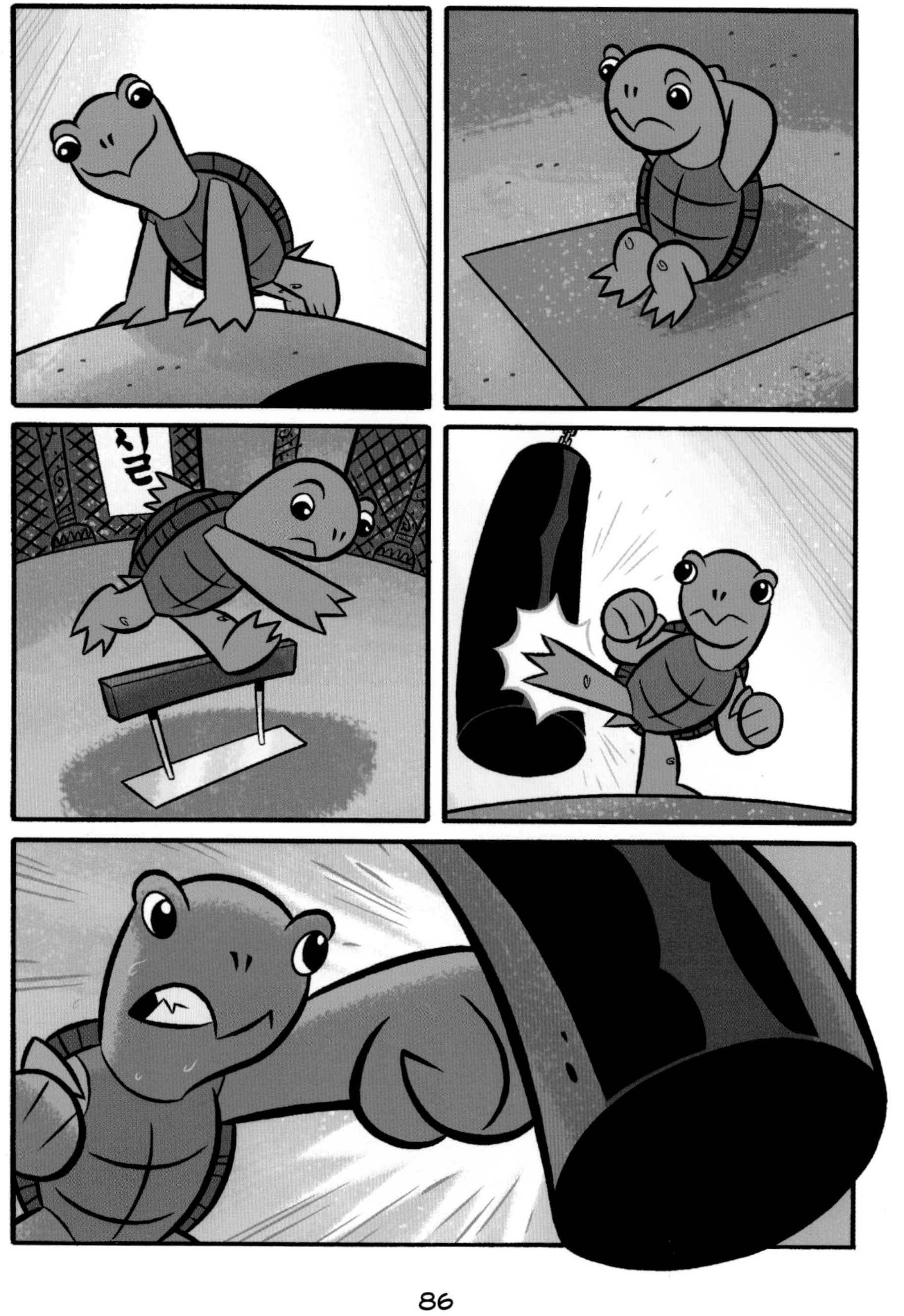

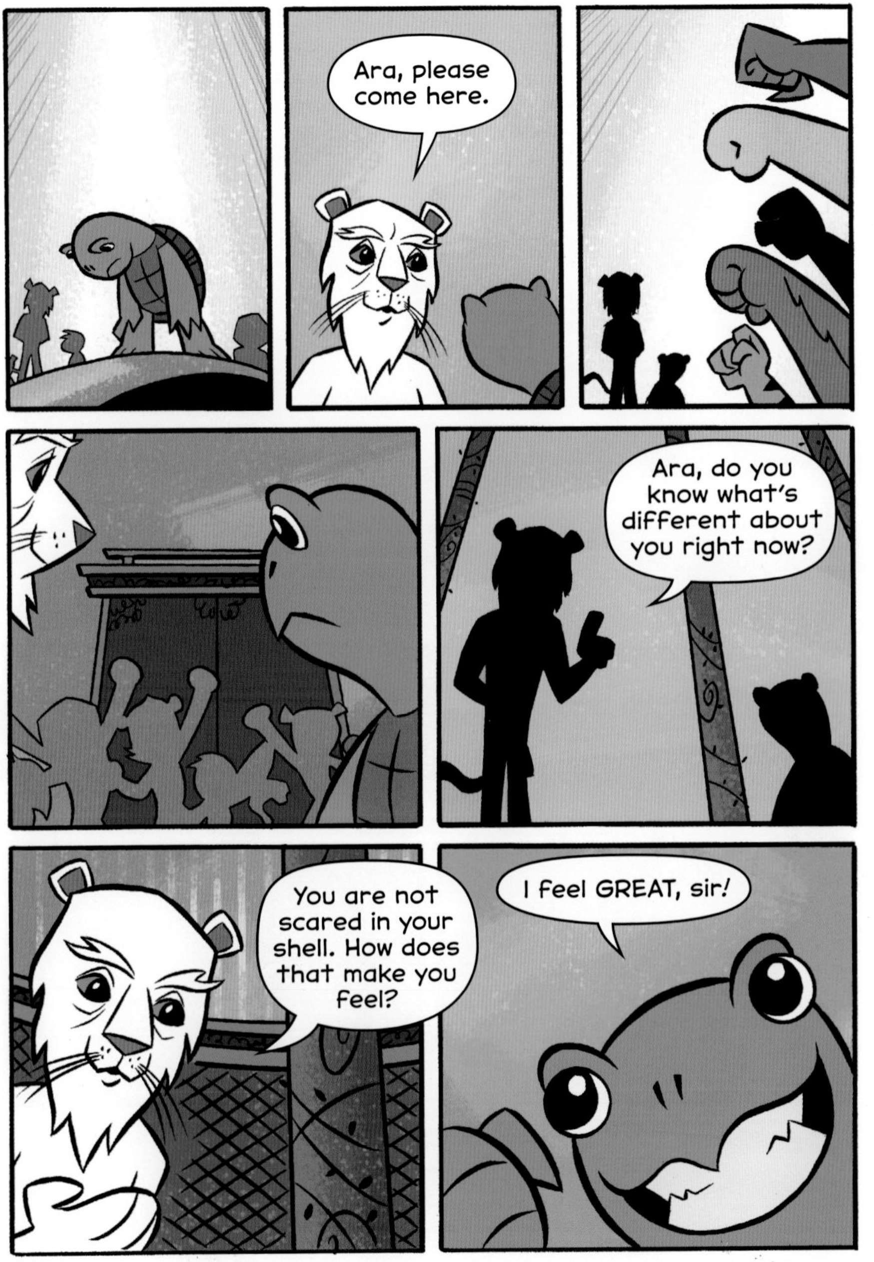
Ara, please come here.
Ara, do you know what's different about you right now?
You are not scared in your shell. How does that make you feel?
I feel GREAT, sir!

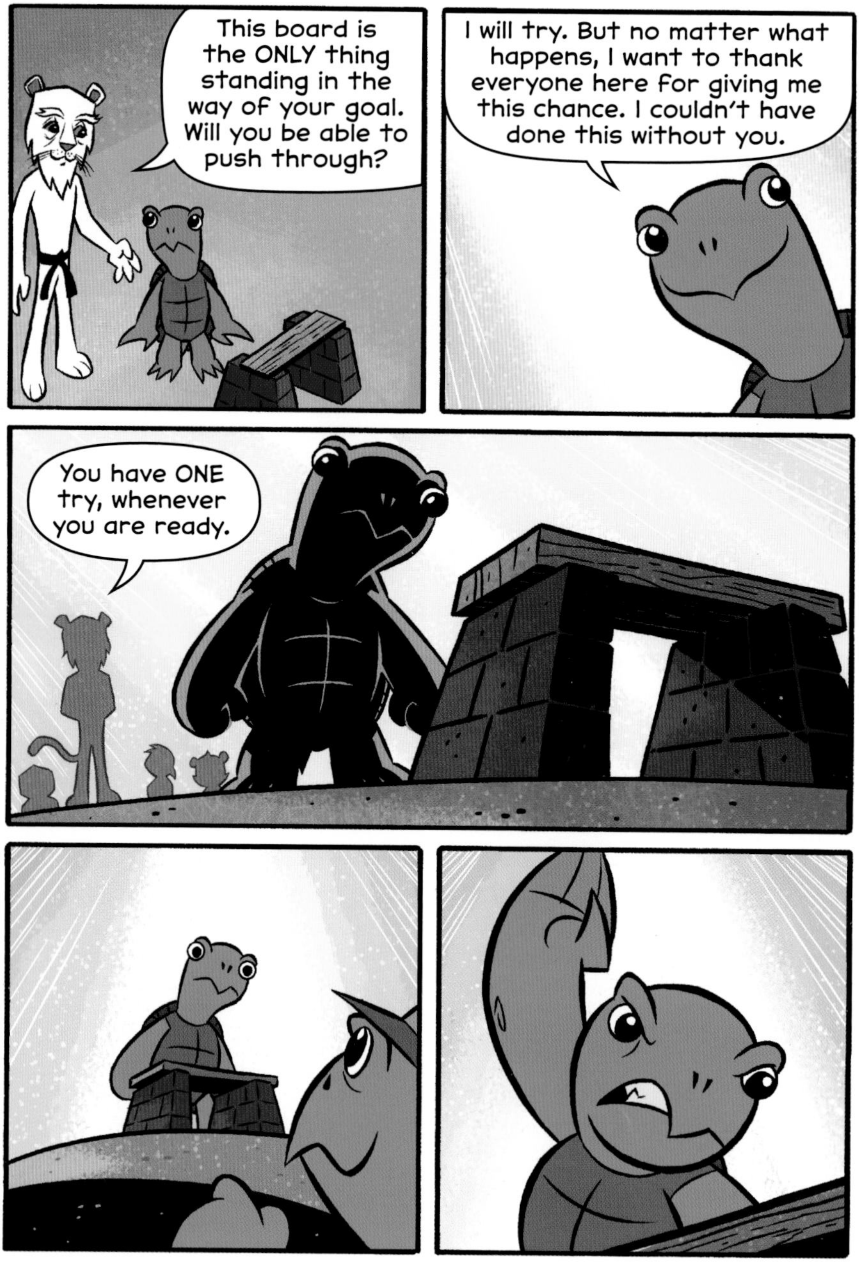
This board is the ONLY thing standing in the way of your goal. Will you be able to push through?
I will try. But no matter what happens, I want to thank everyone here for giving me this chance. I couldn't have done this without you.
You have ONE try, whenever you are ready.

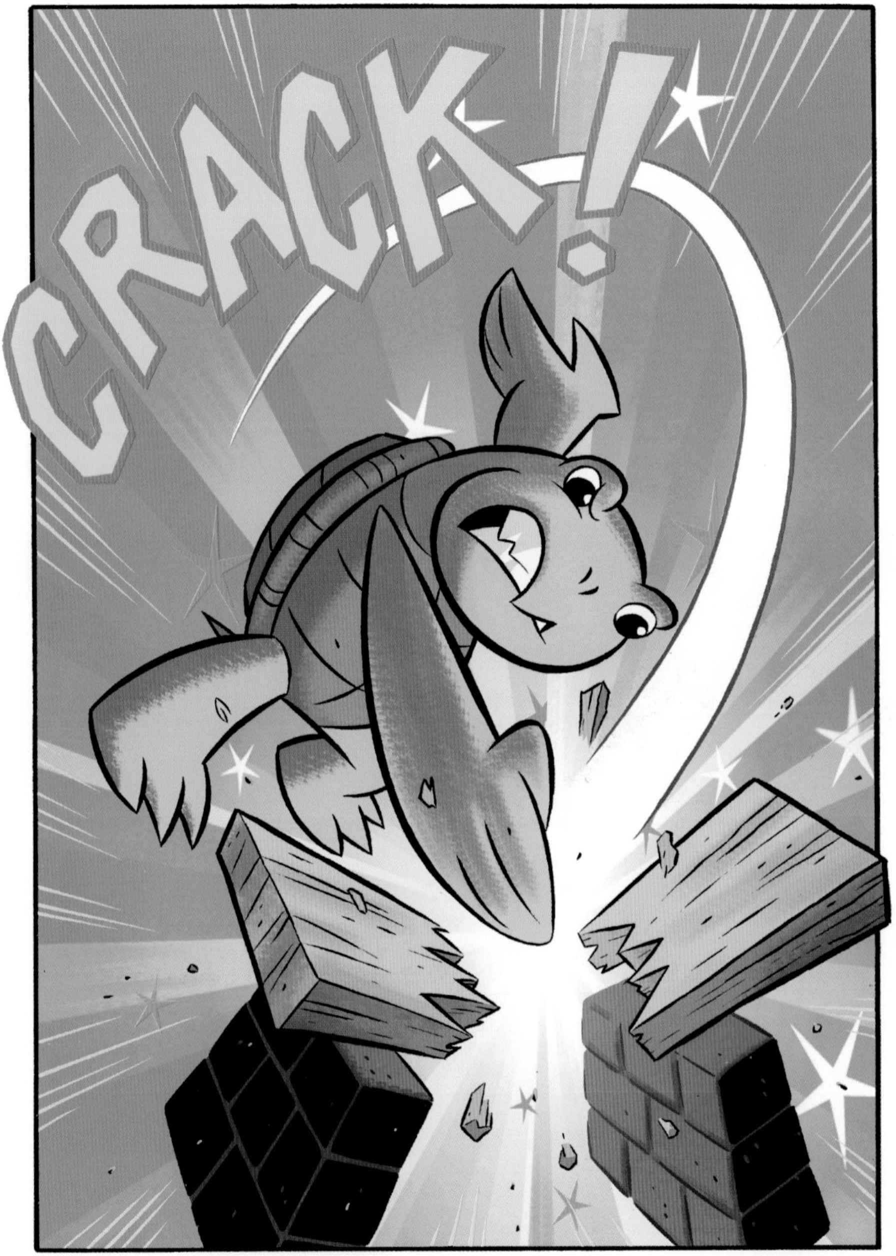
CRACK!

Line up, Tigers!

No, sir. You stay up here with me.

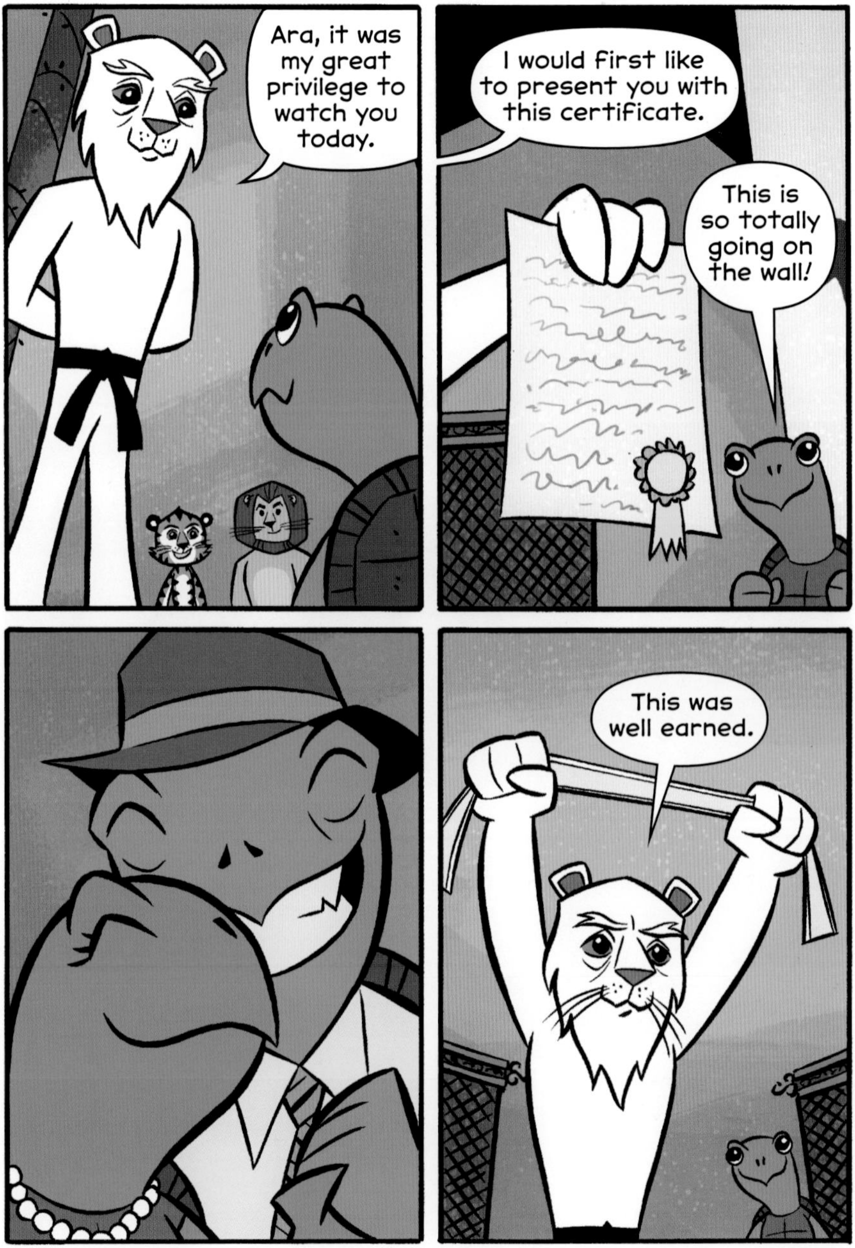
Ara, it was my great privilege to watch you today.
I would first like to present you with this certificate.
This is so totally going on the wall!
This was well earned.

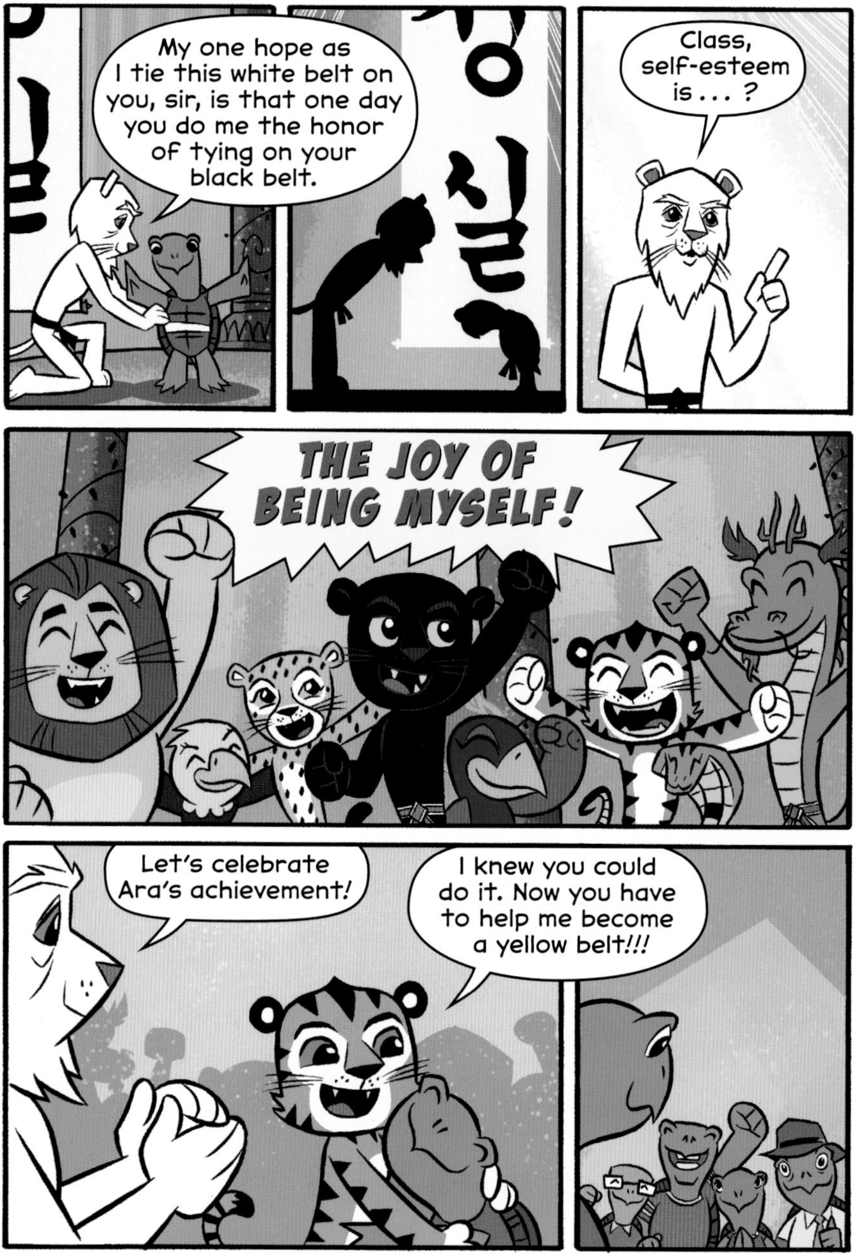
My one hope as I tie this white belt on you, sir, is that one day you do me the honor of tying on your black belt.
Class, self-esteem is . . . ?
THE JOY OF BEING MYSELF!
Let's celebrate Ara's achievement!
I knew you could do it. Now you have to help me become a yellow belt!!!

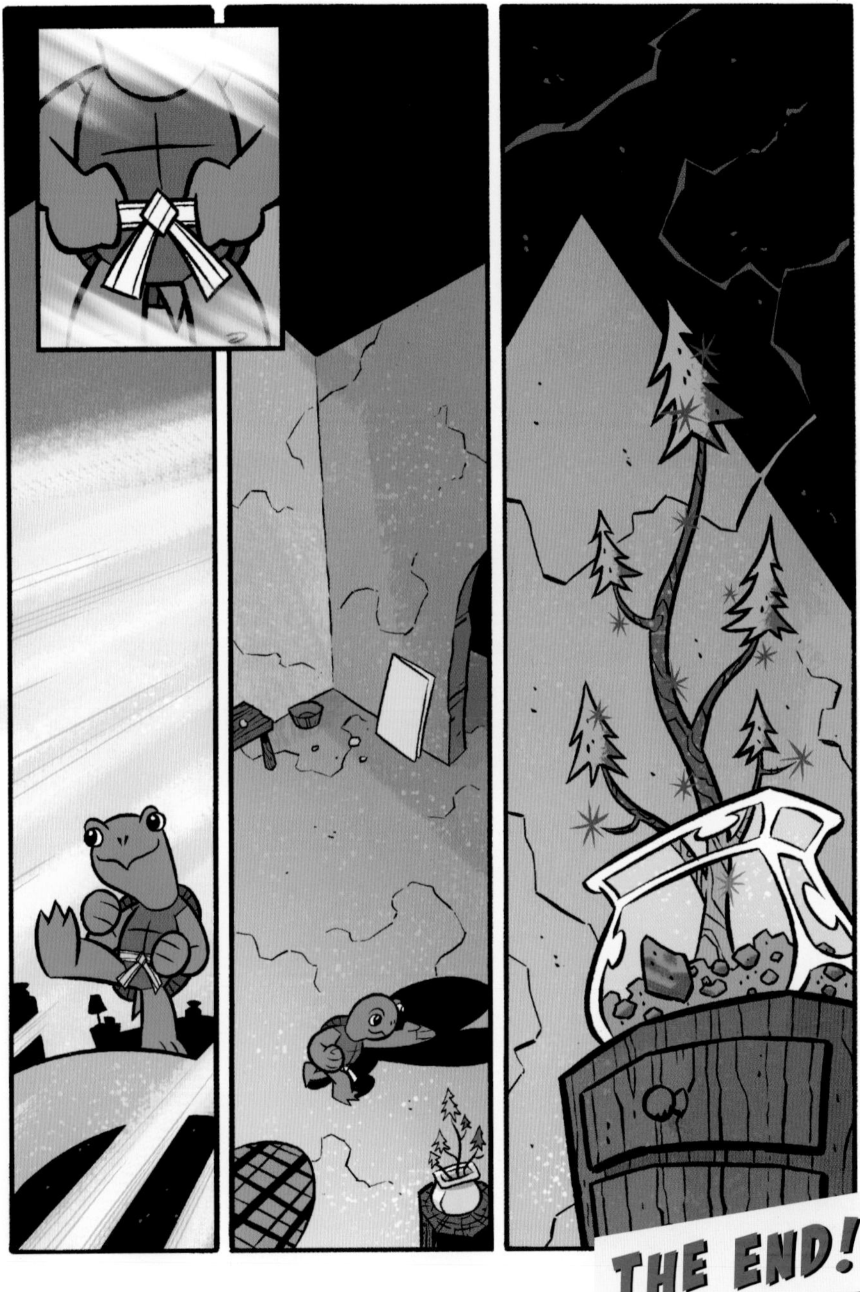
THE END!

I PROMISE:

TO BE A GOOD PERSON,
WITH KNOWLEDGE IN MY MIND,
HONESTY IN MY HEART,
STRENGTH IN MY BODY,
TO MAKE GOOD FRIENDS,
AND...
I WILL BECOME
A BLACK BELT LEADER!

TEAM TAEKWONDO BELT RANKS

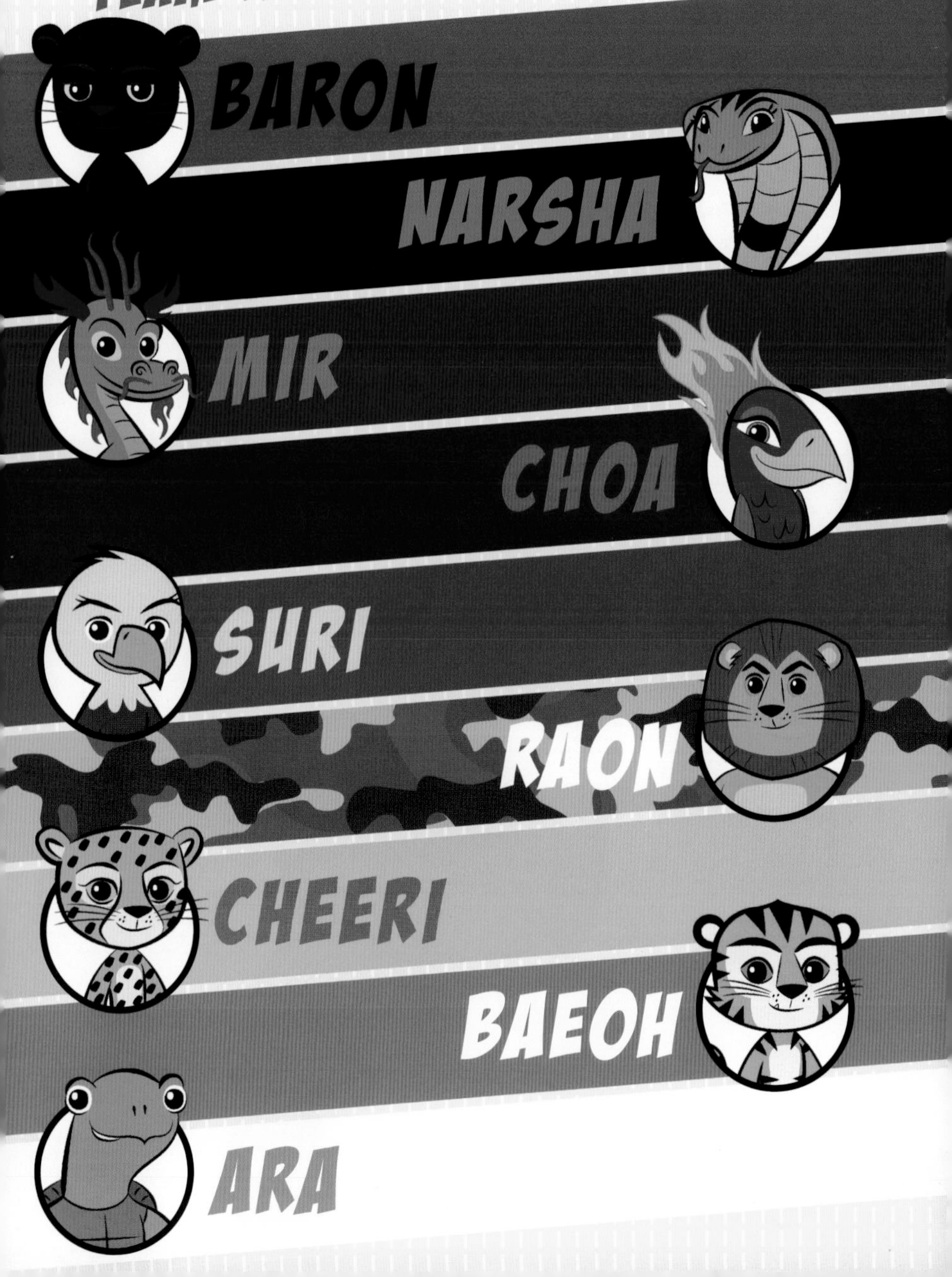
BARON
NARSHA
MIR
CHOA
SURI
RAON
CHEERI
BAEOH
ARA

ARA (A-RA)

Ara is a shy turtle. Before joining Team Taekwondo, he usually just stayed in his shell. Now he is making new friends and loves to do his forms nice and slow.

Name means: "of the sea"

Belt rank: white

Favorite move: knife hand strike

BAEOH (BAY-OH)

Baeoh is the funniest tiger ever. He has a big heart and loves to laugh. He is everyone's friend but sometimes lacks confidence.

Name means: "flying tiger"

Belt rank: orange

Favorite move: side kick

CHEERI (CHEER-Y)

Cheeri is the hardest worker in the class. Even though she always makes straight A's, she is always trying hard to get better, maybe sometimes too hard.

Name means: "to defend"

Belt rank: yellow

Favorite move: round kick

...ION (RAY-ON)

...is the biggest member of Team Taekwondo. He is
...strong and a great athlete. Although he always
...s well, and sometimes he leaps before he looks.

...e means: "lion"

...rank: camo

...rite move: reverse punch

SURI (SUR-Y)

Suri comes from a big family of big eagles. He is small for his age and sometimes tries to act bigger than he really is. He always goes too fast but is working on slowing down.

Name means: "eagle"

Belt rank: green

Favorite move: jump front kick

CHOA (CHO-AH)

Choa is a rare phoenix. She is very pretty and likes it when the other animals do things for her. She is learning to do things for herself, and when she does, she is awesome.

Name means: "light of the world"

Belt rank: purple

Favorite move: double knife hand block

MIR (MEER)

Mir is a super smart dragon. He might not be the most coordinated, but he tries really hard. He is learning to control his strength.

Name means: "dragon"

Belt rank: blue

Favorite move: hook kick

RSHA (NAR-SHA)

...a is the nicest cobra you'd ever want to meet.
...though she doesn't have any arms or legs, she
... of the best in her Taekwondo class. She always
... hard but keeps a smile on her face.

...e means: "flying high"

...rank: brown

...rite move: tail strike

BARON (BAR-ROON)

Baron is the highest rank in his Taekwondo class. He is a great leader; he just doesn't know it yet. He is always willing to help.

Name means: "righteous"

Belt rank: red

Favorite move: palm strike

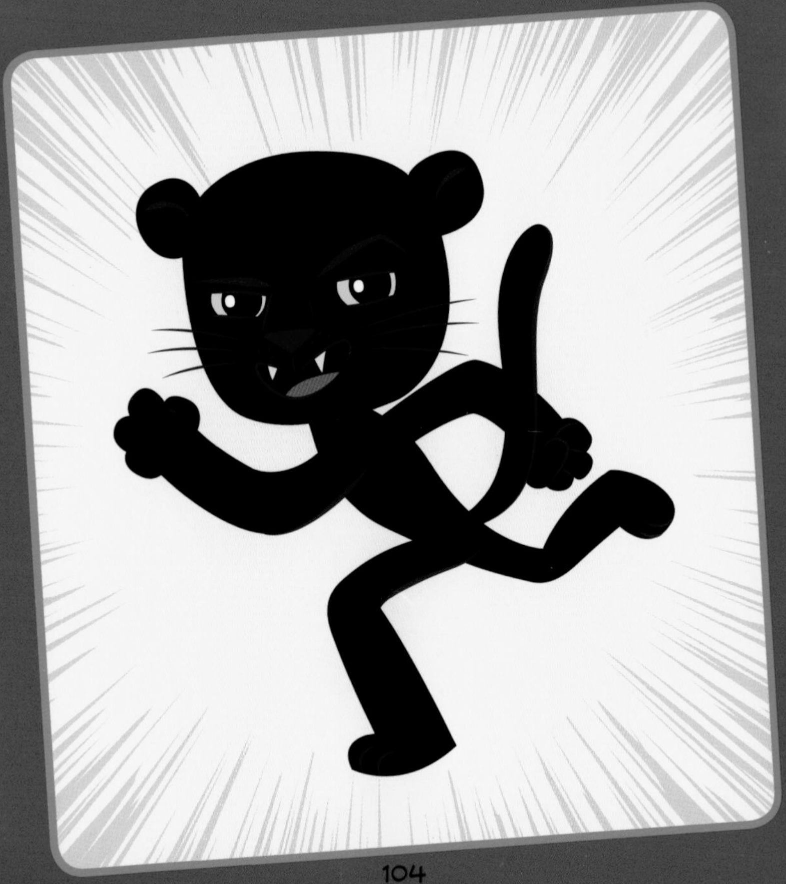

MASTER TAEKWON LEE is a sixth degree black belt and master instructor with many years of experience with ATA International—the world's largest martial arts licensing company. He's also the creator of the award-winning interactive children's video series Agent G. He lives in Little Rock, Arkansas.

JEFFREY NODELMAN is a graphic artist, novelist, painter, and award-winning animator who has worked with Walt Disney, Warner Bros., and Nickelodeon. He is a fourth-degree black belt trained in ATA Songahm Taekwondo and a USA-certified ice hockey coach. He lives in Little Rock, Arkansas, with one wife, two children, and three spoiled rescue dogs.

ETHEN BEAVERS is the illustrator of comics for DC Comics, Dark Horse Comics, and IDW Publishing, as well as numerous kids' titles, including the *New York Times* bestselling series NERDS. He lives in central California. Visit ethenbeavers.com.

THANK YOU FOR READING TEAM TAEKWONDO.

WE HOPE YOU ENJOYED IT!

If you would like to redeem **One Free Class** at a participating independently owned and operated ATA-licensed location near you, please visit:

WWW.ATATIGERS.COM/FREECLASS

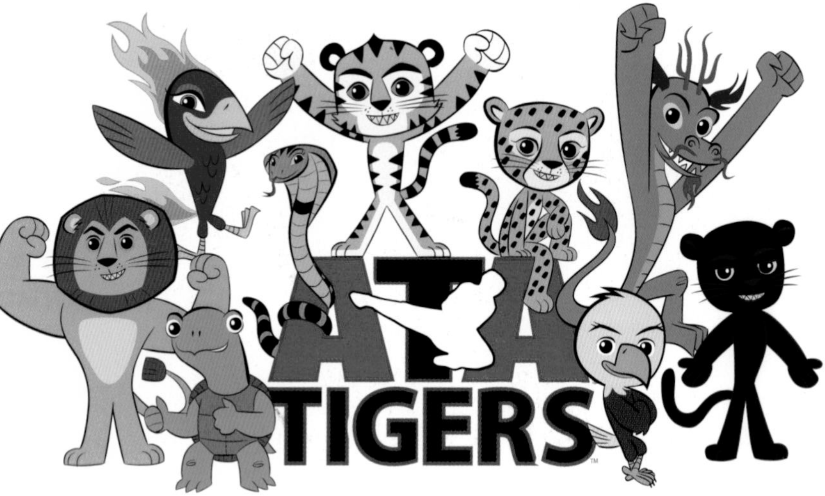
ATA
TIGERS

One Free Class offer may vary.